3650 Summit Boulevard
West Palm Beach, FL 33406

THE
VIOLENT
STORM

Center Point
Large Print

Also by William W. and J. A. Johnstone and available from Center Point Large Print:

Rising Fire
Gold Mine Massacre
The Morgans
To the River's End
A Stranger in Town
Twelve Dead Men
Powder Burn
The Jensen Brand
Hang Him Twice
Evil Never Sleeps
Dig Your Own Grave
Pray for Death

THE
VIOLENT
STORM

A Will Tanner U.S. Deputy Marshal Western

WILLIAM W. JOHNSTONE
AND J. A. JOHNSTONE

CENTER POINT LARGE PRINT
THORNDIKE, MAINE

The text of this Large Print edition is unabridged.
In other aspects, this book may vary
from the original edition.
Printed in the United States of America
on permanent paper sourced using
environmentally responsible foresting methods.
Set in 16-point Times New Roman type.

ISBN: 978-1-63808-288-0

The Library of Congress has cataloged this record
under Library of Congress Control Number: 2021952480

THE
VIOLENT
STORM

CHAPTER 1

Making a journey he had made many times before, Will Tanner guided the buckskin gelding through a gap in a long line of hills that led into the San Bois Mountains. The gap was actually one end of a narrow passage that led through the hills and ended at a grassy clearing at the foot of a mountain. On the other side of the meadow, built against the base of the mountain, stood the log cabin of a man named Merle Teague. A little, gray-bearded man, Merle had become a friend of Will's, just as the original owner of the cabin had. It was built by a quaint elflike man named Perley Gates, who had also become a friend of Will's. But one day, Perley abandoned his cabin and left for parts unknown. Will had gotten into the habit of stopping to camp there whenever he was traveling into certain parts of the Nations. It was on the way and a convenient distance from Fort Smith. And he was always welcome because he usually brought coffee and tobacco. More times than not, he was able to enjoy a supper of fresh venison. So, one of the first things he looked toward was the large oak next to the porch where Perley, and now Merle, hung their fresh-killed venison to skin and butcher. He smiled to himself when he saw the carcass hanging from that tree on this occasion.

Merle spotted him as soon as he left the cover of the trees at the end of the passage. He dropped his skinning knife, picked up his rifle, and brought it to his shoulder before he realized who it was. "Will Tanner!" he exclaimed, delighted. "You musta smelled some of that fresh meat on the fire over yonder." He nodded toward the firepit at the opposite corner of the porch.

"Howdy, Merle," Will said. "That's something new. That firepit wasn't here the last time I came by. You're makin' a regular palace outta this place." He was glad to see the little old man was getting by. He pulled the buckskin and his sorrel packhorse to a stop in front of the cabin. "That's a dandy firepit you built there, with that low wall of rocks around it. You can sit right there on the rocks while you tend your cookin', can't you?"

"You sure you wasn't here since I built it?" Merle asked. "Has it been that long since you was here?"

"Six or eight months, I expect," Will answered. "Anybody up in that cave?"

Merle knew Will was referring to a cave up on one of the mountains that was a popular hideout for fugitives on the run. It had earned the name of Robbers Cave. "I ain't been up that way in a week or so. But if there is somebody holed up there, they ain't stumbled on me yet. And they usually do, so I reckon ain't nobody up there right now."

"Well, the least I can do is help you get rid of some of that deer meat," Will said. "I'll take care of my horses first." He pulled his saddle off Buster and the packsaddle off the sorrel, then turned them loose to go to the stream that cut through the meadow. He put his saddle and the packs up on the porch, then he commented, "I like a good cup of coffee with my venison, and I don't see your coffeepot settin' out anywhere."

"I'm sorry about that," Merle said. "I've been outta coffee beans for three months."

"Did you throw your coffeepot away?"

Merle grinned sheepishly. "No, I didn't throw it away. I knew you'd show up here again, so I kept it ready to go."

"Well, get it out and put some water in it," Will said, chuckling. "Here's a twenty-pound sack of coffee, ground, it ain't beans. That oughta last you a little while." Merle could not speak, for grinning so wide. "I brought you a sack of sugar, too. What about smokin' tobacco? Did you give that up, too?"

"About two days after I gave up coffee," Merle managed, still beaming like a kid at Christmas.

"Well, I reckon you can start again," Will teased. "You didn't throw your pipe in the fire, did you?"

"I swear, Will, if I had the money, I'd be happy to pay you double for this stuff."

"Hell, it's a fair trade for some fresh deer meat,"

Will replied. "I don't get to go deer huntin' like I used to. I brought you some flour. I bet you're outta that, too."

Merle just shook his head as if he couldn't believe his good fortune. Without further delay, he ran into the cabin, came back with his coffeepot, and went straight to the spring to fill it. "I knew this was gonna be a good day when I woke up this mornin'." They enjoyed a big supper of venison and fresh coffee and a long visit while Merle finished butchering his deer and prepared a good portion of the meat to be smoked on a rack that Perley Gates had made for that purpose. It was later than either man's usual bedtime when they finally turned in, Merle in the cabin, and Will in his bedroll on the porch.

"I swear," Lester Camp whispered to his partner, "I didn't think they was ever gonna go to sleep, but I reckon it was worth the wait."

"I'll say it was," Carl Babcock replied. They had trailed the old man after he had killed a deer they had been following for more than a mile. Lester had wanted to shoot the old man and take the deer right then and there, but Carl talked him out of it. He persuaded him to wait and follow the old man to see if he had anything else they could use. He figured the deer was theirs for the taking, even if he didn't have much else they could use. "I don't know if we woulda ever found this place, if he hadn't led us here. Then this other feller comes along, ridin' a dang good-lookin' buckskin horse and leadin' a packhorse loaded with supplies. It can't get much better'n this." He grinned wide with pleasure over the happenstance, knowing it was just plain luck.

"Ain't no trouble takin' care of the feller on the porch," Lester figured. "That old man might be a chore to get outta that cabin. Might have to burn him out."

"I hope not. We could use that cabin," Carl reminded him. "We mighta made a mistake waitin' for dark to take care of that old man."

"I thought it was you that wanted to wait and let him skin that deer and butcher it for us," Lester declared. "Besides, you saw how quick he had that rifle up when the other feller showed up. I don't care how old he is, it don't take much strength to pull the trigger on that Henry rifle he was holdin'."

"I say we oughta wait a little bit longer to make sure they go to sleep," Carl suggested. "And while we do, I'm gonna slip up to that little corral they put the horses in and lead that buckskin over closer to our horses back there. I mean to have that horse, so if anything goes wrong, and we have to run, I'm takin' that horse with me."

"Hell, ain't nothin' gonna go wrong," Lester insisted while he watched Carl sneak back to the horses they had tied on the other side of the meadow to get a rope. He almost chuckled as he watched Carl going to the trouble of sneaking up to the corral, where he removed the two rails that served as a gate. The horses started walking out of the corral, so Carl waited and stopped the buckskin. He quickly fashioned an Indian bridle with his rope, then led Buster halfway across the meadow before tying him to a small bush. Then he returned to take his place beside Lester.

"You ready?" Lester asked, and Carl said that he was. Lester drew his long skinning knife from his belt and tested the edge of the blade with his thumb. "When I cut this jasper's throat, if he don't make enough noise, I will. And when that old coot comes running out to see what's wrong, we'll give him a belly full of lead. All right?"

"Why don't you just shoot him?" Carl asked.

"If I shoot him, that old coot inside will grab his gun and bolt the door, and we'll have to shoot up a lot of cartridges tryin' to get him outta there," Lester explained. "Might have to set fire to the cabin to get him outta there before it's over. But if I cut the other feller's throat, I'll holler like hell, and the feller inside will come a-runnin' to see what happened. He might have his gun with him, but he'll be out of the cabin. And that's when you'll cut him down."

"All right," Carl answered. "You be careful."

"Always am," Lester replied. "Don't worry, I'll leave him with a great big smile, right under his chin." He got to his feet again and, hunkered over in a crouch, he approached the sleeping figure on the porch. Carl aimed his pistol at the cabin door and waited.

Lester paused at the edge of the porch to listen for sounds from the sleeping man. There were none, thanks to a contented belly, Lester figured. *Good,* he thought, *best way to die, with your belly full of deer meat.* He climbed onto the tiny porch and crawled over to his victim, whose back was turned to him. Even though he was on his side, his victim was turned more toward his stomach, so Lester didn't have a clear view of his throat. He laid a hand gently on his shoulder and slowly rolled his body toward him. The sleeping man offered no resistance, but as the body turned, the barrel of a Colt .44 six-gun came into view, and it was aimed straight at his face. "Was there something you wanted?" Will asked, his voice soft and calm. Lester Camp made the last and worst mistake in a long line of mistakes in his life. His reaction was to try to stab Will. With no time to think, Will pulled the trigger at the same time he tried to block the hand holding the knife. The result was a .44 slug sent into the forehead of Lester and a cut on Will's left arm.

Shocked almost to a state of paralysis, Carl nevertheless managed to fire a couple of rounds at the porch, but Will held Lester's body in front of him to catch both bullets. He returned fire then when he saw the spot the shots came from and rolled off the porch to take cover behind Merle's firepit. In a panic then, Carl didn't like the position he now found himself in, so he decided to run when he realized that Will didn't know exactly where he was in the darkness. It was so dark in the narrow valley between the mountains that Will didn't know Carl was running until he caught an image of a dark figure moving across the meadow. He had no way of knowing how many his attackers were before, but now he felt sure there had been only two. So he scrambled out from behind the low rock wall of the firepit and gave chase, ignoring the fact that he was without his boots.

Running as fast as he could manage, Carl was already out of breath when he came to the buckskin he had left tied to a bush. He untied the horse and jumped on his back. When he kicked the buckskin with his heels, Buster kicked his rear legs straight up in the air, with only his front feet on the ground, causing Carl to go flying over his head to land hard on his backside. Stunned for a few moments, he looked back to see the dark form of Will Tanner running toward him, and behind him, Merle Teague jumped off the porch to give chase as well. Again in a panic, Carl reached for his six-gun, only to find it missing from his holster, having lost it when Buster bucked him off. Almost crazy with fear now, Carl looked all around him for his missing handgun, crawling one way, then another until finally he found it. With Will almost upon him, he frantically fired one round and missed before he was struck in the chest by a round from Will's .44. He went down at once and never moved again. Hearing Merle puffing behind him as he ran to catch up, Will said, "He's done for. It's over." He then knelt beside the body and took the pistol out of Carl's hand, then slowly released the hammer. He realized then, that had the man been able to pull the trigger again, he probably would not have missed, for he was so close by that time.

"What in tarnation?" That was all Merle could think to say at the moment. "Was there any more of 'em?"

"Don't think so," Will replied.

"Are you all right?"

"Yeah, I'm all right. That one back there at the porch managed to give me a little cut on my arm, but that ain't my worst problem. I ain't got my boots on and I feel some sore spots on the bottom of my feet from runnin' after this jasper."

"That horse of yours is kinda particular about who rides him, ain't he?" Merle asked.

"Not so much," Will answered. "He'll let pretty much anybody ride him as long as it's me." That prompted him to remember. "The direction he was runnin' in was that way." He pointed to some trees on the other side of the meadow. "So

I reckon we'll find their horses over that way somewhere. I'll go see if I can find 'em."

"While you're doin' that, I'll go back to the cabin and get a lantern, so we can take a look at these two buzzards," Merle said.

"That's a good idea," Will japed. "They mighta been some of your relatives come to visit you."

"If they are, we treated 'em the right way," Merle replied, then turned to go back to the cabin to fetch the lantern. Will walked toward the edge of the clearing until his eye caught the movement of forms big enough to be horses in the darkness of the trees. At that point, he drew his weapon again, confident that he wouldn't need it, but cautious enough to make sure he didn't blunder into a third person left to hold the horses. There turned out to be just the two horses, as he expected, so he untied their reins from the tree branches and led them back toward Merle's corral. He put all the horses in the corral and pulled the saddles off the two would-be assassins' horses. Then he went over and joined Merle, who was taking a close look at Lester on the porch. He picked up his boots, but decided against putting them on, since he had already torn the bottom of his socks and caked them with dirt.

"I brought their saddlebags over," Will said. "Thought I'd throw 'em on the porch, so you can look in 'em to see if there's anything worth something in 'em. I'll bring the saddles up, too, and you can see if you can trade them for something, but I wouldn't get my hopes up on 'em. You recognize him?"

"Never seen him before," Merle said. "He's just another one of those drifters who robbed somebody, or killed somebody, and came up to the mountains to hide. Don't know him, and I don't know his partner, but they were sure fixin' to settle your grits, weren't they?"

"Yep. Neither one of 'em gave me any choice. I had to shoot both of 'em."

"I sure thank the Lord you came along. This was my lucky day when you showed up."

"Well, I'm glad I happened to be in a position to help," Will responded. "Those two weren't plannin' to leave anybody in this cabin alive."

"Oh hell," Merle snorted. "I weren't talkin' about them two tryin' to kill me. They'da played hell tryin' to smoke me outta this cabin. I was talkin' about the coffee and the tobacco you brung me."

"Right," Will replied. "What was I thinkin'? Bring your lantern and let me take a look at the other fellow." They walked back out in the meadow to Carl's body and Will took a quick look. "I don't know him, either," he told Merle. "Did he have anything on him?"

"A Colt .45 Army revolver and a knife, eighty-five cents in his pocket, and that's all," Merle answered. "Oh, and a pocket comb. You want it? You've got hair."

"I don't want it," Will told him. "You feel like diggin' a hole tonight to put these two jokers in, or you wanna wait till mornin'?" Merle chose morning, saying he'd rather go back to bed now. That suited Will fine, so he dragged Lester's body off the porch to lie in the yard till morning. He moved his bedroll away from the puddle of blood Lester had left on the porch and retired to try to make up for some of the sleep the visit had cost him.

They were up early the next morning, in spite of the little interruption in their sleep the night before, and enjoyed another meal of fresh-killed venison for breakfast. They gave their two guests a rather undignified burial on the backside of the mountain before Will set out again on the trail to Atoka. "How long you figure you'll be down that way?" Merle asked. He was wondering if Will might stop by on his way back to Fort Smith.

"I don't know for sure," Will told him. "After I see Jim Little Eagle in Atoka, I'm gonna ride on over to the other side of Tishomingo. Tom Spotted Horse wired Fort Smith about some cattle rustlin' goin' on over near the Red River. So I don't know how long I'll be gone."

"What about all this stuff we ended up with after we stuck these two fellers in the ground?" Merle asked, already pretty sure what Will's answer would be.

"I figured it might be a little more trouble for you, but the next time you ride over to McAlester for supplies you'll have a lot more to trade for 'em. And you won't have to wait for me to show up to have coffee."

"I 'preciate it, Will. That's mighty generous of ya. I might keep one of them horses, that roan. He looks in pretty good shape and that sorrel I've been usin' for a packhorse is gettin' so dang old he ain't gonna be good for much of anythin' pretty soon."

"Yeah, that roan looks like he's got a lot left in him, and you oughta get something for the bay, too," Will allowed. "Well, I'd best get in the saddle. I've got a good day and a half's ride to get to Atoka. Maybe by the time I get there, Jim will have taken care of the problem, himself."

CHAPTER 2

Will and Buster put in a long day after leaving Merle that morning. He wanted to arrive in Atoka around noon the following day because he planned to eat dinner at Lottie Mabry's dining room, which she had recently started calling Lottie's Kitchen. It was next door to a rooming house owned by her husband, Doug, and started out as the dining room for her husband's boarders. In short time, the quality of Lottie's cooking became quite well known, and consequently, the favorite place to eat in the little town. As much as he had enjoyed the fresh venison, he was hankering more toward a good homestyle dinner with some biscuits or corn bread and butter. So after a day's ride that he figured to be close to forty-five miles, he rode into Atoka a little after noon. He decided to eat first, then ride out to Jim Little Eagle's cabin on Muddy Boggy Creek. He knew Jim's wife, Mary Light Walker, would insist on fixing him something to eat, if he had not already eaten. The food would be good but not what he was hankering for on this day.

He pulled Buster up before the hitching rail in front of Lottie's and dismounted, wrapped the reins of both horses around the rail, and paused only a moment to admire the new sign

21

that proclaimed the dining room to be Lottie's Kitchen. "Will Tanner!" Louise Bellone called out when she saw him come in the door. "I thought you musta died."

"Howdy, Lou-Bell," he greeted her by the name she was called by all her friends. "I couldn't die till I had one more dinner at Lottie's."

"So you're sayin' one more dinner here will kill you?" Lou-Bell replied. "I don't know if you oughta tell Lottie that or not."

"You know what I meant," he said. Knowing she was japing him, he gave up immediately. He knew better than to get into a battle of wits with Lou-Bell. "What's for dinner today?"

"Lottie made meat loaf," Lou-Bell said, not willing to give up that easily, "and it's pretty deadly. But if you wanna be sure, we can fix you up with something that's guaranteed to do the job."

"Just bring me the meat loaf and whatever else goes with it and maybe that'll do the job," he said. She shrugged and headed for the kitchen to fill a plate for him, passing Lottie on her way out of the kitchen with the coffeepot. He went into the back part of the room and sat down at one of the small tables, instead of taking a seat at the long table in the center.

"Howdy, Will," Lottie greeted him. "Is Lou-Bell giving you a hard time?" She turned the coffee cup right side up on his saucer and filled it with hot coffee.

"She always does," Will admitted. "I think she knows she's got a sharper wit than I have, and I know when I'm overmatched."

Lottie chuckled and said, "Sometimes I think I oughta put a gag in her mouth, but I'm sure half my customers come in here just to swap lies with Lou-Bell."

"Well, I'm in the other half," Will said. "I come in here because the food is the best in this part of the country."

"Why, thank you, sir," she responded, "I certainly appreciate that." She stepped to the side then to give Lou-Bell room to place his dinner on the table.

"Here you go, Deputy Tanner," Lou-Bell announced as she set his plate down. "Hope it does the job," she japed, and gave him a wink. She turned to Lottie then and said very softly, "Look who's coming in the door. I kinda hoped they wouldn't be back today."

Forgetting Will for the moment, Lottie said, "Well, let's not sit them at the big table today. Go tell Fred to clear the dishes off that table over there by the window. I'll seat them there." Lou-Bell went at once to the kitchen and Lottie turned toward Will again. "I'll check with you in a little bit." She started to leave, pausing only a few seconds when Will asked a question.

"Who's Fred?" During the many times he had eaten there, he had never seen anyone named Fred.

Lottie quickly explained, "You probably remember Lila, the elderly lady who used to work here as our dishwasher. She came down with arthritis so bad she couldn't work anymore. We couldn't find anybody to take her place, so her husband came in to do her job till we found someone else, and he's still here." She hurried away then to intercept the two men coming in the door.

"Good afternoon, gentlemen," Lottie greeted them. "You've come back to see us again."

"You said that like you're surprised," Clyde Vickery responded. He turned to look at his partner. "Didn't she, Sonny?"

"Maybe she's sayin' we ain't welcome," Sonny Doyle answered.

"We try to welcome everyone here," Lottie said. "We hope that everyone who eats with us is considerate of everyone else who's eating here. I'll call your attention to the table we've provided in the corner for firearms and ask if you'll be considerate of the other customers in the room and leave your weapons on the table until you're ready to leave. Yesterday, you refused. I'm hoping that today you'll leave them on the table. How 'bout it, you wanna make the rest of my customers feel more at ease?" Her earnest request failed to wipe the smirks off either face.

"How 'bout it, Sonny? You wanna make her customers feel more at ease?"

"I don't give a fat rat's ass whether her customers feel at ease or not," Sonny answered him. "I just care about how I feel, and I feel uncomfortable when I'm settin' in the back of the room full of sodbusters and my .44 is layin' on a table up front."

"Well, there you go, sugarplum," Clyde told her. "I reckon you've got your answer. Now the smartest thing for you to do is to bring us plenty of food and don't let none of them other customers bother us, and everythin' will be just fine."

Lottie hesitated. She glanced over at the opposite back corner at Will, already eating, apparently paying no attention to the two men she was talking with. She couldn't decide whether to ask him to order the troublesome two out of the building, or not. Maybe these men had no intention of causing anyone any trouble and just wanted to eat and get on their way. Finally, she made a decision. "All right, gentlemen, I'm gonna seat you right over here at a table by the window, best table in the room. It'll be cleaned off and set up with clean knives and forks." She led them over to the table. "Have a seat and I'll go to the kitchen and get your dinner ready."

Clyde and Sonny looked at each other with surprised grins on their faces. "Now, that's more like it," Clyde declared.

Watching from the kitchen door, Lou-Bell

grabbed Lottie's arm when she walked into the kitchen. "What did you tell them?"

"I decided the best way to handle them is to treat 'em like a couple of kings, feed 'em good and fast, and get 'em out of here as quick as we can. Don't give 'em anything to complain about."

Surprised by her plan of action, Lou-Bell was quick to remind her, "We've got a genuine U.S. Deputy Marshal settin' right across the room from them. Why don't we just tell Will to order them out of here?"

"That was my first thought, too," Lottie answered while she set two plates next to the stove and put two healthy slices of meat loaf on each one. "But those two refuse to take their guns off, and if we get Will to throw them out of here, I'm afraid there might be a gunfight. Then we would be endangering the lives of all our good customers in here. I'd rather try this approach first and save Will for the last resort."

Lou-Bell thought about it for a moment, then shrugged. "I don't know. Maybe you're right. It wouldn't be too good if it turned into a gunfight in here. But I ain't sure your idea will work on those two ignorant saddle tramps. I don't think they're housebroke."

"I'll wait on 'em if you don't wanna," Lottie suggested, even though she was of the opinion that Lou-Bell was far more bulletproof to insults and crass remarks than she was.

"Oh hell, no," Lou-Bell came back at once. "I'll serve 'em with a sweet smile, no matter how bad they misbehave." Fred came from the back sink with an empty dishpan and walked around them on his way to clear off the table by the window. "Clear off those dirty dishes, Fred, and we'll set those gents up with enough food to keep their mouths shut."

Out in the dining room, Will cleaned the last little bit of grease from his plate, using a piece of biscuit for a mop. Contrary to what Lottie and Lou-Bell thought, he was very much aware of the guns still riding in the holsters of the two rather raunchy-looking men seated at the table by the window. He knew that Lottie had a policy of no firearms in the dining room, unless you were a lawman. He was curious as to why Lottie was making an exception for them. So he decided to have another cup of coffee and stick around for a while. He made an attempt not to be obvious about his interest in the two drifters. They hadn't broken any laws that he was aware of, just refused to remove their weapons in the dining room. That was Lottie's law, but not one a deputy marshal was called upon to enforce. *Hopefully, they'll just eat and be on their way,* he thought. It didn't take long for him to find out.

"Let me clean up this table a little bit for you fellows," Fred Polk said, and started picking up the cups and dishes left on the table.

27

"Who the hell are you?" Clyde demanded, thinking the old man had been sent to wait on them since they wouldn't surrender their guns. "Where's that sassy gal that waited on us yesterday?"

"Lou-Bell," Fred replied. "I reckon she'll be servin' you. I'm just cleanin' up the table for her."

"He's just the dishwasher and the cleanin' woman, Clyde," Sonny remarked. "Ain't that right, old man?"

"I reckon you could say that," Fred answered. "I'm just tryin' to help Lottie out a little bit till she finds another dishwasher."

"We wouldn't want him handlin' our food, anyway," Sonny continued taunting the old man. "If somebody drops a dish on the floor, he has to clean it up. Ain't that right, old man?"

"I reckon I'd most likely be the one to clean it up," Fred allowed.

"Oops." Sonny grinned and slid a coffee cup to the edge of the table to let it drop off and smash into pieces. He and Clyde both chuckled as Fred tried to clear the rest of the table before any more dishes fell. "You better check this table," Sonny continued. "I don't believe it's level."

"I didn't know you was a carpenter, Sonny," Clyde blurted gleefully. "Maybe you oughta take a look at this table to see if you can see what's wrong with it." He took hold of the edge of the table and came up with it till all the remaining dishes slid off on the floor. "Sorry about that, old man. Looks like you've got a bigger mess to clean up. Come on, Sonny, we're gonna have to move to another table."

"You're gonna be movin' farther than that."

So absorbed in their harassment of an old man, neither Clyde nor Sonny was aware of the man who got up from the table in the opposite corner until they heard him speak behind them. Both turned to discover the dead-serious eyes of Will Tanner. Sonny was the first to challenge the stranger. "Mister, you'd best turn your behind around while you still can and mind your own business."

"This is my business," Will replied. "Now, you and your partner have shown everybody that you're not fit to eat with civilized folks. So both of you start walking toward that door."

Amazed, the two drifters exchanged puzzled glances before Clyde sneered, "And what if we don't? You gonna throw us out?"

"I'm gonna give you the chance to walk out of here peacefully," Will answered him, and pulled his vest aside to show his badge.

"A lawman!" Clyde exclaimed, then broke out with a grin. "This is Injun Territory. You ain't got no jurisdiction in Injun Territory. So you can just go to hell."

"I'm gonna explain this to you just one time," Will said. "This badge says I'm a U.S. Deputy

Marshal. I *am* the law in Indian Territory for every white lawbreaker like you two sorry scabs who think you can do anything you want in the Nations. That ends all the discussion we're gonna have on that subject, so start walking toward that door. You better hope you've got enough money to pay for all those dishes you broke. You're lucky that table ain't broken." He glanced at Lottie, who was standing frozen like everyone else in the dining room now. "How much are those dishes worth, Lottie?"

Still too flustered to think straight, Lottie could only stammer for a few seconds before she blurted out, "It's not that much. Just take them out of here. They don't have to pay for them."

Seeing she was too upset to think, Will asked, "Would a dollar cover it?" She said yes immediately, so Will looked back at Clyde and said, "Put a dollar on the floor beside those dishes." He could almost see the thoughts racing through the crude man's head as he snarled and raised a hand that hesitated over his holstered pistol. "Don't even think about it," Will warned, and drew his .44 to enforce the warning. He had hoped to avoid the appearance of a gun in the dining room, but Clyde had hesitated long enough to warrant his concern. "A dollar," Will reminded him.

His eyes blazing with anger, Clyde reluctantly reached in his shirt pocket and pulled out a small roll of bills. He peeled a dollar off the roll and dropped it to fall in the middle of the broken dishes, then looked defiantly at Will. "I wonder how tough you'd be if we took it outside and you faced me with that pistol back in your holster."

"That would make me as stupid as you," Will answered. "Now, I'm tired of messin' with you two, so walk right on out that door." With little choice, since his gun was already out and aimed at their backs, they did as he ordered. Once outside, he said, "I'm arrestin' you for disturbin' the peace and destruction of private property. That's three days in jail."

"Three days in jail?" Clyde exploded. "Hell, man, I paid for those broke dishes!"

"That's right," Will replied. "The jail time is just for disturbin' the peace. It woulda been five days for both counts." He let them stew over that for a few seconds, then continued. "I'll tell you what, I'm in a pretty good mood today, so I might cut you fellows a little slack. We ain't got no real jail here in Atoka, so I use the Choctaw jail, which ain't nothin' but an old smokehouse they turned into a jail. It's gonna be a little cramped up for ya, dependin' on how many drunken bucks the Choctaw policeman has in there right now. So, I'm gonna give you a choice—the Choctaw jail, or get on your horses and ride outta town right now. What's it gonna be?"

"I reckon we'll ride," Clyde said, and untied

his horse's reins and backed it away from the rail. Sonny, the silent witness to the confrontation between Clyde and the deputy marshal, was astonished by his partner's apparent surrender, especially when they had the deputy outnumbered two to one. And when Clyde's horse backed away from the rail and blocked Will's vision of him for a couple of seconds, Sonny didn't hesitate. He reached for his six-gun and raised it halfway before Will put a round into his right shoulder, causing him to drop his weapon and stagger backward several steps.

"You ain't had time to grow any common sense, have you?" Will asked. "I oughta put a round in your head, so you'd have something inside that empty space." Stunned for a few moments, Sonny clutched his wounded shoulder with his left hand. When he thought to pick up his six-gun and made a motion to do so, Will said, "Leave it right where it is. Can you ride?" Sonny didn't answer, so Will looked at Clyde and said, "Get him outta here, before I decide to throw him in that smokehouse jail and throw the damn key away." Clyde immediately went to help Sonny, and Will watched while he got the wounded man in the saddle. While Clyde was busy with that chore, Will picked up Sonny's .44 and emptied the cylinder. Then he dropped the gun into Sonny's saddlebag. "You gonna be able to take care of that wound?" Will asked.

"Nope, but I know somebody who can," Clyde answered. "Maybe we'll see you again sometime."

"Is that a threat?" Will asked, his six-gun still in his hand.

"No, it ain't no threat. I was just sayin', that's all," Clyde quickly replied.

"Get on your way, then," Will said, and stepped back out of the way. He stood there to watch them ride out of town. Near the end of the street, they passed a rider coming into town, who gave them a concentrated looking-over. Will smiled when he recognized the rider as Jim Little Eagle.

"Will Tanner," Jim called out as he pulled up next to him and slid off his horse. "One fellow back there look like he been shot. Was that you?"

"Yeah, that was me. Couple of drifters makin' trouble in Lottie's. It got outta hand, so I had to ask 'em to leave."

"You not put 'em in jailhouse?" Jim wondered.

"I'll be honest with you, Jim, I didn't wanna burden you with 'em, and I sure as hell didn't wanna take 'em with me. I didn't bring a jail wagon with me, and I've got to go on out to the Chickasaw Nation after I leave here. That's why I decided to run 'em outta town and hope they don't come back for a while."

"Better you shoot 'em. Then they don't come back," Jim said. "I hear one shot just before I get to town."

"I put a bullet in one of 'em's shoulder. He tried to go for his gun when I'm standin' there with mine in my hand. His partner said they didn't have to see the doctor, said he knew somebody who could take care of it. I don't know where he was talkin' about."

"I know where they go," Jim declared. "That's the reason I send wire to Marshal Stone and ask him to send somebody for little problem we got." Will knew Jim always asked Stone to send him, and it was usually for the sale of whiskey to the Indians.

"Has to do with those two fellows?" Will asked.

"Them and others just like them," Jim said, nodding slowly to emphasize the gravity of the problem.

"Don't tell me those women we left to operate Mama's Kitchen down the road have started sellin' whiskey, after all their promisin' to run a law-abidin' eatin' place," Will remarked. It had not been that long ago that he and Jim Little Eagle had worked together to close down an illegal saloon and whorehouse no more than three miles from Atoka. Run by a crude man named Tiny McGee, in partnership with a Texas cattle rustler named Ward Hawkins, Tiny was selling whiskey in Indian Territory to white man and Indian alike.

"No," Jim quickly assured him. "Those women do like they promise, sell food and rent rooms."

He nodded toward the door of Lottie's Kitchen. "They give them some competition. What I wire Marshal Stone about is new place. Man named Reese Trainer build cabin on Clear Boggy Creek, twelve miles east of Atoka. I think he build big house, must have big family, but he not build house. He build saloon, sell whiskey. I tell him no sell whiskey in Choctaw Nation. He tell me mind my own business. I tell him deputy marshal come to see him. He tell me mind my own business."

"I'll take a ride out that way after my horses are rested up. You ready to go with me?" Will asked. Jim said that he was and suggested that Will could leave his packhorse at his cabin, assuming that Will would camp at his place on Muddy Boggy Creek, as he often did. Will was agreeable with that, so he went back inside the dining room to pay Lottie for his dinner. She and Lou-Bell both thanked him for getting rid of their troublesome customers even though there was no guarantee they would never come back.

CHAPTER 3

Reese Trainer talked to Clyde Vickery as they both stood watching Cora Branch dig a .44 slug out of Sonny Doyle's shoulder. "She's really goin' after that bullet, ain't she?" Clyde felt inspired to comment when Sonny grimaced with clenched teeth, straining not to show the pain. "I swear, I believe she's enjoyin' herself the more Sonny bleeds."

Overhearing Clyde's comments, Cora paused a moment to look up at him. "You said you wanted the bullet out. What did you think I would do, sweet-talk that bullet outta his shoulder?" She held the slug up for them to see. "There it is."

"Reckon I coulda gone after it with my hand ax," Clyde answered, "make the job a little quicker and not much bloodier. Whaddaya think, Sonny?"

Sonny bravely showed a smile and some of the color returned to his face when he saw the bullet in Cora's hand. With new strength gained from the fact that he had endured Cora's rough operating technique without emitting a sound, he bragged that it wasn't as bad as they imagined. "I can stand a lot more pain than that little diggin' around she was doin' on my shoulder. Yow!" He howled a moment later when she poured a generous amount of whiskey in the bloody hole she had left in his shoulder. "Son of a . . ." he started but didn't finish due to the loss of his breath. "You oughta tell me when you're gettin' ready to do somethin' like that," he complained.

"We was all wantin' to see how tough you really are," Cora replied. "You needed somethin' on that wound to keep it from gettin' infected." She grinned and added, "And I was sure you couldn't stand up to cauterizin' it with a hot poker."

"How'd he come to gettin' in a gunfight with a lawman, anyway?" Reese asked Clyde.

"Lack of sense," Clyde answered. "He weren't in no gunfight. He decided he'd draw down on a man standin' there, lookin' at him with a gun in his hand, cocked and ready to fire."

Reese looked back at Sonny and shook his head, amazed. "Why did you do that?"

" 'Cause I know I'm faster than that lawman," Sonny boasted. "Tell him, Clyde, even with his gun already in his hand, I had my gun in my hand and had it halfway up when he shot me. If we started even, I'd blow him away before he knew what happened."

Reese just grinned and said, "Pour him a drink, Pug, to make up for the one Cora wasted on his shoulder. Back to Clyde then, he asked, "This lawman, did you say he was a U.S. Deputy Marshal?"

"That's what he said, and he showed us a badge," Clyde answered.

"But he just let you go? Even after Sonny tried to draw on him?" That sounded unlikely to Reese.

"He just wanted us to get outta town," Clyde said.

Pug Murphy, Trainer's bartender, interrupted with a comment. "You sure it wasn't that Injun policeman that was in here the other day? That Jim Flyin' Bird or whatever his name was. And he knew he couldn't arrest a white man."

"Nah, it weren't him," Clyde said. "We passed him comin' into town on our way out. This feller weren't no Injun."

"You didn't tell him nothin' about this place, did you? You know, tell him where you was takin' Sonny to get fixed up?"

"Didn't have no reason to," Clyde assured him. "He didn't give a damn, anyway. He just wanted us to get outta town."

"There you go, all fixed up," Cora announced, interrupting the conversation about the lawman. "You need to keep them bandages dry till that wound starts to pucker up and scab over. Right neat job, if I do say so, myself."

"How much I owe you?" Sonny asked.

"Dollar and a half," Cora answered. "Same price for goin' back to my room for a social visit."

"Too damn high for either one," Sonny grumbled, but dug into his pocket for some money.

"Just for that, the next time it'll be two

39

dollars," Cora declared, aware that he and Clyde were carrying some money from a little holdup of some kind in a Texas town. How much, she didn't know, but the holdup was big enough to cause them to run to Indian Territory to outrun a Texas posse. She looked at Clyde and winked. " 'Course, it would be the old price for you, honey." She and Reese were both intent upon separating the two outlaws from some of that money, and the only solution they could come up with at the present time was to start serving three meals a day. If they did that, there wouldn't be any reason for customers like Clyde and Sonny to ride twelve miles to Atoka to get a good meal. The problem with that was the fact that Cora had to be the cook, and Cora preferred to be a saloon hostess. It was a problem that Reese promised to fix as soon as he could find a good cook. The cheapest option was to induce an Indian woman to take over the job. But the fact that Jim Little Eagle, the Choctaw policeman, lived in the area was enough to discourage the women. In the meantime, Cora reluctantly announced that she had put on a big pot of beans to soak early that morning. And she would be serving them for supper, along with some bacon and corn bread. "That's what you need to get that shoulder healin' up real fast," she advised. She poked Reese on the arm and said, "I thought I heard your little bell."

"Yeah, I heard it," Reese answered. "I'll take

care of it." He left the barroom and walked down the hallway past the kitchen to a small room off the side of the back porch that he laughingly called his Choctaw Room. It was where the Indians came to buy firewater, and he had hung a little bell on a chain beside the door that a customer could ring for whiskey. The door was cut in half, so that the top half could be unlocked and swung open, leaving the bottom half to serve as a counter with a wide shelf built on it. Reese kept a couple of kegs of cheap whiskey in his Choctaw Room. The customer brought a container with him, usually a fruit jar, and Reese filled it with firewater. If the customer didn't have a fruit jar, Reese sold him one. It was a good business, thriving from the start, so he was doing all right. But his goal was to attract the outlaws who fled to Oklahoma Territory to escape the law. He was just getting his business started, but word should get around pretty quickly. When that happened, he knew he'd be sitting pretty. He hoped before long he could satisfy all their wicked cravings right under his roof. He would call it the Clear Boggy Social Club, he decided, but for the time being, he would sell the firewater-thirsty Indians a fruit jar at a time. These were the thoughts occupying his mind when he unlocked the top half of the door and swung it open to find Jim Little Eagle standing there.

"What the . . ." Reese blurted.

"Reese Trainer," Jim Little Eagle announced, "Deputy Marshal Will Tanner come to see you. He go in white man's door."

At about the same time Jim Little Eagle greeted Reese at the back door, Will walked in the front door to a greeting of shocked expressions on the faces of Clyde and Sonny, and open curiosity on those of Cora and Pug. "Well, howdy, stranger," Cora Branch sang out. "What would you like to drink?"

"Shut up, Cora!" Clyde whispered frantically. "He's the damn deputy marshal who shot Sonny!"

Already taking a couple of steps to meet Will, Cora immediately backed up to the table again. With her hands behind her back, she wiggled her fingers frantically until Clyde finally got the message and slid the whiskey bottle into her hand. "We've got creek water and buttermilk," she went on to announce as she skipped like a young schoolgirl across to the bar. "I'll have supper ready in half an hour. If you're hungry, a glass of cool buttermilk goes good with soup beans." With her hands still grasping the bottle behind her, she stopped when she reached the end of the bar where Pug was standing. Then, still facing Will, she wagged the bottle desperately until, finally, Pug realized what she was doing, stepped up behind her, and took the bottle from her hands and put it under the counter.

Will was tempted to give her a hand for her performance. He had to give her credit for her originality, even though he was aware of the bottle behind her back. Instead of commenting on her transfer of the bottle, he addressed Clyde and Sonny. "I see you got your wound taken care of. Looks like a pretty good job of bandagin'. You do that?" He glanced at Cora.

Before she could answer, Sonny growled, "You got your nerve, walkin' in here like this. This ain't none of your business here, and you sure as hell ain't welcome, so why don't you just back your behind right on outta here?"

"Well, I'll have to say I sure am surprised by your attitude, after I decided not to put you in jail. I really didn't expect to see you two here. I came to talk to somebody else."

"That would be me, I expect," Reese said as he opened the door in the back of the room and came into the room to join them.

"If your name is Reese Trainer, it would be," Will said.

"I'm Reese Trainer. What do you want to talk to me about?"

"You've got a nice-lookin' place here, Mr. Trainer. I just rode over from town to find out what kind of business you're plannin' on doin' here." He paused a moment when Jim Little Eagle came in the front door behind him. "Jim, here, was worried. He said he wasn't sure if you knew it was against the law to sell whiskey in the Choctaw Nation. 'Course he's worried about the harm to his Choctaw brothers, but it's illegal to sell to whites, too."

"I don't sell whiskey to anybody," Reese quickly declared.

"Well, I'm right happy to hear that," Will commented, "because when I look around here, it looks like a saloon. Fellow walkin' in off the street for the first time might have a natural impulse to order a couple of shots of rye. Tell me, Mr. Trainer, what kinda business are you plannin' to operate here?"

"Just a regular tradin' post," Reese said. "Ain't no law against that, is there?"

"No, sir. No law against openin' a tradin' post, as long as you ain't using whiskey to buy the pelts," Will answered. "I'm interested to know why you picked this spot on Clear Boggy to build your tradin' post. Never figured this part of the territory was much good for trappin'." He looked at Jim Little Eagle. "What do you think, Jim? Do your people do a lot of trappin' for fur-bearin' critters? Deer, beaver, elk, buffalo, critters like that?"

"One time, maybe," Jim answered. "Not good here now. Most game gone now."

"And that's from a fellow who knows," Will said to Reese. "You might wanna change your mind about a tradin' post before you invest any more of your money in it."

Reese stood there, undecided if Will was that naive, or playing him for a fool. Since he wasn't sure, he decided to end the foolish discussion with a final statement. "You're wastin' your time, Deputy. I ain't sellin' likker and that's the fact of the matter."

"Good," Will replied. "Glad to hear there ain't no whiskey on the premises, and if I was to search your storeroom, I wouldn't find any whiskey."

"I didn't say there ain't no whiskey on the place," Reese came back quickly. "I like a drink of likker once in a while, so I've got some for my use and some to pour a drink for my friends."

"What's your job here?" Will suddenly asked Pug, who had remained standing behind the bar, watching wide-eyed and with gaping mouth at the unexpected interrogation.

When Pug was struck dumb, unable to answer right away, Reese quickly said, "He's a clerk."

"Right, I'm a clerk," Pug echoed.

"A clerk?" Will questioned. "Let me ask you this, clerk, is there more than one bottle of whiskey under that bar you're standin' behind? Or is that bottle the lady sashayed over there with the only one?" Pug looked to be in a panic, not sure what to say. "Never mind, clerk, I think I've got a pretty good idea what's on the shelf under that bar."

"I told you," Reese blurted, "that ain't no bar."

"If this ain't no saloon, let's take a look in your storeroom," Will challenged.

"Hell, no. I don't have to show you nothin'," Reese exploded. "What I got in my storeroom is my private business."

"Today, we're gonna make it the business of the Federal Court for the Western District of Arkansas, of which I am a legally appointed representative. If you ain't got any whiskey in your storeroom, then you ain't got nothing to worry about. Right?"

At this point, the usually unflappable Jim Little Eagle was beginning to get a little on edge. Will was pushing a little too hard, he figured. There were five of them against Will and him. Even though one was wounded, and one was a woman, the odds were in their favor. Consequently, he held his rifle at the ready and waited for the first move by the outlaws. He could feel the tension in the room. Then suddenly, Reese seemed to relax a little, as if he just thought of something. "All right, Deputy, you win. You can take a look in my storeroom. Then when you see there ain't no likker bottles and there ain't no kegs of whiskey, you can get your butt and your Injun friend outta my store. Right?"

"I think that's fair enough," Will replied. "That oughta satisfy my boss and Jim Little Eagle, too. I'll wire Fort Smith and let 'em know I investigated the claim, and that'll be that."

Reese nodded, almost friendly, and led Will and Jim out the back door of the barroom, down the hall, and stopped at a padlocked door, just before the little room where the Indians were served. He unlocked the door and held it open for them to enter. "It's gettin' a little too dark to see. Wait till I light this lantern." He lit the lantern then placed it on top of a stack of crates. "Don't want you to think I'm tryin' to hide anything."

"What's in the crates?" Will asked.

"Fruit jars," Reese answered. "The Injuns buy them." He made a sweeping motion with his hand. "There, now you see there ain't really much in here, and sure as hell, there ain't no whiskey."

Will exchanged a quick glance with Jim before asking Reese a question. "You expectin' to sell the Indians a lot of molasses?"

"What?" Reese blurted at first, then quickly answered, "Yes, sir, Indians buy a lot of molasses."

"I never knew that," Will replied. "But, damn, Trainer, you've got"—he paused and started counting—"fourteen kegs of molasses," he totaled. "Jim, you never told me you Indians love molasses. I'm gonna have to buy a little bit of that. I wanna see why they like it so much." He smiled at Reese, who was obviously in a state of shock. "Let's open one of those kegs and take a sample." Like Jim Little Eagle, Will was again thinking about the raid the two of them performed on Tiny McGee's saloon and the wagonload of whiskey kegs they destroyed, all disguised as molasses. "That one over there, layin' on its side, has got a tap in it. I woulda thought molasses was too thick to draw out of a tap. Shows you what I know. Jim, hand me one of those jars outta those crates."

"Hold on!" Reese exclaimed. "That keg's empty. It had water in it. That's the reason it's got a tap in it." He tried to fake a chuckle. "No, you wouldn'ta got any molasses out of that barrel. Come on, we'll go back in the store and get Cora to fix us up some coffee and somethin' to eat."

Will held out his hand for the jar Jim was still holding, and when he took it from him, he placed it under the tap and opened it, while keeping a steady eye on Trainer. He was not at all sure how the man was going to react. Reese, too stunned to react at that moment, could only stare at the tap and the jar that rapidly began to fill with rye whiskey, realizing now how pitifully weak his bluff had been. Unnoticed by him, Jim moved quietly over between him and the door, as Will sniffed the contents of the jar before taking a sip of it. "I ain't an expert on whiskey, but I'd say this is rye. Am I right?" Like a rat caught in a trap, Reese backed away toward the door, only to bump into Jim. He turned to see the condemning gaze of the Choctaw policeman, and when he turned back to face Will, he found the deputy holding his Colt .44 on him. "This is the risk you take when you break the law and bring whiskey into the Nations. We've got to empty every one of these kegs, and I'm gonna have to place you under arrest, and you'll stand trial for possession and sales of alcohol in Indian Territory. You'll wait in the jail until a jail wagon can be sent to transport you to Fort Smith." He looked at Jim and said, "I'm assumin' Sam Barnet ain't changed his mind about using that jail I made outta that railroad buildin'."

"No, he change his mind," Jim replied. "You have to use Choctaw jail. Barnet say shoot too many holes in railroad building."

"Wait! Wait!" Reese exclaimed, hardly able to believe it was happening. "I could make it worthwhile for you and the Indian." He looked frantically back and forth between the two lawmen, but there was no response from either. "I could cut you in for a percentage of all my sales, both of you. We can make a fortune, and all you'd have to do is look the other way. All I'm tryin' to do is make it possible for a man to enjoy a drink of likker, if that's his pleasure. Where's the crime in that?"

"Firewater make Choctaw man crazy and good for nothing," Jim Little Eagle said, answering his question. "Wife and children have nothing to eat while drunk Indian lay in cabin all day."

Totally frantic now, Reese pleaded. "I can't go to jail. Everything I own is here in this building. What will happen to all my possessions?"

"That's the risk you took when you decided to defy the law," Will replied. "You gambled and you lost. Why is it always such a damn surprise to men like you? I'm tempted to bust all these kegs open right here, throw a match in it, and burn this place down."

Past desperation at this point, Reese tried another tack. "There's four people in the other room that ain't gonna sit still and watch you destroy all that whiskey and haul me off to jail. That whiskey represents a lot of money."

"Yeah, that is a risk that we're takin'," Will conceded, and it was one he was already giving a lot of thought to, since he spotted a coil of rope lying in the corner on the floor. "So, I think I'm gonna hog-tie you right here with your precious barrels while Jim and I go talk to your friends. Put your hands behind your back."

"What if I refuse to?" Reese asked, in one last act of defiance.

"Then you'd be doin' me a favor," Will answered. "That would give me cause to shoot you and save me a helluva lot of trouble. I wouldn't have to take you to jail or have you transported all the way back to Fort Smith. So, go ahead and solve my problems for me."

While Will held his gun on Reese, Jim tied his hands behind his back. Then Will holstered his .44 and helped Jim tie Reese's hands and feet together. Once they were satisfied he was securely tied, Will said, "We'll go back to the other room and talk to the others." Reese made no reply, but he was thinking there was a better-than-average chance that the deputy and his Indian friend were going to find a welcoming party waiting for them. Sonny and Clyde had ample motivation to gain revenge on the deputy. And he was confident that Pug and Cora would join forces with them and cause the disappearance of another deputy marshal in Indian Territory.

Will was pretty much of the same opinion, so when they got outside the storeroom, he told Jim to walk silently, "Like an Indian," he said. Then instead of going back up the hallway, they slipped out the back door and went around the building to the front door. Will's hunch paid off, for as they quietly opened the door, it was to discover all four waiting for the hallway door to open. Clyde and Sonny were poised with six-guns drawn, Pug had a shotgun leveled at the door, while Cora was eagerly awaiting the show. Using hand signals, Will directed Jim to cover the bartender with the shotgun while he took on the two drifters. His reasoning was simple. He was fast enough to have a chance to stop both outlaws, if they chose to fight, especially since Sonny's right shoulder was wounded. If Pug was fast enough, or lucky enough to turn and get off a shot at that close range, both he and Jim would likely catch enough shot to do some serious damage. Consequently,

Will felt that with Jim concentrating on the one man, he had the best chance of stopping him.

When he felt they were ready, and all four were still staring at the hallway door, with no idea there was anyone behind them, Will silently mouthed the word *Ready?* Jim nodded. "Drop your weapons on the floor!" Will demanded. All four acted as one, turning at once, guns still in hand. There was no time for second chances. Will's first shot caught Clyde in the side and dropped him immediately. His second slammed Sonny in the chest, causing him to stagger backward several steps and get off one shot before he collapsed. Fortunately for Will, Sonny's shot was wide of the mark, the shot fired with the gun in his left hand. There was no time for Will to see what was going on between Jim and the bartender. But he and Jim were still standing, and when he did have time to turn and look, he saw Pug on the floor beside his shotgun. He looked at Cora Branch then to find her seemingly stunned, but that didn't last for long.

"Well, that turned out real good, didn't it, Deputy?" she managed to ask after a few moments. "What did you do with Reese? Have you already killed him? Makes it a helluva lot easier than havin' to arrest 'em and lock 'em up, don't it?"

"I gave them the opportunity to drop their guns and surrender," Will told her. "They chose to have it their way, so we had no choice but to accommodate their wishes to go to hell. You're lucky you weren't holdin' a gun."

"You'd shoot a woman?" She hurled it at him as an insult.

"Quicker'n a cat can blink his eye," he answered. "So if you wanna walk away from this mess, you'd best not get any big ideas about settlin' the score. They made a mistake when they decided to defy the law. If you don't make the same mistake, you've got nothin' more to worry about from me."

"What are you plannin' to do with me?" she asked when she realized he really might not be thinking about locking her up.

"I'm not plannin' to do anything with you. As far as I know, you just worked for Trainer. You ain't his partner, are you?" She shook her head. "That's what I figured, so I've got no reason to arrest you. I don't have any facilities to handle women prisoners in Atoka, anyway."

"Could I just stay on here, then?"

"If you want to," he said. "Just as long as you ain't sellin' whiskey. And by the way, that whiskey in the storeroom ain't gonna be here when we leave. I wouldn't recommend a woman livin' in a cabin like this alone, but that's up to you."

"Well, I've gotta say that's mighty decent of you, Deputy Tanner. I 'preciate you givin' me a chance to get on with my life."

"Good luck with it," Will said. "Maybe you can find a better class of people to hang around with." He looked at Jim then and said, "We've got some work to do now. Let's see if Mr. Trainer is doin' all right and we'll just leave him tied up till we get all that whiskey outta there and dumped."

That caught Cora's attention at once. "Are you sayin' Reese is still alive?"

"I never said he wasn't," Will replied. "He's goin' to jail and he'll stand trial for bringin' whiskey into Indian Territory to sell. Are you still serious about stayin' here in this place? 'Cause if you're not, I'm thinkin' about burnin' it down, so nobody else comes along with the same idea Trainer had."

"Yes," Cora quickly answered, "I'm gonna make a home out of it."

Will shook his head, not at all confident that the woman could make a go of it. "All right, then, we'll roll those kegs outside and empty 'em on the ground."

Leaving Cora to finish cooking the supper she had started before they made their appearance, Will and Jim went back to the storeroom and started pushing the whiskey kegs over on their sides and rolling them off the back porch. They had hoped the five-foot drop off the porch might cause the kegs to split, but that was not the case. The heavy barrels landed with a thud and bounced before rolling into a low spot before the creekbank, where they settled. After seeing that the kegs were not going to break apart, Will went back to the storeroom and picked up a brace and bit he had seen on a shelf. There was a trick to removing the cork from the bunghole of the barrel, but neither Will nor Jim knew what it was. So he decided to take the brace and bit and bore a hole in the cork and pull it out. The process worked, so they continued rolling the barrels to the porch, removing the corks, and dropping them off the porch.

Inside, in the kitchen, Cora's mind was racing with many thoughts. One that troubled her was the idea of remaining there alone. She had been honest when she told Will she would be all right there by herself. But now that she knew Reese was not dead, she was thinking it would be better to have a man with her, any man, even one as evil as Reese Trainer. She considered slipping into the storeroom and untying him but knew that was too risky with Will and Jim going in and out of the room as they rolled the barrels to the porch. Then it struck her that if she could free him before they destroyed all the whiskey barrels, he would surely take her with him, wherever he went. With that in mind, she went into Trainer's office and took his Colt revolver out of the top drawer. *Take care of the deputy marshal first,* she thought, *and the Indian would be easy to handle.*

This is a tough one, Will thought as he sat

astride the barrel working with the brace and bit until he bored a hole all the way through it. Then he worked the tool back and forth until he broke the cork free and pulled it out of the bunghole. He backed off the barrel and started it rolling toward the edge of the porch. He stood up straight then, as he watched it go over the edge. About to turn around to take the next barrel, he was suddenly startled by the shot right behind him. He turned quickly, drawing his six-gun as he turned, and confronted Cora Branch, her arm extended, aiming a revolver straight at him. Instead of pulling the trigger, however, she released the gun and let it drop to the floor. She remained standing in that position until seconds later, when she collapsed, shot through the head. Only then did he discover Jim Little Eagle standing behind her, his Colt, Army model .44 still pointed at the fallen woman. "She was fixin' to shoot you," the Choctaw policeman explained. "No time to stop her."

Realizing how close he came to being shot, Will said, "She sure as hell was."

CHAPTER 4

Will walked over to the body to make sure Cora was dead. There was little question of it, judging by the bullet hole just above her temple on one side and the ragged exit hole on the other. It was an unexpected ending to this grim business. He had not come with the intention to kill anyone. His intent was to arrest Reese Trainer and destroy the illegal whiskey. He had no idea that Clyde and Sonny were there. Thinking about it now as he looked at the woman's body, he could not honestly believe he could have prevented the killing. He decided then that it would be best to go with his first idea to burn the whole place down, lest someone else might be tempted to use it for the same purpose Trainer had. With that decided, he took hold of Cora's wrists and dragged her back into the barroom, where the bodies of Clyde, Sonny, and Pug were. *Might as well have a community funeral pyre,* he thought.

He went back to the porch and found Jim still standing in the same place he had been when he came upon Cora with her gun aimed at him. Jim said nothing, but Will sensed the Choctaw policeman was upset by his part in the events that had just happened. It occurred to him that Jim might be upset because he had been forced to

57

kill a woman. Then it struck him that the Indian might be concerned because he had killed a white woman, and not only that, he had killed a white man as well. Indian policemen had no authority to kill, or even arrest, a white person, and they would be severely punished for doing either. He decided he'd better try to set Jim's mind at ease.

"I need to thank you, Jim. There ain't no doubt you saved my life today, and I'll never forget it. And if you're worried a-tall about the fact that she, and the bartender, are white folks, don't give it another thought. I officially deputized you to help me on this job, so you didn't have any restrictions on who you shot. Matter of fact, when I make my report, I won't say who actually killed who." From the look of relief on Jim's face, he knew he had guessed right. "Let's just roll the rest of those barrels into the saloon."

Acutely aware of what was going on, even though tied hand and foot in the storeroom, Reese Trainer struggled in vain against his bonds. The anger he felt upon being arrested was rapidly being overcome by the fear of losing his life. The last gunshot he heard had come from the back porch, and he was certain the victim had been Cora Branch. They had ruthlessly killed everyone but him, and there was no reason to think he would not be next. He heard them roll six barrels off the back porch, but now he could hear them rolling the rest of the barrels up the hallway toward the barroom. It was obvious they intended to burn his building down, and he was afraid that his execution was to be by fire as well. The thought caused him to struggle against his ropes again, and again to no avail. The only weapon left to him was a defiant front, which he found difficult to employ under the circumstances. Still, he tried. When Will came back into the room to get another barrel, Reese said, "Execution is too stiff a penalty for sellin' whiskey. You don't have the right to kill me for bringin' that whiskey here."

"I never said I was gonna kill you," Will said. "I told you, you're under arrest. You're goin' to jail."

"That's hard to believe, after the way you killed everybody else here," Reese charged. "And they didn't have nothin' to do with sellin' whiskey."

"That *was* damn unnecessary," Will allowed, "but that was their own doin'. They didn't give us a choice. I told them to drop their guns and surrender, but they chose suicide. I had no reason to charge any of them until they tried to kill Jim and me." He hesitated a moment, then decided to continue, in case it might mean something to him. "It was only the three men who were waitin' in ambush for Jim and me to come back in the room. The woman didn't have a gun, so I let her go, told her she could do what she wanted to. But she got hold of a gun and decided to rescue you,

I reckon. That's the only reason she got shot." He watched Reese's facial expression and decided Cora's attempt to come to his aid meant nothing to the outlaw.

With a renewed feeling of hope now that Will convinced him he was not to be executed on the spot, Reese asked, "Are you going to haul me all the way to Fort Smith?"

"I'm not gonna take you there. I've got some more business to take care of. I'll wire Fort Smith to send a jail wagon over here to pick you up, and you'll be in the Choctaw jail till it gets here."

"I've seen that place," Reese blurted. "That's not even a jail. That's a damn smokehouse!"

"It used to be a smokehouse," Will allowed, "but now, it's the official Choctaw jail and Jim Little Eagle will see that you're well taken care of. Right, Jim?"

"I take good care of you," Jim assured him. "Make you fat and happy till jail wagon come."

"There, ya see," Will said, "Jim'll take care of you. I reckon I could have rented a room for you at Doug Mabry's roomin' house, next door to Lottie's Kitchen. But I'm afraid Doug might not take as gooda care of you as Jim will."

Reese was not amused, his mind working now on the possibility of escape, since he was reasonably sure he was not going to be executed. "How long are you gonna keep me tied up like this?"

"No longer than right now, I reckon," Will

answered. "I don't see any reason to keep you hog-tied, now that there's nobody else we have to worry about. I think I'll let you out of the storeroom now." He walked out the front door and returned a minute later with a pair of handcuffs. He untied Reese's hands and clamped one wrist in the cuffs, then he untied his feet and pulled him up. With both his and Jim's guns drawn, they marched him into the saloon, where Will sat him on the floor in front of the bar and closed the other handcuff around the brace that attached the footrail to the bar. "There you go. You can just sit there and relax while you watch Jim and me test your whiskey to see if it's watered down or not."

So, under Reese Trainer's gut-sick gaze, barrel after barrel was rolled into the saloon and the bungholes opened. Soon there was a strong fog of whiskey fumes filling the room as the barrels were emptied on the barroom floor. "You damn fool!" Reese finally barked. "You make one tiny spark and this room's gonna be a ball of fire!"

"You know, I expect he's right," Will said to Jim as he rolled the last barrel in and parked it next to the others. "I feel like I'm gettin' drunk just breathin' this stuff. Maybe you oughta take the horses down to that little stable with their horses. I'll stay here and keep an eye on Mr. Trainer." Jim, already thinking along the same lines, didn't bother to comment but turned immediately and went out the front door. At this point, Will was not really sure how volatile the great quantity of whiskey was, but he knew he'd best be cautious when he tried to set it afire. They had already taken the precaution to remove all the firearms and ammunition they could find before they started rolling the barrels. "I reckon I'd better move you," he told Reese when he noticed a little rivulet of whiskey running toward the bar where he was sitting. Not certain how big a reaction he was going to cause, he decided to risk it, took a lantern sitting on the bar, and tossed it into the middle of the barrels. An explosion of flames flared almost to his feet, reaching up to the ceiling. "Damn!" he barked in shocked surprise, and hurried to unlock Reese from the footrail. With his gun against the shaken prisoner's back, and his other hand holding the back of his collar, he hustled him out the front door, dodging churning circles of flame as the fire fed on the fumes in the air.

Outside, they met Jim Little Eagle running to meet them, having been shocked by the sudden explosion. "Will, I think you blown up for sure!" he gasped excitedly.

"I thought I was, too, for a moment back there, but it looks like Trainer, here, was plannin' to sell hundred-proof whiskey. That stuff would be like drinkin' dynamite. Let me find Mr. Trainer a comfortable tree and I'll go see if we can light those barrels in the backyard." He led Reese, who was still in somewhat of a daze, over to a small tree and handcuffed his hands around the trunk.

The new lumber used to build Reese's saloon caught up fairly rapidly as the fire aggressively spread into the smaller rooms and the roof. There was no doubt that the building would be consumed. Using a flaming piece of a rafter, the six barrels in the yard were ignited, making the destruction complete. There was the question now about what to do with the weapons, ammunition, horses, and anything else of value. Jim was not surprised when Will told him to take what he wanted. That was what he usually did, occasionally keeping some extra ammunition for himself, or one of the horses, if he needed an extra packhorse. This was one of the reasons Jim was always eager to work with Will. As for Will, he was of the opinion that Jim earned it. "It might be worthwhile to take a good look in that little barn where the horses are," Will suggested to Jim. "Might be a waste of time, but it strikes me as kinda strange how Trainer sat there watchin' us set his business on fire and he never said anything about any money gettin' burnt up. Makes me a little suspicious. If he's got some money hid somewhere, he must think it ain't in no danger from the fire. So maybe he's got a hidin' place somewhere in that barn."

That piqued Jim's interest at once. "Twenty-dollar rule?" he asked.

"Yep, twenty-dollar rule. We ain't tryin' to recover any big cash from a robbery, so we'll use that rule today."

"I look that barn over good," Jim said with a wide grin. "I think maybe you change that rule now that you have wife to support."

"That's right," Will responded. "I forgot about that. I still ain't used to the idea. But we'll use the rule on this job." Jim Little Eagle had thrived on the twenty-dollar rule. It was a practice that Will's boss, Daniel Stone, would raise hell over, if he knew about it. Whenever Will and Jim worked together to apprehend lawbreakers, if there was unclaimed money left on the scene, Jim got the first twenty dollars of it for himself. Everything over that twenty was split between the two of them. It never amounted to much, but it helped to supplement the modest income of a deputy marshal and it was a considerable boost to Jim's wealth. In Will's opinion, it was well deserved. He got along well with most of the Indian policemen, but he had worked very closely with Jim on a number of occasions. "You can go ahead and look that barn over if you want. I'll watch the fire and the prisoner. It's gonna be a while yet before I'll feel safe in leavin' it. We might as well eat the beans and corn bread that woman started to fix. Before it got too hot to get in there, I got the pot of beans and the corn bread she had already mixed up ready to put in the oven. There's a fryin' pan in my packs. We'll just fry it."

It was well into the shank of the evening by the time Will felt it safe to leave the smoldering remains of the saloon. So it was after midnight by the time they returned to Atoka, and later yet by the time they released Reese into the crude, dark smokehouse that served as the Choctaw jail. It was a bitter man who stood patiently while Will removed his handcuffs, with Jim holding his rifle on him. "Your eyes will adjust to the darkness in a little while," Will told him. "There's a cot straight ahead of you against the far wall, and a little table with a candle on it at the head of it. There's some matches beside it. We'll get you a bucket of water and a waste bucket, and I'll make arrangements with Lottie to feed you till you get picked up to go to Fort Smith. Jim'll take care of you while I'm gone."

"What else is livin' in here?" Reese asked as he looked around him, trying to see as much of his surroundings as he could. As late as it was, there was not much he could see with only the faint light provided by the open door. "This ain't no fit place to lock up a man," Reese complained. "There's gotta be a more humane place to lock me up. Hell, I give you my word, I won't try to escape. You can handcuff my hands around a tree all night. I won't give you no trouble."

"Ya see, Trainer, the trouble is your word ain't no good," Will replied, "like when you told me you didn't sell whiskey. I'm sure you see what I mean, an intelligent man like yourself. Now, I'm fixin' to close this door, so you'd best get your candle lit."

When he saw that his humble pleading fell on deaf ears, Reese dropped the pretense. "You're a dead man, Tanner! You just ain't realized it yet."

Will locked the padlock on the door. "He seems comfortable enough," he said to Jim Little Eagle. "I expect Mary might be limberin' up her tommyhawk, waitin' for you to come home."

"She be all right when I show her this," Jim replied. He held up the small roll of bills he found under a floorboard of Trainer's barn. It added up to thirty-seven dollars and represented quite a bonus for the Choctaw policeman. With their prisoner locked away, Jim rode back to his cabin on Muddy Boggy Creek while Will made his camp on the creek close to town.

One of the first customers to arrive at Lottie's Kitchen the next morning, Will was ready for breakfast. While he was there, he made arrangements with Lottie to provide meals for his prisoner in the jail. It was nothing new for Lottie, having done it before more than once. When he finished breakfast, he took Trainer's breakfast with him and he found Jim Little Eagle waiting for him at the jail. "I don't see any tommyhawk bruises on your head," Will joked.

"No trouble," Jim said. "She say she enjoy peace and quiet. Said stay longer next time."

Will laughed, picturing the tiny Choctaw woman, then he turned his attention back to the prisoner. "Here's what I think you oughta do with this particular prisoner. I brought you my extra pair of handcuffs. I think it'd work out best if you bring him outside to eat his meals. Handcuff one hand to this iron rod on the door latch and he can sit down on this crate and eat his breakfast." He nodded toward a wooden crate that had been left beside the building. "He oughta like a chance to come outside for a little while. And it'll make it easier for you to go in the jail to empty his buckets with him out of the way. Also, it'll be better for anybody from Lottie's who might bring him his meals. They won't have to go inside. Whaddaya think?"

Jim nodded up and down. "That sound like good idea."

So Will pulled the wooden crate over to the door and set the breakfast tray on it. Then he took Jim's key and unlocked the padlock, opened the door, and with his pistol in hand, told Reese to step up to the door. Groggy from his short night in the dark enclosure, Reese stepped up to the door, squinting his eyes against the early-morning light. "We're gonna let you eat your breakfast outside," Will told him. "Stick out your left hand." When he did, Will locked one of the cuffs around his wrist and led him out the door. He then closed the other handcuff around the rod on the door latch. He picked up the breakfast tray and said. "Sit down and eat your breakfast. You don't get first-class service like this in any other jail. Jim will continue to make it easy on you as long as you behave yourself." Reese made no reply but sat down on the crate so Will could set the tray in his lap. Eating with one hand, he eagerly attacked the breakfast prepared by Lottie's Kitchen. Although there were many threats he wanted to make, he was wise enough to realize he would most likely lose the momentary freedom from the dark smokehouse if he did.

After Reese was back inside his prison, Will thanked Jim Little Eagle for taking the responsibility for him and left him then to go to the telegraph office to wire Fort Smith for a jail wagon. He returned to tell Jim that Dan Stone promised to send a deputy with a wagon just as soon as he could. Normally, Will would have transported Reese back on a horse, but the second problem Will was sent to investigate was in the Chickasaw Nation, near the Red River. It was in a little settlement called Waurika, over a hundred miles west of Atoka. As best he could figure, it would take him two and a half days to get there from Atoka, maybe three, because he needed to get more supplies. And he was getting a late start to begin with. So he decided to restock his supplies in Tishomingo at Dewey Sams's store, about thirty-five miles away. By the time he climbed up into the saddle to ride, it was already so late in the morning that he was tempted to wait a little longer and have one more good meal at Lottie's. But he nudged Buster instead, and the big buckskin gelding started immediately at a comfortable pace.

When he reached Tishomingo, the capital of the Chickasaw Nation, his first stop was the cabin of Chickasaw policeman Tom Spotted Horse. The stop was only a common courtesy to let Tom know he was operating in his nation. For some reason Will had never been able to determine, Tom Spotted Horse was an unfriendly sort who seemed to hold a resentment for the deputy marshal's authority over him. For that reason, Will had restricted his contact with the short, broad-shouldered Chickasaw to no more than notification that he was in his area. When he came to Tom's cabin outside of town, he was pleased to find the policeman was not home. So Will told Tom's wife, Sarah Little Foot, to let her husband know he was just passing through town. "I tell," was all Sarah said. She, like her husband, had no use for the white deputy marshal. Will couldn't help thinking of the contrast between Tom's wife and Jim Little Eagle's wife, Mary Light Walker.

Mary would have insisted that she should fix him something to eat. He uttered half a chuckle when he thought about it. He was probably going to be in for a scolding the next time he saw Mary, because he didn't stop in this time. That thought carried over when he rode back into town and stopped at Dewey Sams's store. Dewey's wife, Melva, was as gracious as Sarah was rude. He had a short visit with them before he packed his coffee, flour, bacon, salt, and hardtack. He then continued on toward Waurika.

CHAPTER 5

It was close to midday when Will approached the little settlement called Waurika. It could hardly be called a town. There was a blacksmith, a stable, a harness shop, and a post office, all gathered around a trading post, operated by Jordan Hatfield and his wife, a Chickasaw woman named Bright Dawn. It was a sleepy-looking little settlement, he thought, as he directed Buster toward the large two-story building bearing a sign that read, HATFIELD'S. *That makes it easier,* he thought, since he figured he was going to have to search for the author of the letter he carried in his saddlebags. Buster pulled up at the hitching rail in front of the building and Will stepped down from the saddle. He wrapped his reins loosely around the rail, then took another look around him before stepping up on the wide front porch.

"Howdy, stranger," a large man with curly gray hair greeted him. "What can I do for you today?"

"Howdy," Will returned, and held up the letter for him to see. "I've got a letter here from Jordan Hatfield. It was sent to the U.S. Marshal in Fort Smith, Arkansas. I'm wonderin' if you can tell me where I might find Mr. Hatfield."

His announcement fairly astonished the man

behind the counter. "Lord in heaven, I don't believe it," he declared. "Are you from the marshals' office?"

"Yes, sir, I am. I'm Deputy Marshal Will Tanner." Guessing from the man's reactions, he felt sure in asking, "Are you Jordan Hatfield?"

"I am!" Hatfield replied excitedly. "When those boys had me send that letter, I never thought we'd ever hear anything back from it. And I sure as hell didn't think a U.S. Deputy Marshal would show up here, especially today."

"Sorry it took so long," Will said. "We're spread kinda thin, and it's a big territory. You say you've got some trouble with cattle rustlers?" He wondered just what the trouble might be, since Hatfield was obviously a store owner and not a rancher.

"Like I said, I wrote the letter and sent it off for some of my customers who are pretty good at raisin' cattle, but not so good at writin' letters." He paused then when a cheerful-looking little Indian woman walked into the room and he turned to address her at once. "Dawn, honey, this man is a U.S. Deputy Marshal, come to answer my letter." Back to Will then, he said, "Deputy, this is my wife, Bright Dawn."

"Ma'am," Will said, and tipped his hat. Like her husband, she seemed very excited. Turning his attention back to Hatfield again, he asked, "You say you wrote the letter for some ranchers around here? How can I find them?"

Hatfield looked at his wife and they both laughed. Will was beginning to think they thought it some kind of joke. "You ain't gonna believe this, Deputy, but there's a meetin' right here this afternoon for the four ranchers who have been hit the hardest. And here you show up right on time for the meetin'. If that ain't the dad-burnedest thing I ever heard of. They ain't gonna believe it. We'd all given up on the marshals and the Texas Rangers, too. So, mister, you're mighty welcome. They was hopin' for a whole company of deputies or Rangers, but I hope they'll appreciate the trouble you took to come out here all by yourself."

"And the meetin's this afternoon?" Will asked.

"That's right. They had one meetin' before this," Hatfield said. "They had that one at night, after all the chores were done, and one of 'em lost cattle that night. So this one's at two o'clock this afternoon, so they can be home to try to watch their cows tonight."

"I reckon that makes sense," Will commented. "If that clock is right, it's almost twelve-thirty now, so I'll take care of my horses and fix a little something to eat for dinner. You don't happen to sell dinner, I reckon."

"No, sir, we don't," Hatfield replied. "But we were fixin' to eat when you rode up, and Dawn always cooks up too much. That's the reason my belly's as big as it is. Why don't you just have some dinner with us? You fix enough stew, honey?"

"I fix enough to feed three more people," Bright Dawn answered. "What you wanna drink?"

That was what he was hoping to hear. "I'm partial to coffee, if that's what you're havin', but water will do, if you don't drink coffee."

"I make big pot of coffee," she said.

"I'll be glad to pay you for my dinner," Will offered, but his offer was refused. Things were working out in his favor. He hoped the woman could cook good stew. "Well, thank you kindly for your hospitality. I'll go give my horses a rest and a drink of water, and I'll be right back." He went back outside and led his horses down behind the store, which was only a dozen yards from a lively little stream. He pulled Buster's saddle off and unloaded the sorrel's packs. Then he hobbled the sorrel, but left Buster free, knowing the buckskin wouldn't wander off anywhere without him. Then he went back and tied a lead rope on both horses to restrict the distance they could move after he noticed a vegetable garden between the back porch and the stream. He figured it wouldn't do for his horses to get into that garden.

Bright Dawn turned out to be a good cook, and the stew proved to be as good as he had ever had anywhere else. He figured the vegetable garden between the back porch and the stream had a lot to do with the taste of the stew. After dinner was over, Bright Dawn cleared the table, but Hatfield and Will remained seated, since this was where the meeting was to be held. Hatfield began to paint a general picture of the trouble the small ranchers were suffering as a result of a gang of rustlers from Texas. "To me, it seems pretty obvious how these rustlers are workin'," Hatfield said. "They ain't crossin' the Red and drivin' a man's entire herd back into Texas and wipin' him out. That ain't their style. The way they do it is they just cut out part of a man's herd. That way, they don't put him outta business. They leave him some cows to raise and build up his herd again, so he thinks they won't be back. There's enough small ranches around here that the rustlers can cut out a portion here, a portion from another ranch, and so on until they have enough to drive to market in Fort Worth. I suspect they've got some bigger outfits they're robbin' on the Texas side of the river. Indian Territory is just gravy for them."

"That sounds like a regular steady business for somebody," Will commented. "They've got your friends raisin' cattle for them to take to market and collect the money for 'em."

"That's what it amounts to," Hatfield said. "They work over the brands with their Full Moon brand. That's what they actually call it. It's just a big round brand that burns out the real brand."

"And you don't know who's actually stealin' the cattle?" Will asked.

"I do and I don't," Hatfield replied. "We're pretty sure who's behind it, but we ain't sure who's actually doin' the rustling." The conversation was interrupted then with the arrival of one of the participating ranchers. Hatfield saw him through the open door and yelled, "We're in the kitchen, John, come on back."

"Am I the first one here?" John Dillard asked, but paused when he saw Will sitting at the table.

"Yep," Hatfield answered, "you're the first. This is Will Tanner. He's gonna sit in today. Will, this is John Dillard, owns a ranch three miles from here."

"Mr. Dillard," Will greeted him, and shook his hand. He figured Hatfield wanted to wait and tell everybody at once who he was and why he was at the meeting, so he was fine with that.

Dillard gave him a friendly nod, then announced to Hatfield, "I saw Clayton coming down the west road. He'll be here in a minute or two. As he said, Clayton Hill arrived shortly after and got the same introduction to Will that Dillard had gotten.

Bright Dawn made another big pot of coffee, while the men made small talk, awaiting the other members of their little group. She took a pan of biscuits out of the oven and placed it in the middle of the table with a jar of molasses. Her efforts were cheered by the men already seated at the table when the last two came in. "I told you Bright Dawn would bake some biscuits and I didn't wanna be late for the coffee," Sonny Wiggins complained to his brother.

His brother started to respond but stopped to stare at Will. "I know you!" he exclaimed, and looked at his brother. "We know him!" Back at Will, he said, "You're that deputy marshal that captured Ward Hawkins. You remember us? I'm Cal Wiggins and that's my brother, Sonny."

"I sure do," Will answered with a grin. "You're the ones who were fixin' to shoot me one night. Will Tanner's the name. You told me how to find the Hawkins ranch, so I reckon I oughta tell you I'm much obliged for your help. I was lucky to get Ward Hawkins away from there."

His planned surprise already sprung at this point, Jordan Hatfield got to his feet and made his announcement anyway. "This is U.S. Deputy Marshal Will Tanner and he's come out here from Fort Smith in answer to your letter." That served to generate a buzz of conversation among the small group of ranchers. And it also caused Cal and Sonny to repeat the story about the night they came upon Will's camp and mistook him for a cattle rustler.

"I heard you arrested Ward Hawkins," Cal said, "and you killed Lemuel and Arlie Hawkins when they came after you. Now Fanny Hawkins ain't got but one son left, Caleb."

Clayton Hill, by nature a skeptical man, was as surprised as the others to hear who Will was and why he showed up at Hatfield's today. He listened patiently to the Wiggins brothers reciting the story of their first meeting with the deputy marshal until he got a chance to speak. "That was a helluva thing, goin' into Fanny Hawkins's stronghold and arresting her oldest son. But I don't see how one deputy marshal ridin' out here is gonna stop that gang of outlaws from rustlin' our cattle. There ain't no doubt who's leadin' that gang of rustlers—Fanny Hawkins. That old witch has been givin' the orders ever since the old man died. Everybody knows that and the work was bein' done by her three sons, but nobody was able to catch 'em in the act. Now she ain't got but one son left, but we're still missin' cattle, so she musta got some men to take their place." He paused to look directly at Will. "Now, don't get me wrong, Deputy, I appreciate the fact that you rode all the way out here from Fort Smith to try to help. I'm just sayin' it's a waste of time sendin' you out here by yourself. We need a troop of deputies, if we're ever gonna stop them from ridin' across the Red to rustle our cattle."

"Well, I can see why you feel that way, Mr. Hill," Will said. "And I'm sorry we ain't got a standin' army of deputies available for times like these. But I'd like to take a look at the situation and see if there's anything we can do right away to stop the rustlin'. Which one of you has gone the longest without gettin' raided?"

"I reckon I have," Clayton Hill answered.

Will smiled. "I can see why you were doin' the talkin'. What kinda shape is your herd in?"

"They're in good shape. I had a good breedin' season and I've made up a lot for the cows I lost last season when they cut out fifty head."

"Is that a typical number they steal?" Will asked. When they all nodded, he said, "I understand now how Fanny Hawkins was operatin' with just her sons doin' the stealin'. They just cut out what they could handle. So now, you're thinkin' it's about time your turn came up again, right?"

"That's what I'm thinkin'," Clayton answered.

"Have you seen any sign of anybody lookin' your herd over lately?"

"No, I haven't," Clayton said. The question seemed to irritate him. "I can't set out there and watch for anybody snoopin' around. I don't have a crew workin' my farm, none of us do. That's why we joined up to help each other. When the cattle are ready for market, we drive 'em all together."

"That sounds like a good plan," Will said. He was getting the picture now. These men were farmers, basically, with a partial investment in raising cattle. They were easy pickings for the cattle rustlers. "I'd like to see if I couldn't do a little scoutin' and maybe catch somebody checkin' on your herd, since yours is likely to be the next target."

Clayton shrugged indifferently. "Fine, but it might be a waste of your time, if they decide to raid somebody else's cows."

"Ain't nothin' guaranteed," Will replied. "But I agree with your thinkin'. The odds sound like your cattle might be the next on their list." When Clayton still looked less than enthusiastic about it, Will said, "I came out here to see if I can do anything to help. I ain't gonna be in your way. I'll make my own camp. Just tell me who have I got to look out for from your house. Who helps you run your farm?" When Clayton told him all the work was done by himself and his two boys, aged fourteen and twelve, then Will knew who was supposed to be around the cattle. "Good enough," he said. "I'll start at your place tonight."

With that settled, there was a sense of optimism from the group of small-time ranchers, in spite of Clayton Hill's pessimism. It was hard to expect one deputy to put a stop to all the rustling, primarily because the rustlers were in Texas, and Will had no authority there. But he had responded, and they appreciated that. So the meeting continued to address the original purpose it had been called for. And that was to discuss the possibility of raising their cattle together in one large herd, share the work and the guarding of the herd, and split the profit equally. The general objection was the fear of losing their crops if so much of their time would be spent taking care of the cattle. Also, there was a reluctance to lose their work independence if they became an association. When the second pot of coffee was gone and the biscuits were finished, there was no definite decision other than to see if the deputy marshal could make any difference at all.

When the meeting was over, Will informed Bright Dawn that she baked the best biscuits in the whole territory. It was a practice he routinely employed in case he should ever eat there again. It was always wise to be on good terms with the cook. He saddled his horses then and rode back to Clayton Hill's ranch with him. John Dillard accompanied them about halfway before dropping off to go to his place. When the road cut through a long ridge running down toward the river, Clayton told Will that his cattle were on one side of the ridge and John's were on the other, south of the road. "But your houses and fields are on the north side of the road?" Will asked.

"All the decent grazin' is between the road and the river," Clayton explained. Then, anticipating Will's next question, he added, "But there ain't no decent place to build a house."

The situation became more and more under-standable to Will. The small herd of cows were down near the river, while the house and the barn were north of the road. It made it a simple operation to cross the river and drive the cattle back across to Texas. They rode about fifty yards farther up the road before they came to the path that followed a wide creek up to Clayton's house. Winding up through a forest of runty oak trees, they followed the creek to a clearing and the house, barn, and outbuildings that comprised the Hill ranch. A pleasant log house with a wide front porch, it stood on one side of the clearing, opposite the barn at the other edge. There was a gradual rise in the land behind the house and Will got a glimpse of a cornfield directly behind the barn.

When they came out into the clearing, they were spotted by a small boy near the barn, and he ran to meet them. "Who's that, Papa?" the boy asked when they met him halfway to the barn.

"Mind your manners, son," Clayton corrected the boy. "That ain't very polite to meet a stranger like that. Where's your brother?"

"Hoeing the bean patch," the boy answered, still staring at Will.

"Run and get him," Clayton told him. "Tell him I said come here." The boy turned and ran out behind the barn. "That's my youngest," Clayton said to Will. "Stanley, he was named after his grandpa on my wife's side. We call him Stan. He's twelve, his brother's fourteen. His name's Clayton, Jr. We call him Clay, and he'll stand beside you all day and match you stroke for stroke."

They continued on to the barn and stepped down from the saddle. "I'll take you to the house to meet my wife," Clayton said. He wasn't sure what Will wanted to do, so he hesitated to suggest anything. His two sons arrived at the barn in the next moment, so he introduced Will. "This is Deputy Marshal Will Tanner. He's gonna be scoutin' around the place tonight, mostly down by the cattle. Take a good look at him, so you don't go takin' a shot at him. Will, this is my eldest, Clay." He turned to his son then. "Clay, take the saddle off my horse and put him in the corral."

"Yessir," Clay responded. "You want me to unsaddle his, too?"

"No, thank you anyway, Clay," Will said. "I'll take Buster down that creek with me tonight, in case I need him. I would like to leave my packhorse here, though. I'll get a couple of things out of my packs to fix some supper." He started to loosen the packsaddle on the sorrel, but Clay interrupted.

"I can take care of that for you," he said. "I'll leave your packs over yonder in the corner of the barn, and I'll turn the horse out in the corral."

"Why, that's mighty neighborly of you," Will said. "Thank you kindly." He handed the packhorse's reins to the boy and led Buster as he walked with Clayton toward the kitchen door. By now, Louise Hill had spotted her husband and the stranger coming from the barn, so she wiped the flour off her hands and stepped outside on the little back porch to greet them.

"Clayton," she said in acknowledgment when they reached the back steps, while she looked Will over and waited for an introduction.

"This is U.S. Deputy Marshal Will Tanner, hon. We had a drawin' at the meetin' today and I won him. I knew we didn't have one, so I brought him home with me. Will, this is my wife, Louise."

Will was astonished by the sudden appearance of a sense of humor in the heretofore humorless man. Louise was obviously not. She brushed a wayward strand of hair from her forehead and smiled at Will. "Well, I suppose we'll have to find a place to put him," she returned the japing. "How do you do, Mr. Tanner? Or should I say Deputy Tanner?"

"How 'bout just plain Will?" he answered. "I'm pleased to meet you, ma'am."

She smiled at him a moment longer, then turned to address her husband. "Anytime now, Clayton. Who have you brought home with you?" Back to Will again, she asked, "Are you really a deputy marshal?"

"Yes, ma'am, I am," Will said, waiting patiently for her husband's little game to be over. Clayton reverted back to his former serious disposition then and explained Will's purpose there.

When she heard what he planned to do that night, she immediately invited him to supper. "The least we can do is give you something to eat before you spend the night in the woods."

"Oh no, ma'am. Thank you just the same, but I don't wanna put you to that trouble. You didn't have any notice, and I'll just camp like I usually do."

"Won't be any trouble at all," she insisted. "Tell him, Clayton." Clayton shrugged. She continued. "I'll just roll out some more biscuits and peel a couple more potatoes and we'll be ready to eat in about an hour. You can just make yourself comfortable on the porch, or wherever and I'll call you when it's ready."

"Well, I'll certainly accept your invitation, but I've got to take a little ride down that creek and pick out a good place for my camp. I should be back in time for supper."

"You do whatever you need to do, and don't worry if you're a little late. I'll keep the food warm in the oven."

"Thank you, ma'am, I'll try not to be late." He turned around to look at Clayton, nodded, and said, "Shouldn't take long." He stepped up into the saddle and turned the buckskin back the way they had come, leaving the clearing at a comfortable lope.

"What a polite young man," Louise remarked as she and her husband watched him ride out toward the road. "I wonder if he's tough enough to do the job you said he was going to try to do."

"I don't know," Clayton replied. "I hope so. He must have some bobcat in him somewhere. Accordin' to Cal Wiggins, he crossed over the Red River, went into Texas, and pulled Ward Hawkins right outta their ranch house. Then when old Fanny Hawkins's other three sons went after them, he killed two of 'em."

"My Lord . . ." Louise gasped. "He was the one?" She shook her head slowly and recited, "You can't judge a book by . . . I'd best get in there and roll out some more biscuits."

Will followed the creek approximately a quarter of a mile before he caught sight of the cattle. Most of them were grazing close by the creek, so he continued on until he came to the last of them. He turned Buster around then and looked at the ridge just east of the creek. About halfway up the ridge there was a shelf that ran the length of the ridge. It looked wide enough to ride on, so he nudged Buster again and headed the big horse up the side of the ridge. When he reached the shelf, he found it even wider than he thought. It was high enough to afford a good view of the little valley below where the cattle were grazing. He could even see the house in the clearing, and it occurred to him that it was a good spot to look the place over, not only the cattle below him, but anyone coming from the house or barn.

It couldn't be much better, he thought as he stepped down from the saddle, so he could take a better look at the ground. Finally, he found what he was convinced had to be there: hoofprints. They were difficult to see since the ground under the trees was covered with a thick carpet of leaves, but he found a clear hoofprint where the leaves had been blown away. The question was, how old was the print? He couldn't say. He continued on for several yards before he came upon the ultimate calling card, horse turds. Fresh droppings—the scout was there on the ridge, looking things over. He must have just missed him. He wondered if he had been spotted by the scout. He took another long look at the scene below the ridge. What would the scout's report be? Everything peaceful, the cattle bunched nicely, nobody working the cattle, they're ready, he decided. And unless the scout saw him riding down the creek and got spooked, there were good odds that the raid was on. He would have to assume he hadn't been seen and prepare to meet rustlers that night.

There was one more thing to do before returning to the house for supper and that was to select a spot to lie in wait for the rustlers, if Clayton's cattle were in fact the target. There were a couple of good spots for his camp where he could watch the cattle, unlikely to be seen by the rustlers. He decided on the one that put him between the main herd and the river. Satisfied that he had made a good choice, he turned Buster back toward the house.

CHAPTER 6

Caleb Hawkins walked over to the fire and poured himself another cup of coffee. He stood there to sip it for a few minutes, gazing out across the Red River. He was thinking about a time not long ago when his brothers Lemuel and Arlie were still alive. Most of the time, it was just the three of them on these little rustling parties. Back then, he didn't have much say about what they did, or how they did it, because he was the youngest. But since the Hawkins family had crossed paths with Will Tanner, that was all changed. Their little raiding party was now four, instead of just three. He had hired three men, but he was now the boss. He liked being the boss. It was just bad luck for his brothers. He had felt some guilt for running away from the fight that killed Lemuel and Arlie, but he had justified his actions in his mind. They had ridden into an ambush. That was what he had told Fanny. Her boys had always called their mother by her given name. She seemed to prefer it. To keep her from grilling him too heavily about the ambush, he told her there was a posse, not just Will Tanner, that descended upon them. He was lucky to have escaped. His thoughts were interrupted then when he caught sight of a horse and rider approaching the river from the

Oklahoma side. "Yonder's Ringo," Spence sang out at almost the same instant.

"I see him," Caleb replied. The other men didn't bother to get up but craned their necks around to see. He remained by the fire, watching Ringo's progress as he crossed the river. Spence and Welch got up from their seats on their saddle blankets when Ringo's horse came out of the water and approached the fire. "Well, whaddaya think?" Caleb asked as Ringo stepped down.

"Any more coffee in that pot?" Ringo replied.

"A little bit," Spence answered him.

"What the hell do you think?" Caleb repeated with a little more heat.

Ringo displayed a wide smile for him and said, "Everything's just right. Ain't nothin' goin' on at the Hill place, and the cows are just waitin' for us to come get 'em. I could almost hear 'em beggin', *Come get me, Ringo, these dad-burned sodbusters don't know nothin' about workin' cattle.*" He took the coffee cup Spence handed him.

"Are they scattered?" Caleb asked. He didn't like the idea of spending a lot of time rounding up stray cattle.

"No, right now they're bunched, so you could part 'em with a comb and cut out ever how many you want," Ringo said. " 'Course that could change before dark, but I doubt it will." He waited for Caleb to give the official word, and when Caleb said nothing for a few moments, Ringo pressed. "So I reckon that means we're goin' over the river tonight, right?"

"I reckon," Caleb replied. His reply brought forth grunts of satisfaction from the three men riding with him.

"In that case, I think I'll cook me up a little of that bacon we brought," Welch declared. "It's gonna be a couple of hours before dark, so we got plenty of time for supper."

"You got time," Caleb told him. "I wanna wait till hard dark. It's a lot easier to move 'em then."

"I might even catch me an hour or two of shut-eye, too," Welch said. "It's gonna be a long night." The others followed suit and pretty soon they were all circling the fire, baking bacon on branches, like the spokes on a wheel.

At approximately the same time the outlaws were roasting bacon around a campfire, Louise Hill, using an iron bar, rang the triangle beside the back door to summon everyone to the supper table. Will heard the signal as he rode back into the clearing, but he decided he would give Buster a little rest since Louise had given him permission to be late. He rode the buckskin to the corral, pulled his saddle off, then turned him loose in the corral. He left the saddle on the top rail of the corral just as young Clay came out of the barn, on his way to the house. "We'll both have to take a scoldin' for bein' late for the table," he said to the boy as he joined him. It was good for a polite chuckle from the boy.

"Well, I'm glad to see you were able to make it to supper while the food is still hot, mister"— Louise caught herself then—"I mean, Will," she said, and smiled warmly.

"Yes, ma'am, I didn't wanna miss it," he responded, and turned his plate right side up.

"Clayton usually asks the blessing," she said. "Since you're our guest, maybe you'd like to ask it."

I almost reached for a biscuit, he thought. To her he said. "Ah no, ma'am. The Lord already knows how thankful I am to be able to eat with you folks, and I feel like your husband will use better words than I can." Clayton laughed in appreciation of his response and immediately recited the same blessing he always said. When Clayton said, "Amen," Will paused just a moment to make sure he wasn't jumping the gun again. And when everyone started passing the bowls, he reached for that biscuit that had caught his eye before it had been blessed. He held it up over his plate for a few moments while he admired it. "I'll be honest with you, Mrs. Hill, if this biscuit tastes just half as good as it looks, I'm gonna have to say you're the biscuit-bakin' champion of the whole territory. And I'd appreciate it if you didn't mention that to Bright Dawn Hatfield, if you're in the store, because you won the title from her."

"Are you married, Will?" She chuckled when she asked. " 'Cause, if you are, you'd best not let your wife know you're bragging about everybody else's biscuits."

He had to stop and think for a moment before he answered. "Ah yes, ma'am, I'm married. I got married this past Christmas. Her name's Sophie, and I honestly don't know if she can bake biscuits or not. I surely hope she can, 'cause I'm a plum fool about biscuits." He turned his attention to the bowls being passed to him then, but he couldn't help thinking about his recent marriage. He wasn't sure what kind of cook Sophie was. Margaret did the cooking for the boardinghouse. *Hell,* he thought, *I ain't even sure I'll still be married when I get back to Fort Smith.* Sophie was never pleased when work kept him away too long. He was happy to be distracted from those thoughts when Clayton asked him a question.

"You haven't said anything about your ride before supper. Did you pick out a good spot to camp tonight?"

"Yes, sir, I did," Will answered. "I think it'll be all right."

Clayton sensed a hesitation on Will's part to talk about the possible raid in front of his wife and boys, especially at the dinner table. "Feel free to tell me what you're thinkin' about the possibility we might get raided. Louise and the boys know what's goin' on."

"Well, I found out you had a visitor today, on that shelf that runs along the ridge. Judgin' by the sign his horse left, he hadn't been gone long when I got there."

"You think they'll hit us tonight?"

Will could see Clayton's jaw set rigid when he asked the question. "To be honest, I think there's a good chance they will. It depends on whether or not whoever was up on that ridge saw me comin' from here this afternoon. And it may not. But I still believe there will be a small group of thieves, if they do make a try for the cattle."

Clayton's fist tightened around the butter knife he was holding. "Well, by God, we'll be ready for 'em this time. I've got plenty of shells for my shotgun and Clay has his rifle . . ."

Will interrupted him. His reaction was what Will was afraid it would be. "Mr. Hill, I know how you feel, and I respect you for it. But I don't wanna take a chance on us shootin' at each other in the dark tonight. And I definitely do not want any harm to come to your fine family. I have a strategy to work against the rustlers that I think will keep you from losin' any of your cattle. What I would like to ask of you is to stay here and protect your family in case things do go wrong. Then all I'll have to worry about is the cattle. Can I count on you to do that?"

"That seems to me like you're takin' on too big a risk," Clayton protested. "You don't know how many you'll be up against."

"I think I have a pretty good idea. I've handled situations like this before, Clayton. It's my job, and I don't want to take a chance on you and me shootin' at each other."

"Listen to him, Clayton," Louise pleaded. "He knows what he's talking about."

"Listen to your wife," Will said. "Give me a chance to take care of it. I won't let 'em take your cattle, if you won't let 'em harm your family."

"All right," Clayton finally yielded. "We'll do it your way."

Louise breathed a sigh of relief. "Now, let's all eat our supper, so I can get the kitchen cleaned up before it gets too late tonight." The meal was resumed then with little conversation and everyone, including the two young boys, thinking about what might take place in the pasture below the road. Clayton knew that he would not sleep that night. He planned to spend it on the front porch, keeping watch over his family. Clay and Stan wanted to stand watch with him, and because of that, Louise knew she would not be able to sleep, even if she tried. Will finished his supper, thanked Louise once again for her hospitality, and said good night. Clayton walked with him to the front porch.

"You know, if there are too many, if you need

help, I'll be right here on the porch. All you have to do is just holler and I'll come a-runnin'."

"I know that," Will said. "And it's good to know I've got the backup. If things go like I want, we shouldn't need it. I'll see you in the mornin'." He walked down to the corral to saddle Buster and rode out of the clearing in the fading light of the evening. He had no real concern that Clayton's family might be in danger. The rustlers were after only the cattle. He just wanted to know that Clayton and his son would not be riding around in the dark with him and the rustlers shooting at each other.

It was already pretty dark in the trees by the creek as he walked the buckskin slowly along the way he had ridden in the daylight. For a few minutes, he thought he wasn't going to find the spot he'd decided on because of the darkness, but he kept going for he could still see cattle in the open pasture across the creek. Finally, he found his spot, and he liked it even more since it was so hard to find. He dismounted and led Buster down to the creek and let him get a good drink before he led him a little way back to a washed-out area in the bank. It had been caused by a flood at some point, he figured. For now, it offered some protection for his horse and himself. "Sorry, boy, I'm gonna have to leave your saddle on you. I think we're gonna have work later tonight, and

I won't have time to saddle you." Buster seemed to understand, so Will took his bedroll from behind his saddle and placed it on the side of the washed-out area to sit on. "Nothin' to do now but wait," he told the horse.

He wasn't sure how long it was before they showed up. It was Buster who first alerted him when the buckskin acknowledged the arrival of horses. Will moved to the edge of the trees and watched the open area they would surely approach through. In a short while, four dark forms of men on horseback emerged from the black of the moonless night. *About what I figured,* he thought, *but I was hoping for only three.* He let them continue to come forward until he could hear them talking in hushed voices. Although he couldn't understand what they were saying, he could tell that one of them was sending two of the other men to circle around the herd. Evidently, he meant for them to determine how much of the herd they could comfortably handle and push the selected cows forward, and the remaining two men were to act as flank riders and guide the cattle toward the river.

When the cattle started slowly moving toward the river, Caleb and Ringo, who were at the head of the herd, remained where they were and watched the cattle move past them. And when the cows continued to head in the right direction, they dropped back to flank positions on each side to keep them moving. Since cattle rustling was a hanging offense, the same as horse stealing, Will had considered lying there on the bank and cutting down as many of the four as he could with his rifle while they were riding up in a group. There would have been no questions asked, had he done so, by Marshal Dan Stone, or the Texas Rangers. But to suit his own conscience, he felt it his duty to give the rustlers the chance to surrender, even though it would give him a hell of a problem to transport them or hold them until the Texas Rangers picked them up. He thought of what Fletcher Pride had told him when he was first hired. *There ain't nothing more useless than a deputy marshal with a conscience.* With that in mind, he climbed aboard Buster and drew his Winchester from the saddle sling. Remaining in the cover of the trees, he rode up ahead of the lead cows before coming out ahead of the herd.

As the leading cows approached him, he yelled at them, and when that didn't deter them, he dropped Buster's reins and fired two quick rounds in the air. This effectively got their attention and caused them to veer off toward the west and the rest of the cows blindly followed. Back on the flank of the herd, when they heard the shots, Ringo shouted across the moving mass of hides and horns, "What the hell? Somethin's turned 'em!" He kicked his horse hard and galloped toward the frightened lead cows, which were now turning the whole herd away from the river. Seeing the dark figure on the horse, pressing the cows to stampede, Ringo shouted, "What the hell are you doin', ya damn fool? They're goin' the wrong way!"

Will reined his horse around to face the irate man, his rifle ready to fire. "I'm turnin' 'em back and arrestin' you for rustlin'."

Ringo couldn't believe what he was hearing. It was too dark for him to identify the man making the ridiculous statements. "The hell you are!" he roared, and pulled his pistol. The bay gelding he was riding made for an unsteady shooting platform for a .44 revolver at that distance. So his shot was wide of the mark, while Will planted a round in the middle of Ringo's chest with his rifle. The shots caused the cattle to stampede in earnest, and not in the direction the rustlers intended.

With the simple planned raid suddenly gone haywire, Caleb Hawkins didn't know what to do. When the stampeding herd turned in the wrong direction, he had to turn with them or get run over, so he turned his horse and galloped toward the leaders, with no idea if he could turn them back on course. His thoughts were confused and scrambled in his head. He heard the shots and knew they started the stampede, but who fired them? How did they know the raid was planned to happen? Marshals? Vigilantes? Who had ambushed them?

Behind him, Welch and Spence had been forced to hightail it to each side to keep from being run over by that part of the herd that had been left for another time, when they stampeded. Spence, who had been on the same side Ringo had flanked, rode forward to join him, only to pull his horse to a sliding stop when he came to Ringo's horse with an empty saddle. He spotted Ringo's body on the ground at the same time he saw the man on the horse waiting for him. His reaction was to go for his gun. It was the last reaction he would ever have in this world. *That leaves two,* Will thought as he turned Buster's head toward the leaders of the stampede, which was showing signs of slowing down. He cautioned himself to be more careful now, since the two remaining thieves were well aware of what was happening to their plan to steal cattle.

More gunshots and no word from Spence or Ringo were enough to tell Welch there was nothing to do but get the hell away from that valley. He knew that Caleb was ahead of him somewhere, so he concentrated on finding him as soon as possible. Then the two of them could stand off the party of ambushers, or better yet, make a run for it. That little herd of cows wasn't worth getting killed over, so he pressed his horse for more speed.

Breathing nearly as hard as his exhausted horse, Caleb pulled the tired roan to a stop, knowing he'd kill him if he didn't. There had been no more shots for quite some time now, and there were no riders in sight, so he stepped down from the weary horse. He suspected that he must have outrun the danger. He thought at once of how he could explain their failure to Fanny. She would be furious. His thoughts of reporting this failure were suddenly interrupted almost at once, for he heard the sound of hoofbeats pounding the grassy meadow behind him. *They had seen him run!* The panic of being killed gripped him immediately. He started to climb back on his horse, but one look at the roan and he knew he could not outrun any horse at this stage. Trembling with fright, he thought of his only hope. He drew his rifle from the saddle sling and cranked a cartridge into the chamber just as the dark image emerged from the heavy darkness, and he was thankful to see that it was only one rider. He pulled his horse around in front of him to use for cover. Then he laid the barrel of the Winchester across the saddle to steady his aim. *This would be better,* he told himself. *When I kill him, then I'll take his horse.* He figured it had to be fresher than his roan because it was coming on pretty fast. He decided to start shooting as soon as the rider was in the Winchester's range. And if he missed, he'd have time to shoot again as he got closer.

Sighting on the rider, he waited, his finger nervously tracing the contour of the trigger. Finally, he could wait no longer, and he squeezed the trigger. Within a hundred yards now, the rider jerked straight up in the saddle when the bullet struck him in the shoulder, and he cried out, "Caleb!"

He knows my name! Caleb panicked. *How could he know my name?* He cranked another cartridge in the chamber and fired again. This time, his target reared backward in the saddle, then fell forward on the horse's neck. The horse slowed to a walk, came up to Caleb's horse, and stopped. The rider, Jim Welch, slid off on the ground. "Oh hell, oh hell," Caleb muttered to himself, his hands trembling as he held the rifle and stared at the body. "It's not my fault. I didn't know who it was comin' after me. It's your fault for not lettin' me know it was you." It occurred to him then that the people who laid the ambush were still out there in the darkness somewhere and he didn't have time to lament Welch's poor decision to chase after him like that. He hurriedly stripped Welch of his gun belt, then checked his pockets for any money before he climbed on Welch's horse. Holding the reins of his horse, he continued in a westerly direction, thinking that was his best chance of escape. When he figured he had gone far enough, and there was no sign of pursuit, he turned south and rode to the river. It would take him a couple of days to get home, so he needed to go back to get the packhorses they had left at their camp on the Texas side of the river.

CHAPTER 7

There were four riders that Will had seen when they came into the herd. He could account for only three dead. But the last body he found was not shot by him, so he could only figure that it was an accidental shooting by one of the man's partners. "That's a helluva way to go," he commented to Buster. "He put two rounds in him." The dead man's horse was nowhere around. Will figured it might show up somewhere tomorrow, or possibly the fellow who shot his partner took the horse with him. The cattle were already bunching up near the creek again, so there were no casualties there, and that oughta please Clayton Hill. Thinking of Clayton, he knew he told him he would see him in the morning. But with all the shots fired, Will thought it might be best to go on back to the house now and give Clayton the report, since he said he was gonna spend the night on the front porch. Will would have to take care of the three bodies, but he thought that could wait till morning, and he might even get some help with the grave digging. So he tied a rope around Welch's boots and dragged his body back closer to the creek and left it with the other two bodies.

There was one other thing he had a mind to do.

The freak killing of this last raider by one of his own gang prompted him to think about the one man who got away. He was willing to bet the four men had made a camp somewhere close by on the Texas side of the river while they waited for darkness. Probably left some packhorses there, since they showed up here without any. If that was the case, then there was a possibility the one who escaped might come back for the packhorses. He decided it was worth a try, even though he couldn't do much searching until daylight. Odds were the man would have come and be long gone by the morning. But even so, he might leave him a trail to follow. And it wouldn't be the first time he had trailed a man into Texas. "But right now, we'll go take the word to Clayton," he said to Buster. "I might even take that saddle offa you tonight."

After taking one last look to make sure the cattle had calmed down, he started back toward the house. As he rode through the grove of oak trees just before the clearing where the house sat, he thought about Clayton's determination to protect his family. He also thought a little about the death of the last rustler, shot by his friend. The front porch was a long way from the edge of the clearing, and as dark as it was, it might be hard to identify friend from foe. "A little caution couldn't hurt," he said, and turned the buckskin into the grove of trees to slowly walk around the clearing until he was behind the barn. He paused to take a look at the barn and the yard before he rode out of the trees. He found a lantern in the barn and lit it. He had given Buster a good drink at the creek, but he took him to the trough in the corral before leading him into a stall that obviously had been prepared for his use by fourteen-year-old Clay. There was even a bucket with grain hanging on a nail right outside the stall. *If Sophie and I ever have a boy, I'd like one like that one,* he thought.

He still had some concerns about getting shot by Clayton, if he came walking across the yard to the porch. So he walked to the back of the house and went around the other side. When he got to the edge of the porch, he saw Clayton sitting in a rocking chair, his shotgun lying on the floor beside it, with Clay and Stan asleep on a blanket on the floor, next to the wall. So he climbed up on the porch, then very softly, he said, "Clayton." Soft though it was, it was enough to light Clayton's fuse. He came out of his chair like a cannonball, grasping the air behind him for his shotgun on the floor, causing the chair to rock wildly. "Clayton." Will spoke a little louder. "It's me, Will, Will Tanner," he reminded him.

Clayton regained his senses right away. "Will, damn! You gave me a start. I musta fell half asleep there for a minute. I heard the shootin', but then it got quiet for a long time, so I wasn't sure who shot who. I wasn't sure who might come up to the house."

"Well, I wanted to let you know that everything's all right, and you didn't lose a cow that I could see."

"You were able to scare 'em off then?"

"No, they decided to fight it out," Will said. "There were four of 'em. Three of 'em are dead and one of 'em got away. I'm gonna go in the mornin' and see if I can track him. It's too dark to track him tonight." He gestured toward the two sleeping boys. "I think you and the boys can finish out the night in your beds."

"I swear," Clayton replied, "I reckon you knew what you were talkin' about when you said you could handle it by yourself. You killed three of 'em?"

"No, I didn't shoot but two of 'em 'cause they fired at me. The other one was shot by one of his own gang, the one that got away. It ain't so unusual that he shot one of his partners when you think about how dark it is down there, with the cattle stampedin' and everybody shootin'. That's why I didn't want you and Clay out there. It mighta been me that shot one of you. Then Louise wouldn't bake me no biscuits."

"Well, I reckon I need to say I'm sorry for what I said in Hatfield's," Clayton said. "I believe I was dead wrong. You are the same as sendin' a whole troop of deputy marshals."

Will laughed. "I don't know about that. Sometimes you just get plum lucky." He turned then, when he heard the front door open, and they were joined by Louise. "I'm sorry, ma'am, I didn't mean to wake you up."

"Are you serious?" Louise replied. "Do you think I could possibly go to sleep with all that's happening? Guns going off in the middle of the night, my husband and sons out on the front porch, I'll be lucky if I ever get my eyelids to close again." She closed her robe up tightly under her chin against the cool night air. "Did I hear you say some men were killed?" Her husband repeated Will's accounting of the incident. When he finished, she looked at Will and said, "You've had quite a night of it, haven't you? Maybe I'd best go ahead and start some breakfast."

"Not on my account," Will said. "I reckon that's up to you and Clayton. I'll catch a couple hours' sleep before first light. Then I'll need to borrow a shovel. I've got graves to dig, and you might wanna tell me where you'd rather have them," he said to Clayton.

"I reckon I can at least take care of the buryin' for you," Clayton volunteered at once. "I know you wanna see if you can pick up that other fellow's trail as soon as it gets light enough to see."

"I appreciate that, Clayton, it'll save me a lot of time in the mornin'."

"I'll make up that bed for you in the spare room," Louise said, "so you can get some sleep."

"Ah no, ma'am," Will quickly replied. "I'll be sleepin' in the barn with my horse. Clay fixed his stall up so nice with plenty of fresh hay, so it'll be softer than a feather bed. Besides, Buster sometimes gets a little melancholy when I leave him in a strange place, and I want him to be in good spirits in the mornin'."

She laughed politely at his attempt at humor. "I guess you know best," she said, then took a look at her two sleeping sons. "I think I'll leave those two right where they are." To Clayton, she asked, "Are you coming to bed?" He said he was, so as she turned to leave, she called back over her shoulder, "I'll be fixin' an early breakfast, Will, so you don't need to ride off hungry."

"Yes, ma'am. Thank you, ma'am."

He had Buster saddled the next morning and was in the process of loading his packhorse when Clay came in the barn to tell him breakfast was ready. "Mama said to tell you she just pulled the biscuits out of the oven."

Will smiled and said, "Well, you can tell her I'll be right there, soon as I tighten this pack down." He figured she sent that message to lure him to eat before he left. He smiled to himself and gave himself credit for causing her to bake fresh biscuits after he made such a big fuss over them.

"I'll go tell her," Clay said, but he paused for

a moment as he watched Will fixing his packs. "How come you're takin' your packhorse? Ain't you comin' back?"

"I might, but I might not," Will answered. "It depends on whether or not I can pick up a trail to follow. If I do, and I go to trackin' that last fellow, I don't know how long it'll take, and I'll need my packs." When he noticed a distinct look of disappointment in the boy's face, he said, "But I'll be comin' back to tell your pa what happened, just maybe not tonight.

"I appreciate you taking care of the burials, Clayton. I really do." He thanked the Hills again for their hospitality, and said he'd let them know if there were any results. But he didn't get out the door before Louise handed him a couple of biscuits wrapped in a cloth.

He took a small amount of time to scout the trees below the pasture where the cattle were grazing, and he easily found where the four riders came out into the pasture last night. It was a good three miles to the Red River at this point, over nothing but scrubby trees and tall grass. He would expect the rustlers' trail would be easy to pick up. But before following it, he rode back up to find the spot where he had found Welch's body, so he could take a look at it in the daylight. By the tracks he could find, he was able to confirm what he had speculated on last night. The man who got away did take the dead man's horse with him, and he could see the tracks of two horses leading off to the west. Now he had to decide which trail to follow. He thought it over for no longer than a minute before he had to go in favor of the tracks of the four original riders coming up from the river. It was bound to be the shorter of the two, for it probably came straight up from the river. And surely the one who escaped would have circled back to return for the packhorses. Besides that, the back trail from the camp where they left the packhorses would be a double trail now, if he returned the same way they had come. He thought that if he could find out where the rustlers came from, he would turn the information over to the Texas Rangers or the Texas marshals and let them take it from there. He was without authority to make arrests in Texas, anyway.

His course of action decided, he returned to the lower end of the pasture and followed an obvious trail into the brush and scrub oaks that lay between the road and the Red River at this point. There had been no attempt to hide their trail for the simple reason the rustlers had planned to drive a herd of cattle back over the same ground. And they were not worried about that because they had planned to drive that herd well up into Texas before Clayton Hill knew they were missing. Since all the ranchers he had talked to in Indian Territory had no doubt that the boss calling the shots was old Fanny Hawkins, herself, Will was anxious to see if this outlaw he was trying to track would indeed lead him back to the Hawkins ranch. When he reached the river, his thoughts were brought swiftly back to the trail before him at the present. Where he saw their tracks come out of the water was where he entered it, figuring the footing to be fine for his horse, since they made it across. He cautioned himself that from this point on, it was wise to be alert to what he was riding into in case the surviving rustler might now be sitting on the riverbank waiting for him.

The river was shallow enough for Buster to walk across, except for a narrow channel that required him to swim about fifteen feet. That would have been the trouble spot for the rustlers, had they been successful in their raid, but it wouldn't have stopped them. With no idea where the camp was that he searched for, he felt like a helpless target until Buster climbed up the other bank. Once again, the tracks of the four riders were very easily seen as he followed them up the other side of the river. Looking up ahead, he could see where they had come out of a grove of trees that looked to be a likely place to make a camp, so he headed toward it. When he was within about thirty yards of the first trees, he reined Buster to an abrupt stop. A few yards before him, he saw more tracks from horses. But these tracks were at an angle to intercept the tracks he was following. Then he realized who they belonged to when he looked back toward the way they had come. It was clearly the man he was trailing and it was obvious that he had crossed the river some distance to the west of there and ridden along the riverbank until he came to the tracks leading out of the woods. Will climbed down from the saddle to take a close look. The tracks didn't look very old. He would have liked to have Jim Little Eagle with him at this moment. Jim could tell him how old the tracks were and the blacksmith who did the shoeing.

Getting serious again, he guessed the rustler was not that far ahead of him, maybe even still in this camp. He took Buster's reins and led him into the trees, his drawn pistol in his hand. He did not go farther than twenty yards before he found it. He was too late. There was no one there. He could see where the packhorses had been tied in the trees. No doubt they were pretty thirsty by the time the lone survivor made it back here. The man had made a fire when he finally made it back here, for Will found the ashes still plenty warm. Why, he wondered, would a man on the run take the time to build a fire and probably cook something to eat? Unless, it occurred to him, his horses were spent, and he had no choice but to rest them. Everything kept adding up to the conclusion that he was not that far ahead of him. *Now, I'm wasting time,* he thought, and promptly started a search around the campsite until he found multiple tracks leading away from the campsite but generally following the Red River.

He stayed on a trail left by four horses. At least, that was his guess. He knew the rustler was leading one horse carrying an empty saddle, and he guessed that there were two packhorses. And the outlaw was generous in leaving tracks. It appeared to Will that he had no thoughts that anyone might be trailing him. He made no effort to hide his trail, so Will thought he had to be gaining on him. It now appeared that the rustler was heading for Wichita Falls, for when he reached the point where the Wichita River emptied into the Red, he promptly cut onto the trail that followed the Wichita River. It was a trail that Will had ridden when he was last illegally pursuing a felon on the Texas side of the Red River. He was reluctant to stop when he could feel it in his bones that he was gaining on the outlaw, and he knew he was only about seven miles from Wichita Falls. But he knew he had to rest his horses pretty soon. So, when he came to a bend in the river where a little grassy meadow ran down to the water, he decided Buster and the sorrel deserved that spot. He guided the horses close to a wooded area at the edge of the meadow and dismounted. Then he stripped them of their packs and saddles and let them go to the water. "It's dinnertime, so I reckon I'll cook up a little bacon to go with my biscuits," he said aloud as he gathered up some wood to cook over.

With horses and rider fed and rested, Will rode on into Wichita Falls. It was an automatic reaction to check the saloon first when chasing an outlaw, but as he rode by the establishment owned by Howard Blaylock, he couldn't see that the man had made much improvement on the saloon. And since there were no horses tied to the rail out front, he decided he might get more information from someone else. He began pressing his memory in an effort to remember names he had learned the last time he was here. He saw the blacksmith, whose shop was next door to the stable, and the name popped into his mind, Clive Smith. Since Clive was working close to the street, he should see everybody that passes.

"I declare," Clive exclaimed, "the Oklahoma deputy, right?" He laid his hammer aside and walked out closer to the street.

"How you doin', Clive?" Will returned the greeting confidently.

Clive didn't hesitate. "The word we got here in town was that you went out to Fanny Hawkins's ranch and snatched Ward Hawkins right from under their noses. Is there any truth to that?"

"I reckon, more or less," Will replied. "I arrested him and took him back to Fort Smith." He let it go at that, feeling it unnecessary to discuss Ward's final hours.

116

"Mister, that took some doin'," Clive said. "There's talk that Lemuel and Arlie ain't around no more, either. You have anything to do with that?" Will shook his head. It was a lie, but he saw nothing good to come of building a name for himself as an executioner. Clive continued, "They say the only one of them boys left is Caleb. I know he's the only one of 'em I've seen in town lately. Matter of fact, I saw him ride past my forge about an hour ago. He was leadin' three horses. One of 'em had a saddle on him. The other two was packhorses."

"Caleb, huh?" Will remarked casually, although it took great control, for he remembered that it was Caleb who put a bullet through his shoulder on that night last Christmas when the three brothers attempted to free their eldest brother, Ward. They weren't successful, and two of the three were killed, but the youngest, Caleb, managed to get away. Forcing himself to seem only casually interested still, Will asked, "He didn't stop anywhere?"

"Nope, just rode out the other end of town. He was headin' home, I reckon."

"Probably so," Will agreed. "Well, I'd best get along. I'm gettin' behind in my work." He didn't give Clive a chance to ask what that work was. Instead, he pulled Buster's head around toward the south end of the street and left Clive to wonder. He felt pretty sure the blacksmith couldn't recall his name, and he preferred to keep it that way. He couldn't afford to have Texas law enforcement contacting Marshal Dan Stone again with complaints about him. On the positive side, he had the outlaw he was trailing not only spotted but identified as well. It was definitely Caleb Hawkins, and he didn't have to show his hand by asking about a rider leading three horses. He should have known his target was either the last Hawkins son or someone who worked for Hawkins. So now he knew who was behind the rustling of Clayton Hill's cattle, and most likely, the cattle of the other three ranches who had been repeatedly struck. The question before him was, what should he do about it? His original thought was to give the identity of the persons responsible for the cattle rustling to the Texas Rangers or the U.S. Marshals in Texas and let them take it from there. Now, when he was sure it was the Hawkins clan, he wondered if they had enough to take action against them. After all, he could give them only his opinion that one of the rustlers was Caleb Hawkins. It didn't help matters any that Texas officials were still complaining to Dan Stone about an Oklahoma deputy marshal making arrests in Texas. He found himself in a troublesome position. Now that he knew who the fourth man was in the attempted rustling, he could not deny his usual bulldog-like tendency to seek punishment, if at all possible.

To ensure that, he would have to arrest Caleb Hawkins, himself, instead of relying on someone else's authority. Sometimes he wished he was in another line of work, something where he wouldn't be faced with so many decisions like this one. If he somehow found a way to capture Caleb Hawkins, it wouldn't be any good unless he transported him all the way back to Fort Smith for trial. That thought caused him to think about the man he already had, waiting for transport. He had no idea how long it would have been before a jail wagon and a deputy were available to fetch Reese Trainer. He hoped it was already on the way. He was nowhere close to a telegraph line, so there was no way to find out. Chances were, he would be the one to transport both prisoners to Fort Smith, if he managed to arrest Caleb Hawkins.

"I'm already damn near there," he finally decided. "I might as well ride on out to the Hawkins ranch and snoop around a little bit. If I get lucky and Caleb wanders away from the house, I'll ask him real politely to ride back to Fort Smith with me." Buster looked at him as if he understood and Will decided the buckskin agreed with that plan. So he headed for Bobcat Creek.

CHAPTER 8

"Maudie said you wanted to see me," Robert Baines said when he walked around the house to the front porch, where Fanny Hawkins was seated in her rocking chair, indulging in one of her favorite pastimes. He approached the cranky old woman rather timidly because he knew that Fanny did not like to be disturbed when she sat down with her corncob pipe after supper. A slow-witted man of middle age, Robert did most of the chores around the ranch, since all of Fanny's sons were dead but Caleb. He had been recommended to Fanny by Maudie, Fanny's cook and house-keeper. Robert was her brother and needed a permanent job. Maudie was the only person left that Fanny trusted, so she hired her brother to keep up with the chores. She had found no reason to regret it, for she soon discovered that he was not bothered by deep thoughts. He could see what needed to be done and he did it. He was a far cry from the other hands she had hired since she lost Lemuel and Arlie. Spence, Ringo, and Welch were all hired to carry on the Hawkins' family business of stealing other people's cattle and horses.

She took her pipe out of her mouth long enough to tell him the latch on the outhouse door needed

121

fixing. He said he'd take care of it right away and hurried away to take a look at it. She smiled to herself over his quick response, no questions, just go do the job. Why couldn't most men she hired be like that? Too bad he didn't know one end of a rifle from the other. She sighed and took a deep drag from her pipe, content at least to know that Caleb and the boys should be driving in a good little herd of cattle to add to those presently grazing on her ranch. She paused in her thoughts when she caught sight of a rider on the Bobcat Creek trail, coming from the direction of town. He was leading three horses. She squinted her eyes in an effort to identify him, thinking it might be Jack Coffey. But it would be a bit early for Coffey to show up, since he would be riding all the way from Texarkana, and she had sent her letter only a couple of weeks ago. Then as the rider approached the front gate, she recognized him. "What the hell?" she muttered. It was Caleb, and he had no business back here so soon, and by himself. Then she noticed one of the horses he led was carrying an empty saddle. "What the hell?" she repeated, and jerked the pipe out of her mouth, so she could repeat it once more, only louder. The last time he came limping in from an important job, it was to report the deaths of two of his brothers.

She got up from her chair and walked to the edge of the porch to await his explanation. Her action did not go unnoticed by her son. *Damn,* he thought, *I was hoping she'd already be finished smoking her pipe.* He knew he had no choice, so he guided his horses up to stop in front of the porch. Before he could speak, she said, "Don't come draggin' your sorry ass home and tell me you ain't brought no cattle back with you."

"We run into a real bad piece of luck . . ." he started, only to be interrupted.

"I told you not to come home tellin' me nothin' about no bad luck," she howled. "Where's the other boys? They'd best be with my cows!"

"Wasn't nothin' we could do about it, Fanny, just pure bad luck. They was waitin' for us, a whole posse of riders, like they knew we was comin'. Ringo scouted the place and said the cows was just waitin' for us to come get 'em. Said there weren't nobody watchin' 'em."

"You just said there was a posse waitin' for ya," Fanny charged. "How come he didn't see none of them?"

"That's what I was wonderin'," Caleb answered. "I figured they didn't get there until after dark, or he'da seen 'em. Like I said, we didn't have a chance. They was waiting on both sides of that herd. We put up a helluva fight, but there was just too many of 'em, till there was just me and Welch left fightin' 'em. Then Welch went down, and I could see there weren't no use in me gettin' killed, too. So I fought my way outta that valley, just so I could tell you what happened, just low-down bad luck."

He had hoped to give her an account that would generate some compassion for his narrow escape from death. Instead, it fueled her frustration and disappointment in him. She found herself unable to believe his story. Except for the circumstances and the players involved, his little scene was the same as the first one when Lemuel and Arlie were killed by a big posse, and he was the one who happened to get away. "Bad luck, huh?" She glared at him and charged, "You ain't nothin' but bad luck. Yellow to the bone. I wish to hell I'd stuck a knife in my belly when I was carryin' you. I'da stuck a knife in your pa, too, if I'da knowed his seed weren't no better'n that."

"It was just like I told you, Fanny, they was just too many of 'em for us to whip," he pleaded earnestly. "I hated to have to come tell you, but I thought you needed to know."

She looked at him for a long moment, thoroughly disgusted. Maybe they had some men waiting for them. Somebody killed Ringo, Spence, and Welch, but Caleb got away, just like he got away the time before that. She would have been proud of him if he had been killed, too, but she had the picture in her mind of him running for his life. She looked at him now, dejected, his head hanging down, hoping for compassion. "Well, go on in the kitchen and get somethin' to eat. Then get all your stuff outta the house and move it to the bunkhouse. You'll be stayin' out there. I don't allow no cowards in my house." She turned her back and walked to the front door, pausing a moment to knock the ashes out of her pipe on the arm of the chair before going inside.

"Maudie!" Fanny yelled when she walked through the parlor, on her way to her room, and by the time she reached her bedroom door, the solemn cook was there in the hall to meet her. "Caleb's back. He'll most likely be lookin' for somethin' to eat. After that, he's gonna be movin' his stuff outta the house. He'll be sleepin' in the bunkhouse with Robert."

"Yessum," Maudie replied. "Will he be eatin' in the dinin' room with you, like before?"

"No," Fanny said. "He'll be eatin' in the kitchen with you and Robert and any other hands I hire."

Since she normally cooked for the family and the hired hands, Maudie wanted to know how many mouths she had to feed now. "The other three men, are they comin' back to the house tonight, or are they staying with the cattle?"

"They ain't comin' back," Fanny said. "And there ain't no cattle. All three of them men are dead, and Caleb came home with his tail between his legs. So there won't be nobody to fix breakfast for but me, you, Robert, and Caleb."

"All I need is the number to cook for," Maudie declared. It was an unusual arrangement for a cattle ranch, but Maudie had been doing all the cooking for family and ranch hands for quite some time. For years after Fanny's husband died, the boys lived in the house, so they ate with the family. And since the sons made up the crew, there was no sense to hire a bunkhouse cook to serve the occasional two or three hired hands. She hoped Fanny hired a bunkhouse cook when she hired men to replace the three that were lost. She had talked about hiring men who knew how to work cattle before it became time for the branding. Her sons used to take care of that. Now there was no one to do it, and according to what Robert told her, the cattle she already had were scattered all over the range.

There was another soul who had an interest in Fanny's youngest son. Now in the fading light of day's end, he lay on the bank of Bobcat Creek, about one hundred yards away, scanning the house and barn with his field glass. He had hoped to overtake Caleb Hawkins before he reached the ranch. Perhaps if he had not taken so much time deciding whether to arrest him or not, he might have caught him. Then he wouldn't have left himself with the delicate problem he was now faced with. He had kidnapped Fanny's oldest son right out from under her nose, but that was because he was bunking in the bunkhouse. He was not confident in his odds of going into the ranch house and arresting Caleb. He was going to have to catch him outside the house somewhere.

He hoped to get an idea of how many men were left on the ranch after the elimination of the three that Clayton Hill buried today back on the other side of the Red River. He would have thought if Fanny Hawkins had more men, she might have sent them to rustle the cattle with the four. Surely, she had to have men to work the cattle she stole, but the ranch seemed almost deserted. He thought of the strays he saw on his way up Bobcat Creek. It was a disgraceful way to operate a cattle ranch. He scanned back to the bunkhouse with his glass. The light was rapidly fading now, but he saw a man come out of the bunkhouse and walk toward the barn. It was hard to tell, but he appeared to be an older man than Caleb would be. Will had not gotten a close look at Caleb on that night last Christmas when the young Hawkins brother shot him, but he thought he had to be younger than the man he was looking at now. *Might as well give it up for tonight,* he thought. *Maybe I'll catch him alone tomorrow, riding out to check on the cattle, or something.* He took one last look at the house before putting his glass away just as the kitchen door opened and another man came outside. His arms were filled with what appeared to be clothing or bedsheets. Will followed him with his glass across the yard, and he knew for certain. "That's my man. That's Caleb Hawkins."

And he was going to the bunkhouse. It occurred to him that Caleb might be taking his belongings out of the house to move into the bunkhouse. "Nah," he muttered. "That would be too much of a coincidence to ever happen. Lightning never strikes in the same place twice." What were the odds of two brothers being snatched from the bunkhouse on two different occasions? He was not prepared for such an opportunity to present itself. It was getting late, he had no camp made, he had not taken care of his horses, and he didn't have a horse for a prisoner to ride. "Unless I put him on my packhorse." Another thought occurred to him then. *This place is deserted, there's no one to chase me.* It was too good an opportunity to pass up. He decided to make it work, whatever it took. *I might be a deputy marshal for twenty years and never get another chance like this.*

He looked around him on the creekbank then. "This'll have to do for our temporary camp," he announced to Buster, "but you're gonna have to wear that saddle a little longer tonight." He tied the packhorse in the trees, the packs still on it. "I'm so low on supplies, there ain't much in the packs, anyway." He took another good look at the trees along the creekbank to make sure he would recognize the place when he returned in the dark. It was getting fairly dark by then, so he decided to make his way over to the bunkhouse to get a look in the window before they blew the lamp out and went to sleep. He had to satisfy himself that he was not going to attack the wrong person. He knew for sure that the man he thought was Caleb went into the bunkhouse but had not come out again. So he climbed aboard Buster and headed the big buckskin across the dark prairie toward the back of the bunkhouse. When he reached the bunkhouse, he climbed down and went to the window at the end of it. He carefully wiped the dirt away until he cleared a hole big enough to peek through.

Inside, he could see the older man already on his bed, while Caleb was sitting on a stool, at a small table, eating a biscuit. The sight of it reminded Will that he was hungry. After a few minutes, Caleb suddenly got up from the stool and appeared to be making some bodily noises. The man in the bed turned away from him, causing Caleb to laugh. He picked up his hat then, plopped it on his head, and headed for the door at the other end of the bunkhouse. *Oh hell,* Will thought, *he's heading back to the house.* He couldn't afford to let him get to the house, so he ran to the other end of the bunkhouse just as Caleb came out. But instead of going to the house, he headed toward the outhouse. Thinking of possible problems that could occur, Will decided to let him do his business and catch him on the way out. So, as soon as the outhouse door closed, he hurried around behind it.

While he waited for Caleb to finish answering nature's call, he thought about the sanity of what he was attempting to do. At last Christmastime, he had brazenly walked into the bunkhouse and arrested not only Ward Hawkins, but Tiny McGee, who was with him, as well. He had been shot at and followed, but this time, he thought there was a chance he could escape with his prisoner in the darkness and not be seen. Then he remembered, last time he tried this, he had gone to the barn and saddled two horses for his two prisoners to ride. It would be much better this time if he had a horse and saddle for Caleb, instead of his packhorse. The problem was he needed the horse ready to go now, as soon as Caleb was contented. If he ran to the barn to saddle a horse now, Caleb would, in all likelihood, be finished and have gone back to the bunkhouse. And then there would be the concern of dealing with the other man in the bunkhouse. He shook his head, perplexed. A horse and saddle would make the ride to Fort Smith a great deal easier. As it now stood, he would either have to walk Caleb back to Bobcat Creek where the packhorse was tied, or ride double on Buster. And he didn't like the idea of that at all. A decision was forced upon him at that moment when he heard the latch on the outhouse door go up. Will drew his six-gun. *In for a dime, in for a dollar,* he thought, and walked up to the door.

Caleb stepped out of the outhouse to encounter a gun barrel inches from his face. Stunned, he let out a little yelp of surprise. "I don't wanna hear another sound outta you," Will warned. "If I do, it'll be the last sound you'll ever make. I'll have no choice but to shoot. You understand that?" Caleb nodded vigorously, frightened out of his wits. "I'm arrestin' you for cattle rustlin'. If you do as I tell you to, and come peacefully, I'll take you to jail and a fair trial. If you don't, I'll shoot you. Do you understand that?" With eyes as big as saucers, Caleb shook his head rapidly again, helpless to do otherwise. He knew without being told that the menacing gunman was Will Tanner, and he was convinced he would do as he threatened.

"Now, we're gonna walk to the barn," Will told him, and turned him in that direction and gave him a little tap behind his head with the gun barrel to get him started. He went straight to the barn with Will behind him and Buster following along behind Will. When they got to the barn, Will said, "Pick any horse you want and put your saddle on him. And remember, I'll be right behind you watchin' every move you make. The first wrong move you make, I'll blow your brains out." Caleb did as he was told, selected a blue roan horse, and put his saddle on it. Will pulled the rifle out of the saddle sling and tossed it in the stall the horse had occupied. Then Will handcuffed Caleb's trembling hands behind his back before helping him up into the saddle. With the horse's reins tied to a post, Will cut a short length of rope from a coil hanging on a peg beside the stall and used it to tie Caleb's feet together under the horse's belly. He turned the lantern off and with Caleb's reins in his hand, he climbed up on Buster and walked the horses out of the barn. Not willing to risk being seen by anyone at the house, he rode behind the bunkhouse again, holding the horses to a steady walking pace, hoping not to attract any attention.

He found the spot where he had left his packhorse with no trouble, so he tied a lead line on the buckskin's saddle while he still held the roan's reins in his hand. Having kidnapped another Hawkins without alerting anyone at the ranch this time, he started back toward the Wichita River, anxious to put some distance between him and the ranch. He was not really concerned about anyone coming after him, for he honestly believed there was no one there to come after him. The older man in the bunkhouse was a possibility maybe, but he didn't expect so. It would have to rank as the most ridiculously easy arrest he had ever made. The young man was so obviously afraid, Will almost felt sorry for him. He had to remind himself that Caleb was the jasper who put a bullet in his shoulder.

Once he struck the Wichita River, he followed

it toward the Red and the Oklahoma border, making a stop to make camp after bypassing Wichita Falls. He wanted to give his horses a rest and he thought he could use some coffee and maybe a little bacon, so he built a fire after handcuffing Caleb to a tree. When he asked his prisoner if he was hungry, Caleb said that he wasn't, he had eaten just before he was captured. It was the first time he had dared to speak since then. Even though he was only about ten miles from the Wichita's confluence point with the Red River, he decided to stay there overnight and start out fresh in the morning. He planned to stop by Clayton Hill's ranch to let him know the threat of cattle rustlers had been stopped, at least temporarily. There was no way to guarantee it wouldn't resume again by Fanny Hawkins or some other outlaw. He knew Dan Stone would appreciate some proof of closure on the request for help from the ranchers in that Red River community. Will figured three rustlers buried somewhere below the east–west wagon track and the final Hawkins son on his way to jail in Fort Smith should be proof enough that the U.S. Marshal responded to their needs.

When Robert Baines heard his sister ringing out the signal that breakfast was ready, he walked up to the house to eat. Maudie said good morning and when she saw that Caleb was not with him, she asked if he was coming to breakfast. "Blamed if I know," Robert answered. "I thought Caleb would be sleepin' in the house just like he always did before his brothers all got killed."

"Kinda surprised me, too," Maudie said. "Miz Fanny is pretty strict in her ways. But she might let Caleb move back in the house again." She glanced toward the back door. "Where is he, anyway? Ain't he gonna eat breakfast?"

"I don't know where he is," Robert said, busy consuming the breakfast on his plate. "He said he was goin' to the outhouse last night. He never came back before I went to sleep, and when I woke up this mornin', he weren't there. I figured he mighta snuck back in the house last night. You sure he ain't in here asleep?"

"I walked down the hall past the boys' bedroom on my way to the kitchen. The door was open. There weren't nobody in there. Reckon where he is?"

"Beats the hell outta me," Robert replied. "Let me finish my breakfast and get outta here before you tell her. Maybe he'll be back in the bunkhouse directly."

"I gotta take her breakfast in to her in fifteen minutes and I'll have to tell her Caleb didn't come to eat. She'll be fit to be tied. She don't want nobody to make any decisions but her, and she never told Caleb he could go anywhere."

Maudie was accurate in her opinion that

Fanny would be furious to find that Caleb had disappeared. She was close to a stroke after Robert later returned to the house to report that the blue roan was missing from his stall, as was Caleb's saddle. But his rifle was lying in the empty stall, and his gun belt was still in the bunkhouse. For a long few moments, Fanny was too enraged to make a sound. What Robert had just told her was enough to paint a picture for her of another brazen visit to her ranch by Will Tanner, a deputy marshal out of Fort Smith, Arkansas, who thought he could go anywhere he wanted to make an arrest. "Where the hell is Jack Coffey?" Fanny demanded.

It was close to dinnertime when Clay Hill called out from the loft of the barn, "Hey, Papa, look who's comin' yonder!" Clayton looked up toward the hayloft to see his son pointing toward the lane through the trees. "It's Will Tanner, and he's got somebody with him."

Clayton immediately put down the harness he was mending and walked out in the yard to meet Will. He stopped halfway and waited for Will to come to him when he saw the man on the horse Will was leading was handcuffed. "That the other one?" Clayton asked. "The one that shot one of his partners?" Caleb cringed when he heard him. He didn't know they knew it was him who shot Welch. Will had said nothing about it. It was

135

enough to bring him to the verge of panic. He had gotten nervous as soon as he realized Will was taking him back to the ranch they had attempted to rustle. Seeing the angry face of Clayton Hill now caused him to wonder if Will had brought him back here with the intention of hanging him.

"This is Caleb Hawkins," Will said, answering Clayton's questions. "He was the fourth man on that party of rustlers. I'm takin' him to Fort Smith to trial, but I wanted to let you and your neighbors know that Fanny Hawkins hasn't got anybody to steal for her anymore. My boss, Marshal Dan Stone, will be talkin' with his counterpart in Texas to investigate the Hawkins ranch and take over that responsibility."

"Well, that's good news, I swear. It's about time somebody gave us some help. Next time, if there is one, we'll just send for you. Wait till I tell Dillard and the Wiggins brothers. Matter of fact, Jordan Hatfield would like to know about it, too. You know, it would be a mighty good thing if we could have us another little meetin' at Hatfield's store and tell everybody at the same time. We could have it tonight. My boy Clay can jump on his horse and go tell the others to come to Hatfield's tonight after supper. Whaddaya say, Will, just set you back half a day?" When Will hesitated, Clayton pressed, "In the meantime, I can tell Louise to throw some extra taters in the pan for dinner." He took a long look at Caleb and said, "We'll throw some in for your prisoner, too."

"You'd best check that with your wife," Will said. "We ain't givin' her much notice."

"Stanley, go tell your mother she's gonna have company for dinner," Clayton told the twelve-year-old. He turned at once and ran to the house. Clayton looked at Clay then. "What are you waitin' for, boy? Go get your horse."

Stanley was gone for only a couple of minutes before he came out of the kitchen door and ran back to them. "Mama saw Will ride in the yard, and she was already rollin' out some more biscuits."

"I'll need a place to park my prisoner," Will said at once, causing Clayton to chuckle.

"I figured that would make your decision for you," he said. "We can put Mr. Hawkins in the corncrib. I'll put a padlock on the door. That oughta suit him for a little while."

"Want me to go get the padlock outta the barn, Papa?" Stanley asked, eager to help with Will's prisoner.

"Yeah, run get it, Stan," Clayton answered. Back to Will, he said, "Really don't need a padlock. Just stick a screwdriver in it and that'll do the trick. The lock is to keep people out of the corncrib, not to keep 'em from gettin' out of it. But since this is such an important guest, we'll put the lock on it."

Caleb could hear the conversation and nothing

he heard gave him any encouragement. Will had told him he would take him to trial in Fort Smith, but instead, he brought him here where he had tried to steal cattle. And now they were planning a general meeting of all the farmers in this part of the territory that Caleb and his brothers had rustled more than once. It sounded to him that he was going to be turned over to these small ranchers he had robbed, and their decision was undoubtedly going to be for hanging. Even if Tanner tried to dissuade them, he would not likely be able to deny them their revenge. *I should not have surrendered so easily,* he thought, even though he knew he had surrendered because he had been afraid to die.

When Stan came back with the padlock, Will untied Caleb's feet and helped him down off the roan, then took him to the crib. He opened the door and said, "Here, gimme your hands." Caleb held them up and Will unlocked the cuff on one of Caleb's hands. "Now, crawl up on that corn." The corn in the crib was only about knee-high, so Caleb crawled up on his hands and knees. "I'll bring you something to eat, soon as it's ready," Will said as he put the lock in the hasp. He went to take care of the horses then, relieving them of their packs and saddles. And he stood there a short while, watching Buster and the roan drink from the creek until he heard Clayton come up behind him.

"I was wonderin' how you captured that man," Clayton remarked. "You musta caught him before he got back to Fanny Hawkins's ranch."

"Almost," Will replied, and tried to drop it right there.

Clayton wanted details, however, so he could tell the story in detail to others. "Whaddaya mean, almost? You mean he was just about there?"

"He made it home before I could catch him," Will said. "I had to arrest him after he got home. The ranch looked almost deserted. They lost their cow thieves right here at your place, so there wasn't anybody there to help him. I surprised him and he didn't put up a fight. End of story. I wish they were all that easy."

Clayton nodded his head thoughtfully. He believed there was a lot more to the story than Will wanted to tell. It figured. He had already seen that Will was not a bragging man—modest, in fact, was his guess. The man had single-handedly cut down three cattle rustlers and driven the other one off, all by himself. There was bound to be more to the story of Caleb's capture. If he wouldn't give the details, Clayton decided he might have to fill them in when relating the story.

CHAPTER 9

When Louise signaled that dinner was ready, Will filled a plate and took it, along with a cup of coffee, out to the corncrib. Since the corn ears that Caleb was perched upon were not a level surface, Will handed him the plate of food first, so he could set it down while he arranged the ears like a shallow hole to put the cup in. "I'll check on you later," he told him, and went back inside to eat his dinner. As he had before, he made a big fuss over the biscuits, pleasing Louise no end. Dinner was over and Will was still drinking coffee with Clayton when Clay returned. "Here comes Paul Revere now," Clayton japed. "Mama, reckon there's anything left to feed the messenger?"

"Sit down, son," Louise said. "I've got your plate in the oven."

"Did you see all of 'em?" Clayton asked. Clay said he did and that they were all going to be there. "After supper, right?"

"Right," Clay answered. "Mr. Dillard said after supper was all right, now that there ain't no more rustlers."

"You told Hatfield, didn't you?" Clayton asked. " 'Cause if you didn't, he's liable to be closed."

"Yessir," Clay answered, "and he said thanks for includin' him."

Will thanked Louise once again for the dinner for him and his prisoner then tried to convince her that they wouldn't need any supper. He was afraid he and Caleb were costing them too much. She quashed his protest and told him she was going to cook enough for everybody, so he'd darn sure better be at that supper table. He claimed he didn't want Caleb to get used to fancy fare. She laughed and declared that no one had ever called it fancy before. Will looked at Clayton and Clayton winked, proud of his wife's manner as well as her cooking. "I'll go and check on my prisoner and my horses. You folks go on with whatever you were doin'. If there's anything I can do to help, I'd be glad to pitch in, as long as it's somewhere I can keep an eye on Caleb." He wasn't comfortable just waiting around for supper when he was plenty full from dinner. He was never any good at wasting time. *I might as well be sitting in the corncrib with Caleb,* he thought.

He had already collected Caleb's dishes and returned them to the kitchen, but he went back over to the corncrib again because he had nothing else to do. "You doin' all right?" he asked when he walked up. Caleb answered with nothing more than the most forlorn look Will thought he had ever seen. "I saw an old bucket outside the barn when I took the horses to water. I'll go get it for you, in case you have to pee. We're gonna be here for a while yet, so I doubt you can hold it that long, and I don't want you to go on the corn."

"I'd appreciate it," Caleb finally spoke. Will nodded, turned around, and headed for the barn. He was back in a few minutes with the bucket, banging on the sides of it to shake out what looked like dirt caked in the bottom of it. He inspected it again and decided there were no holes in it, so he opened the door and passed it in to Caleb, who said, "Thank you." Will started to walk away again when Caleb suddenly asked a question. "Are you really gonna take me to Fort Smith to stand trial?"

"That's my intention," Will answered. "Why are you askin'?"

"Why are you takin' me to that meetin' tonight with those other ranchers? Why don't we start out for Fort Smith?"

"Well, we are killin' a lotta time waitin' around for that meetin'," Will allowed, thinking Caleb sounded like a little kid asking why he had to go to bed. "But it's what we in the Marshals Service call a courtesy. The owners of these farms you and your brothers have been hittin' on a regular schedule need to be assured that you ain't gonna hit 'em no more. And also, the Marshals Service needs to show 'em evidence that we responded when they asked for help. We'll be headin' to Fort Smith first thing in the mornin'. You ain't got nothin' to worry about. They just wanna see an arrested rustler in the flesh. All right?"

"All right," Caleb answered, but he was convinced more than ever that it might be all right for Will Tanner, but it was going to be a lynching for Caleb Hawkins. Will, on the other hand, was certain now that Caleb was actually weak in the brain, like maybe it stopped developing after he reached a very young age. He was not looking forward to the long trip to Fort Smith with the simple person he was getting to know. Maybe he'd be better when they got to Atoka and picked up Reese Trainer, if he was still there. Surely someone would already have picked him up, though. Will hadn't thought about Reese Trainer for some time, and he wondered now how long Jim Little Eagle had to take care of him before a jail wagon from Fort Smith showed up.

Over one hundred miles east of Clayton Hill's farm and cattle ranch, twelve miles from the town of Atoka, a grim-looking man, tall and thin, with a dark mustache, stood gazing at the charred ruins of what had once been a trading post. He might have wished this was not the place he had come from Texas to find, but he knew damn well it was. Reese's letter had been highly detailed in the directions. He shifted his gaze to the small barn still standing when a man walked out the door and stood looking at him. So he led his

144

horses over to talk to him. The man, an Indian, said nothing, watching the white man carefully as he approached. "What happened here?" he asked, and gestured back toward the charred remains of the saloon. He could see a woman and some children inside the little barn.

"Place burn down," the Indian said.

"No foolin'," the white man responded sarcastically. "Where is the man who built it?"

"Gone. This my house now."

"Where did he go?" The Indian shrugged. The white man could see he wasn't going to get much help from the Choctaw man, so he tried one last thing. "Atoka? Which way to Atoka?"

"Atoka, that trail." He pointed to a narrow trail leading away from the creek. It was a continuation of the trail that led him to this point. It seemed to be heading in the right direction, so he nodded to the Indian and climbed back on his horse. Reese's map said Atoka was twelve miles in that direction, so he figured he'd make it there by suppertime.

He rode the length of the main street of the little town, turned around, and went back to the building beside what looked to be a rooming house. There was a sign over the door that read, LOTTIE'S KITCHEN. It was evidently his only choice for supper, so he tied his horses at the hitching rail and went inside. "Welcome," a smiling woman greeted him as he stood just inside the door, looking the place over. He nodded in return to her welcome. Noticing the table near the door and the sign on it, he unbuckled his gun belt, rolled it up, and placed it on the table. He got another smile from Lottie then, one of appreciation. "This is your first time to visit us, isn't it?"

"That's right," he answered.

"Well, I hope we make it a pleasant experience for you. I'm Lottie. Lou-Bell will be taking care of you. Sit wherever there's an empty chair." She signaled Lou-Bell then as he walked over to a small table against the wall and sat down, facing the front door.

"Evening, my name is Louise. They call me Lou-Bell because my last name's Bellone. What do they call you?"

He looked at her for a moment before answering, "Frank."

"Well, glad to meet you, Frank. What would you like to drink?" When he hesitated for a moment, she asked, "Is it Frank something, or something Frank?"

"It's just Frank," he answered. "I'll drink coffee."

"Right, Frank, coffee it is. I'll go get it while you're decidin' if you're gonna eat meat loaf or baked ham. You get your choice tonight." She left to get his coffee, thinking that her usual charm wasn't going to be enough to thaw this customer.

When she returned with his coffee, he told her he would try the baked ham, so she went back to the kitchen to get his plate. "Who's the sinister-looking customer that just came in?" Lottie asked her as she sliced some of the ham for his plate.

"All I know is his name is Frank, and I think that's about all I'm gonna know about him," Lou-Bell answered. "He ain't the chatty type."

"He looks like an undertaker," Lottie japed. "Maybe he's in town to take over Tom Murdock's old business." They both laughed at that. Tom was the town barber who also handled the undertaking business before he was shot by a man named Luke Cobb. "Shut my mouth," Lottie said then. "That was not nice to joke about poor Tom like that."

Lou-Bell took the plate and a couple of biscuits out and placed them before Frank. "How's that look? Can I get you anything else to go with it?"

"Maybe you can answer a question for me," he said. "On my way to town tonight, I passed a burnt-down buildin'. Do you know anything about the man who owned that and what happened to him?"

"About twelve miles from here, on Clear Boggy Creek?" Lou-Bell asked. Frank nodded. "That was a man named Reese," she continued. "He was sellin' whiskey to the Indians until Will Tanner closed him down."

"What happened to Reese?"

"Will arrested him," Lou-Bell replied. "He's still in jail here while he's waitin' for a jail wagon to take him to Fort Smith, Arkansas." Even in a nearly 100 percent expressionless face, she could see that her remark definitely registered with him.

"In jail? I didn't see any jail when I rode in," he replied.

"You have to know where to look for it to find it," she explained. "It's an old smokehouse the Choctaw policeman uses to lock up drunks and rowdy Indians." She could tell she had his interest, so she said, "We're fixin' his meals for him. Jim Little Eagle is taking care of him while Will's out of town. Jim oughta be in here anytime now to pick up Reese's supper."

Frank nodded his head but said nothing in response, so Lou-Bell left him while she responded to another customer's call. In his brain he was rapidly processing what she had told him while he ate his supper in time with his rapid thoughts. His plate was emptied by the time Jim Little Eagle walked in the door and stood talking to Lottie while he waited for Lou-Bell to bring Reese Trainer's supper to him. When Jim turned to leave, Frank got up from the table and headed for the front door. He handed Lottie the money for his supper and quickly strapped on his gun belt. "I hope your supper was satisfactory," she said.

"It was good," he allowed.

"Well, come back to see us, mister"—she paused—"Frank. I forgot, we don't know your last name."

"Trainer," he said as he went out the door, leaving Lottie to turn to look at Lou-Bell, her hand pressed over her wide-open mouth.

Outside, Frank saw Jim Little Eagle walking past Brant's store. Frank untied his horses and led them as he followed the Choctaw policeman down toward the stables. But before reaching them, he turned in an alley. When Frank reached the alley, he saw the small square log building. *Good,* he thought when he saw Jim's horse tied at the corner of the building. *I'm going to need a horse.* He tied his two horses at the rail in front of the barbershop, which was on one side of the alley, and appeared to be closed. Then he walked down the alley just as Jim unlocked the padlock on the door and drew his pistol when he lifted the padlock from the latch. Unaware of the man behind him with his .44 leveled at his back, Jim opened the door and stepped back to let Reese come out for his supper. "Drop it or you're dead," Frank demanded, and jammed the pistol against Jim's back. Startled, Jim had no choice but to obey. He dropped the revolver on the ground. "Pick it up, Reese!" Frank said.

"Frank?" Reese blurted, scarcely able to believe it was his brother, but then he recovered quickly

149

enough to reach down and grab Jim Little Eagle's pistol. "Now, you damn savage," he threatened, and aimed the gun at the Choctaw.

"Hold it, Reese!" Frank commanded. "Don't do it. We don't want the whole damn Injun nation down on us." He gave Jim a shove through the open door. "We'll just let him take your place for a while." He closed the door and put the padlock back on the latch, but he didn't lock it. "Besides, he ain't the one who put you in this rathole. That's the one we're gonna go after."

"Maybe you're right," Reese conceded. "The Injun didn't treat me bad while I was in here, but I wouldn'ta been in here if he hadn't wired the damn marshal and he sent Will Tanner over here to burn up everything I had. He wiped me out, Frank. I'm gonna kill him!"

"Yes, you are," Frank told him, "and I'm gonna help you do it." Although he appeared calmer about the threat, he was hurt just as badly as his brother. Just as Reese had been, Frank was very much invested in the business just burned to the ground. He came from Texas eager to see the building Reese described in his letter only to arrive at a pile of ashes and charred beams, and an Indian family living in the barn. He wanted to see Will Tanner dead as badly as Reese did. "Where is Will Tanner?"

"I don't know," Reese answered. "From what I could figure out, hearin' him talkin' to that

Injun in there, he rode out past the Arbuckles somewhere to settle some cattle rustlin' problems. I'm lucky I was still here when you got here. He wired Fort Smith for a jail wagon to ship me to Fort Smith."

"Well, we need to get outta here before somebody finds out it's the Injun policeman shut up inside this damned smokehouse instead of you. I brought you a nice-lookin' horse and saddle to ride. That ain't no Injun saddle, either, that's a fine-lookin' rockin' chair settin' on that gray geldin'."

"That's that Injun's horse," Reese said. "How the hell can he afford a horse and saddle like that?"

"Probably what he picks up helpin' that deputy that put us outta business. What happened to all that whiskey I sent you?"

"That's what he used to start the fire that burned us out," Reese answered.

"You mean he didn't carry that whiskey off to sell somewhere else?" Frank couldn't believe it. "That woulda set him up for a pretty good payday. I swear, there ain't nobody I got less respect for than a damn honest lawman." He spat on the jailhouse door to punctuate his ire. "Now, we'd best get the hell outta here before somebody starts wonderin' where the Injun policeman is."

"Where are we goin'?" Reese asked. "They took everything I had. They took my gun belt, my rifle, all my cartridges, even took my blanket. I need to get some stuff."

"You ain't gotta worry. I took a big hit, too, but I'm still pretty well fixed. I've got two extra cartridge belts in them packs. That pistol you picked up looks like it's in good shape. Smith & Wesson, ain't it? And there's a rifle in that saddle sling. You'll be just fine."

"Where are we goin'?" Reese repeated. "I wanna know where to find Will Tanner."

"You ain't gotta worry about that," Frank insisted. "When he gets back here and finds out you're gone and you left this Injun friend of his in the smokehouse, he'll find you. So here's what we need to do. Before I left Waco, I got a letter from Brady Thompson. He asked me if you and I wanted to go in with him on a saloon and whorehouse in Injun Territory. He said he'd already got halfway set up on Blue River, near Tishomingo. The building's already there. It was the old tradin' post owned by Lem Stark before him and his two sons were killed. Remember that? Lem had a wife named Minnie Three Toes. She left there. And some say it was Minnie that killed Lem. When I got his letter, it was too late, even if we was interested in goin' into business with Brady. You already had your place built here, so I never bothered to write him back. We can go to Tishomingo and see what ol' Brady's got goin' for himself over there. Whaddaya think? Maybe we might wanna go into business with him. We get a few drunk Injuns raisin' hell over that way, we're liable to have the Injun police cryin' to Fort Smith about it. That's in Chickasaw Nation, so it won't be the same Injun that lives here. He won't know us, but chances are the deputy they send will be Will Tanner."

"That sounds good to me," Reese said. "Let's get movin' outta this damn town." He stepped up into Jim Little Eagle's saddle and pulled the gray gelding up close to the smokehouse door. "Hey, Little Eagle, behave yourself in there and maybe they'll bring you some breakfast in the mornin'." Then the two brothers galloped their horses up the main street, heading for Tishomingo about thirty-five miles southwest of Atoka. It was already dark, and they knew the general direction the town was in but were not sure what trail would take them there. So they decided to take any road that looked like it might be heading in the right direction and put Atoka behind them. They would look for a place to camp, then in the morning, they could ask somebody for directions to Tishomingo.

CHAPTER 10

The afternoon had dragged by until suppertime and Will was surprised that he was hungry enough to eat after not having done a lick of work since dinner. But he knew he had to make a show of it for Louise's sake, especially when it came to the biscuits. Thankfully, it was finally time to express his appreciation to her once again for her hospitality and bid her and the two boys farewell. He got Caleb settled on his horse again and with Clayton Hill leading, they headed for Jordan Hatfield's store. When they got to Hatfield's, they found that they were the last to arrive. The others, Dillard, Kemp, Cal and Sonny Wiggins, and Hatfield as well, were that eager to get a look at one of the rustlers who had caused their grief. Their curiosity was enough to make Caleb even more frightened and jumpy than before, as they crowded around him and Will in the process of dismounting. Will immediately regretted agreeing to the meeting, but it was too late by then. "You said you needed a secure place to hold your prisoner while we had our meeting," Hatfield said. "We can put him in my storeroom, and I'll lock the door. There ain't no windows or no way to get out. You can even keep him in there all night if you want to, and you can make your camp here tonight. Then Dawn can fix you up with a good breakfast to start you out right in the mornin'."

"Thanks just the same," Will said. "But I think it'll be better if I camp down the river a ways. We won't be at this meeting long and I can make camp and be started early in the mornin'. I like to get a real early start before breakfast and cook breakfast when I have to stop and rest my horses. That'll be better, anyway, and the rest of you can carry on as late as you like, and we'll be out of the way." When Dillard and Kemp looked kind of disappointed, Will said, "You've all had a chance to see one of the rustlers, and I expect you got a look at the other three before they were buried." He could tell by their reaction that they had. He figured Clayton must have waited awhile before burying them, knowing that all of the ranchers wanted to see the dead rustlers. "So now you've seen the last one. That was what you wanted, wasn't it?" Will heard a few grumbles, and he couldn't imagine what their problem was, but he thought they'd seen all they needed to see, so he had Hatfield lock Caleb in the storeroom and hand him the key.

"What else have we got to meet about?" Henry Kemp asked. "I figured we was gonna hang him, and that's what we was really meetin' about."

"I thought the same thing," John Dillard spoke up. "So we could send a message to any future Texas cattle rustlers who think we're easy pickin's. Let 'em know what happens to rustlers in Oklahoma Territory."

Their comments warmed the conversation up to a higher pitch, so Will held up his hand and asked for their attention. "Before this goes any further, I need to tell you that there ain't gonna be no hangin'. I'll be takin' my prisoner back for trial, just like I was assigned to do by U.S. Marshal Daniel Stone. There ain't no doubt he'll be found guilty, but if his punishment is hangin' or a prison sentence, we'll leave that up to the judge." His position was disappointing to some of them, but after seeing what he did when he fought four outlaws all by himself, no one wanted to challenge him.

Hatfield was the first to back him up. "Will's right. If we're ever gonna have law and order out here in this part of the territory, it's gonna be up to men like us to obey the laws of the land."

His statement was met with shrugs of indifference and still some signs of disappointment, but no real objections, so Will continued. "Now, the reason I came to this meetin' was, first, to let you see that the fourth rustler did not get away and he is in custody. And, second, I thought you would want to know what the possibility was for more attempts by Fanny Hawkins to raid your cattle." He went on then to paint them a picture of the large cattle ranch with no one to take care of what cattle they already had, and certainly no one to raid other ranches. "The whole place looked deserted. I was able to slip in and confront Caleb Hawkins without anyone at the house even knowin' I was there." He summed it up by saying, "There ain't no guarantee that you ain't ever gonna get hit by cattle rustlers, but I don't think you'll have to worry about Fanny Hawkins for quite a while. And my boss is gonna go to his counterpart in Texas to ask for some action on his part to put a stop to Fanny Hawkins and the like. I hope none of you have any more trouble like this, and I wanna thank you for your help and your hospitality."

His little speech was good for a softening of the feeling of vengeance that some had brought with them. So Will lingered awhile longer than he had at first intended, encouraged by Bright Dawn, Hatfield's wife, who served coffee and corn bread. Before it became much later, however, he said it was time for him to leave. "I wanna be sure my prisoner and I get some sleep tonight. We've got a long ride ahead of us." So all the men wanted to shake his hand and thank him for responding to their call for help. All done, he went to the storeroom to tell Caleb it was time to go. As a precaution, having been in similar situations with a prisoner locked up, he prepared himself for any surprise upon his opening of the door. He had looked around the room when he put Caleb in it and had not seen anything that might be used as a weapon. Besides that, Caleb was almost a frightened mess by then and didn't look capable of any resistance. He would actually have been very surprised if Caleb made an attempt to attack him.

Not sure what to expect as well, Hatfield and the other men followed Will to the storeroom door but stood back out of the way when he unlocked the door and opened it. Caleb didn't come out, so Will went in. After a minute or so with no sound from inside the room, Hatfield's curiosity overcame his caution and he stepped inside the door to find Will standing there, staring at Caleb's body hanging on a rope tied to a rafter overhead. "I swear," Hatfield muttered.

Aware of Hatfield behind him only after he spoke, Will turned around and confessed, "I didn't think of that possibility. I didn't see any rope."

"It was in a cabinet, right there in that corner," Hatfield said, as the other men, hearing them calmly talking, filed in the room to look at the corpse. Will found it hard to explain, but he couldn't help feeling a little compassion for a young man so filled with fear that he would take his own life to prevent someone else from taking it.

One person feeling no compassion for the young man, Cal Wiggins said to his younger brother Sonny, "Now ain't that somethin' to find hangin' in your storeroom?" He stuck his head out the door and yelled to Bright Dawn. "Hey, Dawn, you left somethin' hangin' in your storeroom." She came at once to the door to see what they were talking about.

"Dawn, honey, you don't need to see this," Hatfield told her, but it was too late to prevent her from seeing it.

"Bad luck!" Bright Dawn cried out. "Get him out of there! Bad luck, dead man in house!"

"Dad-gum it," Hatfield said. "Now you've got her all upset. We'll get him outta here, Dawn," he called out to her, and went to help Will get Caleb down from the rafter.

Cal cupped his hand beside his mouth and whispered to Sonny, "Now you know why Hatfield calls her Dawn instead of Bright."

While Will put his arms around Caleb's legs, in position to catch him on his shoulder, Hatfield stood up on the overturned keg that Caleb had stood on when he tied the rope to the rafter. Will lifted the body so Hatfield could untie the knot, then let it drop on his shoulder, and walked on out the door with it. He laid the body across the saddle of the blue roan and untied it as well as Buster and his packhorse. He turned to the party of men who followed him outside. "I reckon I'll be goin' now. Maybe I'll see you fellows again, if I'm out this way again."

"With what's just happened, maybe you might stay over a little longer," Clayton Hill suggested, making one last attempt.

" 'Preciate the invite, Clayton, but I've got a prisoner waitin' in Atoka for me to pick up, so I'd best be gettin' along." He climbed up into the saddle, tipped his hat to them, and rode away into the night.

"Well, we had us a hangin', anyway," Henry Kemp remarked.

Will rode out on the same path that brought him to the tiny settlement of Waurika. By any standard, he had to say he had successfully taken care of the problem he had been sent to resolve. The Hawkins' cattle operation had been stopped, maybe forever, maybe not. It would depend on how important it was to the state of Texas and whether or not they took action against Fanny Hawkins. In spite of his success, he still wasn't satisfied that it had been done by the book. Caleb Hawkins might have been sentenced to death for his part in the raids, or he might have been sent to prison. It had been Will's job to transport him safely to court, and he didn't do that. "I'm startin' to think like an old married man, worryin' about the young 'uns," he commented to Buster. "Things don't always happen the way they're supposed to. At least I'll give this poor tortured soul a decent burial. I reckon I owe him that.

Scared to death, that don't sound like a good way to die."

He figured he had ridden about four miles in the dark when he came to a lively stream and decided he'd make his camp beside it. But first, he'd try to get Caleb into the ground before rigor mortis began to set in. So he turned off the trail he had been traveling and rode down the stream until he found a spot of ground that looked to be free of a lot of roots. He picked a spot to dig that was not close to the water and pulled Caleb's body off the horse. He was glad to see that rigor mortis had not started to set in as yet and he could lay the body out flat on the ground. Next, he led his horses back upstream about forty yards and unloaded them, hobbled the roan and the packhorse, then returned to Caleb with his short spade that he carried on his packs and began to dig.

He wasn't sure how long it took him to dig enough of a grave with his short shovel to feel like an animal wasn't likely to dig it up again. It seemed like a hell of a long time, and when he finally rolled Caleb over into the grave, he noticed he was already showing some stiffness. When the grave was filled in, he disguised it as best he could with dead limbs and leaves, and then performed a casual eulogy. "Here lies Caleb Hawkins. I hope his soul is on its way to a better place than where his brothers are." He paused, then added, "And where his mama will be goin'."

With that finally finished, he went back to his horses and started collecting wood for a fire. He wasn't hungry. He'd already had plenty to eat, but after digging the grave, he had begun to cool down a little and he thought a fire would feel good. When he sat by his fire, he started thinking about Reese Trainer and wondered if he was still in Atoka or if he was on his way to Fort Smith. Surely Stone had sent a jail wagon by this time. But if he hadn't, he planned to transport Trainer on the blue roan that now wore an empty saddle. He might even meet the jail wagon somewhere between Atoka and Fort Smith, he thought. He allowed himself a quick mental picture of Sophie Bennett, then immediately amended it to Sophie Tanner. He hadn't been married long enough to make that sound right. He shook his head then and thought of the snit she was bound to be in when he did get home. As he had learned to do, he put thoughts of her away in the back of his mind when he was on the job. Had he only known of the violent storm that was on his horizon as he made his way across Indian Territory, it might have occurred to him that he might never see Fort Smith again. Even pushing his horses a little harder than usual, he had two and a half days of riding to reach Atoka, then at least two and a half more from there to Fort Smith.

• • •

"Hey! Where can a man get a drink of likker around here?" Frank Trainer yelled out when he and Reese walked into the trading post on the Blue River. Then he stood in the open door, grinning like a dog eating yellow jackets while he waited for Brady Thompson to come storming out of the back room. He didn't have to wait long.

"Who the hell is hollerin' out here?" Brady wanted to know, his voice sounding like a wire brush scraping rust off a piece of iron, the result of a .44 bullet that went through his neck in a saloon gunfight in Dodge City. He stopped short when he saw who it was. "Frank Trainer! I swear, and Reese, too. Well, I'll be go to hell," he rasped. "Did you get my letter?"

"Sure, I got your letter," Frank said. "Why the hell do you think me and Reese are here?"

"Well, I'll be . . . I thought you just wasn't interested enough to answer it. I'll tell you the truth, it riled me a little to think you didn't answer, and now here you are."

"I figured I could get here as quick as a letter, so I just decided to come on down here and see what you've got yourself into," Frank said. "I'da been here quicker, but Reese had built him a business down here and ran into trouble with the law, and they burned him down. So I went up there to get him to come with me."

"I heard about it," Brady rasped, "over toward Atoka. I knew when you built that place you was bound to have some trouble outta that damn Choctaw policeman," he said to Reese. "Tough luck, though. He got Will Tanner sent out here from Fort Smith, didn't he?"

"That he did," Reese answered.

"I knew it," Brady rasped. "It ain't like that over this way. This is Chickasaw territory, and there's a Chickasaw policeman in Tishomingo, but he don't care about nothin' outside of town. And he'll send a wire into Fort Smith once in a while, if he starts seein' too many drunk Injuns in town. But he ain't never been out this far to cause me no trouble."

He paused while they thought about that, then asked, "You remember this place? Lem Stark ran his business here for years before him and his family started killin' each other off. It's a good piece from town and a good place to hole up for a while, down here on the river. I've already got a good Injun trade in the short time I've been here. I expect to see some of the outlaws on the run pretty soon, as soon as word gets around that I've reopened it. Everybody already knows where this place is." That reminded him. "Speakin' of outlaws, you know who was in here day before yesterday and stayed overnight?" He paused, then said, "Jack Coffey." He paused again to wait for their reaction.

"Jack Coffey," Frank echoed. "What was he doin' over here? I heard he was holed up in Texarkana. Where was he goin'?" Jack Coffey was a name well known by most men who made their living on the wrong side of the law. Coffey was a killer for hire, as friendly as a rattlesnake and with a strike just as deadly.

"He was headin' to Texas to talk about a job," Brady rasped. "Some old lady over near Wichita Falls, he said. And that's all he would say about it. He asked me about the best way to get there from here. But, hell, what are we standin' here yakkin' for? Come on in and set down. Whaddaya want to drink? I've got corn and rye, whatever suits your fancy."

"I didn't think you was ever gonna ask," Reese said. "Let's try the rye and see if it's as good as what Will Tanner burnt up at my place."

"Well, you ain't my competition no more," Brady said, chuckling, "so I reckon I'd be happy to pour you one." He went behind the bar, got a bottle, and put it on the table. Then he got three glasses. They sat down at the table and he rasped, "Now, let's talk some business. I know you two boys didn't come to Blue River just to visit ol' Brady. Least, I hope to hell you didn't."

"You're right, Brady, we came to talk business. Reese and I have a little money plus the best source of molasses in the territory at the best price. What we need to know is just how much you've got here and what plans you're thinkin' about makin'. If we invest in it, we'll be doin' it because we wanna build it to be the only place a man on the run from the law wants to go to."

"Sounds to me like you just said everything that I'm thinkin' about doin' with this place," Brady replied. "I could use some help, somebody to invest money in the place to get it to where it's makin' the money it can. I'm tellin' you boys, there ain't gonna be no other place around here where a man can spend his hard-earned money. We ain't that far from the Arbuckles, where there's a couple of outlaw hideouts that I know of. Think about those ol' boys settin' around in some little ol' shack back in them mountains when they find out there's whiskey and women waitin' to help 'em get shed of that money they stole." He paused and took a drink of whiskey while he let them get that picture in their minds. "Whaddaya think, boys? You interested?"

Frank looked at his brother and nodded. "Yeah, I think we are, ain't we, Reese?"

"I reckon," Reese answered. "I'd like to look around the rest of the buildin', though, see how much stock you've got, so we could see what we'd need right away." He looked around the room then. "Ain't you got anybody workin' for you? Are you runnin' it by yourself?"

"I got Loafer Perkins, he does just whatever I need to have done. He's down at the stable right now. And I got a cook in the kitchen," Brady rasped defensively. "And she's a jim-dandy one, too. I don't have to pay her much. She's a Chickasaw woman. I call her Sally 'cause her Injun name sounds more like Sally to me, and I can't pronounce her Injun name. A couple of the men in her family keep us supplied with fresh game, too, deer meat, rabbit, coon. I pay 'em with whiskey. Even get some beef and goat meat sometimes." He winked at them, knowing they could guess where that came from. "So whaddaya think?"

"I think you're gonna be thankin' your lucky stars Reese and I came down here to see you," Frank answered him. "It looks like you've planted a nice little sprout of a business here. You just need me and Reese to fertilize it. Let's go see the rest of the place."

"All right!" Brady rasped. "Lemme go tell Sally she'll need to cook for two extra mouths, and I'll show you the upstairs."

When he hurried to the kitchen, Frank commented quietly to Reese, "We'll use him for everything we can till we get a handle on it. Then he's liable to have an accident. He never was a very careful man." Reese nodded and smiled. When Brady came back, Frank said, "Let's see what kinda stock you've got before we go upstairs. All right?"

"Sure thing," Brady rasped. "Right this way."

He led them down a hallway, past the kitchen where the plump little Indian woman was working over the stove, to a room just short of the back porch. Brady stopped and said, "Poke your head in the door and say howdy to Sally." Sally turned to look at them, then promptly turned back to her stove. "She ain't much on visitin', but she's a doggone good cook." He proceeded on to the storeroom, pulled out a key, and unlocked a padlock on the door, then swung it open for them.

The two brothers walked into a large, half-filled room of various supplies, most of which were for the kitchen, like barrels of flour and coffee beans, lard, and so forth. On one side of the room there were three unmarked barrels and several cases of fruit jars. Frank walked over and placed a hand on one of the unmarked barrels. "Whiskey for your Injun trade?"

Brady shrugged. "Whiskey for whoever wants it."

"You sayin' these three barrels is all the whiskey you've got?" Reese asked.

"Well, yeah," Brady rasped. "I'll be buyin' more when I get down to one barrel. I like to keep at least three on hand all the time."

"How much you payin' for that whiskey?" Frank asked, and when Brady told him, Frank said, "You ain't buyin' it the smart way, Brady. You need to buy it by the wagonload. I've got sixteen barrels settin' in Fort Worth, waitin' for me to tell 'em where to haul 'em. I paid half what you're payin' for these barrels. Those sixteen were gonna go to Atoka to Reese's place, but he weren't in no hurry for 'em, so they're still settin' in Fort Worth. As soon as I can get in touch with 'em, I'll have 'em haul that whiskey here." Brady's eyes grew wider and wider as they went through the building and Frank continued to build on the promise of new and bigger business for the trading post on Blue River.

"I got one more question that's botherin' me," Reese said. "What's gonna keep Will Tanner or some other hard-ass deputy from hittin' this place, like they did on my place?" He and Frank both looked at Brady for an answer.

"I don't know," Brady answered honestly. "I can tell you why I think Tanner ain't ever gonna give me no trouble. And he's been in here since I took it over, but it's always to ask me if I've seen one feller or another. I told him that I don't allow no Injuns in here at all, and I don't sell whiskey to Injuns. And I think he believes me because I don't have any back door or window where they come to buy whiskey. Loafer handles the Injun business in the back of the barn. You mighta noticed the barn's backed right up to the trees on the riverbank, so you don't see 'em comin' and goin'. Loafer makes it plain to them bucks that come lookin' for whiskey, if the law finds out we're sellin' it, then that's the end of their whiskey. And like I said before, we're a good ways from that little town of Tishomingo—nobody pays attention to us. And them deputy marshals have got so much ground to cover, they don't worry about us if we don't cause any big trouble."

Their little business discussion was interrupted then when a couple of young men who looked like cowhands, came into the store, and Brady had to excuse himself while he waited on them. "That's a couple of young fellers who work for a little farm and cattle ranch up the river. Lemme go sell 'em a shot of whiskey." He left Frank and Reese sitting at a table while he tended bar.

"It's good he gave us a minute to talk," Frank said. He had been thinking about their decision to go into business with Brady, as well as his brother's business with Will Tanner. "Are you still hot to settle up with that deputy?"

"You're damn right I am," Reese snapped. "I aim to kill him on sight." Frank could see his brother's neck getting red with anger.

"I want you to listen to what I'm gonna say, all right? Will you listen?" Reese calmed down just a hair but said that he would listen. "First, lemme say I want to see he gets what's comin' to him, same as you. He cost us one helluva lot of money, and I'll help you settle with him."

"I don't need any help," Reese interrupted. "I don't want any help. I plan to have the pleasure of doin' for that pain in the butt personally."

"Listen to me, damn it. I'm talkin' about a gold mine right here, if we play our cards right. When Tanner finds out you broke outta that smokehouse, he's gonna come after you."

"That's what I'm countin' on," Reese interrupted again, "and I'll be ready to welcome him."

"Yeah, and if you do kill him, that'll bring every deputy marshal in Fort Smith down on us. And you can say good-bye to everything we put into this place, because they'll close down every business like this. I'm thinkin' he'll search this whole territory lookin' for you. And it's in our best interest that when he searches up near Tishomingo, he doesn't find you on Blue River. Then we've got a good chance we won't see him around here again, especially if he decides you've left the Nations."

"Are you sayin' I should just forget about what he did to me? 'Cause if you are, you're wastin' your breath."

"All right, listen to me. This is what I'm sayin'. We go into business with Brady. But right now, we leave here and go to Fort Worth, where that wagonload of whiskey sits waiting for me. We'll just sit on it for a while. Enjoy ourselves in Fort Worth for a while till Tanner's had time to find out you've left the territory. Then we come back with the whiskey, and we can hunt Tanner down when he ain't got no idea he's bein' hunted."

Reese hesitated for a moment while he considered what Frank proposed. Frank always was the smarter brother, but Reese had never resented it. He decided it would be better to do it like Frank said. It especially appealed to him that Will Tanner would think he had fled the territory and would be totally unaware that he was being stalked. All at once, he calmed down. Then he nodded his head as if thinking deep thoughts, and finally he said, "You're right, that would be better. We'll go to Fort Worth."

CHAPTER 11

Reese and Frank Trainer drank a toast to their new partnership with Brady Thompson and told him they would be leaving right away to make arrangements for delivering sixteen barrels of whiskey to Blue River. Meanwhile, another business arrangement was about to be agreed upon over 125 miles away, as the crow flies.

Riding one of the spotted Palouse horses bred by the Nez Percé Indians in the Palouse River country, he entered the main gate of the Hawkins' Full Moon Ranch. He guided the Appaloosa, as they were now called, toward the front porch of the ranch house, curious as to why there seemed to be no one about the place. With an eye well practiced in noticing details, he unconsciously made mental notes of the layout of the barn and bunkhouse in relation to the house, itself. It was always healthy to decide where trouble might come from and where the best cover was, if trouble did spring upon you. He had been invited into ambushes before, and there was something about the deadness of this ranch headquarters that warned him to be cautious. Someone here was mighty desperate for his services, either that or desperate enough to kill him, and wire one hundred dollars just for him to come hear their proposal. The message was supposedly sent by a woman. That fact alone made him suspicious, but it was also enough to entice him to check it out. The wire said that if he came out here and didn't accept the job, he could keep the money. That thought caused a wry smile on the rugged clean-shaven face. He had no intention of returning the money, if he turned the offer down. He figured that was their cost for having him ride all the way from his place in Texarkana just to hear their offer.

After he stepped down, he dropped the Appaloosa's reins on the ground, knowing the horse would remain there as long as they were on the ground, and his packhorse's reins were tied to his saddle. As he walked up the steps to the porch, he eased his Colt .45 up and down a couple of times to make sure it was ready to go to work if called upon. He knocked solidly on the front door, then stepped back and waited. Just before he started to knock again, the door opened, and a chubby-cheeked little gray-haired woman stood waiting for him to state his business. "Fanny Hawkins?" he asked.

"No," Maudie said. "What's your name, and I'll tell her you wanna see her."

"Jack Coffey," he answered. "She sent for me."

"Come on inside, Mr. Coffey," she said at once, held the door open for him, and led him into the parlor. "You can wait right here, and I'll get

Miz Hawkins." Then she hurried away. In a few seconds, he could hear the two women talking in the back of the house. They were too far away for him to understand what they were saying, but it sounded to him like an argument. A couple of minutes later Fanny came into the parlor.

"Mr. Coffey," she barked in her usual caustic tone. "I was wonderin' if you was ever gonna show up. Maudie was tryin' to tell me I oughta put on a blouse before I come talk to you. But I just came up from the barn where I was helpin' her brother get a sow ready to have pigs. I told her you'd most likely seen a woman in her petticoat before. And, hell, I got my boots and trousers on. Maudie!" she yelled then.

"I'm comin'!" Maudie yelled back at her, and came in the parlor, carrying a tray with a whiskey bottle and a couple of glasses on it.

Fanny poured the drinks and said, "Now, let's talk some business."

There were very few things that could cause Jack Coffey's face to create a smile, but Fanny Hawkins's entrance came close to making the list. He took the drink from the tray and tossed it back. "All right, let's talk some business. Why did you get in touch with me?"

"My late husband, John Henry Hawkins, said he used to ride with you back in the day when you was just startin' out," she said. "He said you went on your own way about the same time he went into the cattle business. He said he could always get in touch with you if he needed to because you kept a woman in a house near Texarkana, and you always went back there when you weren't travelin' somewhere."

He didn't respond at all until she finished, but when she paused, he smiled and said, "John Henry Hawkins . . . Well, I'll swear, I heard he had gone under, but I never thought when I got your message that you were that little woman John Henry used to go to see."

She took a moment to study him. A well-built man, she decided, but not what she would call husky. By his dress, she assumed he was partial to the color black, for his hat was black, as were his trousers, vest, and bandanna, right down to his boots. "I hope you're as good as your reputation," she said.

"Have I got a reputation?" he asked plaintively, as if it were news to him.

"I expect you know the answer to that," she said, never one to beat around the bush. "I've got a job that needs takin' care of and it's right in your line of work."

"Is that so? And what line is that?" But before he gave her time to answer, he asked another question. "Where are the men who work this spread? I ain't seen a man anywhere. You ain't got that smallpox sickness on this ranch, have you?"

"Ha!" She snorted. "We had somethin' worse than that. We had Tanner sickness."

"What the hell is that?" he responded. He'd never heard of that.

"That's what I sent for you for. You're the cure for it. You ain't seen any ranch hands on the place because Will Tanner killed 'em all. Deputy Marshal Will Tanner, to be exact, and I want him dead, and I'm willin' to pay for it."

"Will Tanner," he repeated the name. "A lawman, huh?"

"That's right," she said, "a U.S. Deputy Marshal. Does that bother you?"

"Not particularly. Where's he work? Wichita Falls?"

"No, he ain't a Texas lawman, and that's another reason I want him dead. He works in Oklahoma Territory, but he made it his business to come into Texas to wreck my cattle business. He killed all my sons and my hired men, too. You see the shape he left my ranch in. I want him dead."

"If he works in Indian Territory, then he works outta Fort Smith, Arkansas. I might have to go that far to track him down. It might take some time."

"I think he spends most of his time in Indian country," she said. "They sent him all the way over here to try to stop some cattle rustling."

"Did he stop it?" Coffey asked.

She hesitated before answering, and when she did, she said, "Well, temporarily."

She earned one of his smiles then. "So he broke up your rustlin' business, did he?"

"You got any problem doin' the job?" she asked.

"You realize I'm gonna be travelin' all over Oklahoma Territory, trying to find the son of a gun. That's gonna take time, and it's gonna cost money."

"I'm willin' to pay you five hundred dollars to do the job." She couldn't tell by his expression if he was pleased or disappointed. "But I want proof of his death. I'll give you another hundred on top of the one hundred I already gave you right now, today. When you bring me proof of his death, you get the other three hundred. Have we got a deal?"

"Yes, ma'am, we've got a deal," he said, since it was more than he had expected to be offered when he rode out there. He was also thinking that in the unlikely event he was unable to find this deputy, Will Tanner, he would give it up while he was still ahead of the game by two hundred bucks. Like the old hag said, however, he had a reputation, and to add this deputy to it sure couldn't hurt.

"Let's have another drink to seal the deal," Fanny proposed, and filled the glasses again. After they tossed those down, her rock-hard facade melted just slightly enough to ask, "You really do feel like you can track him down?"

"Ain't no doubt in my mind," he assured her. "Unless he's found a way to get up on the moon, I'll find him. And when I do, I'll get the job done, and I'll bring you a souvenir to let you know he's dead."

"When will you get started?" she asked as she reached into the pocket of her trousers and pulled out the one hundred dollars she had promised.

"About five minutes ago," he answered, and got on his feet to leave. She walked him to the door and watched as he climbed aboard the unusual-looking horse and rode away. When she backed up to close the door, she bumped into Maudie, who had listened to the meeting from the hallway.

"That man looks like cold death," Maudie remarked. "When you decide it's time to get rid of me, I hope you don't send him to do it."

"Ha," Fanny snorted. "When it's time to get rid of you, I'll do it myself."

Will pushed his horses a little harder than usual to reach the Washita River in one day after he left Hatfield's store in Waurika. His original plan was to reach Jim Little Eagle's cabin on Muddy Boggy Creek at the end of the second day. But Buster was showing signs of fatigue a little earlier than usual, and the packhorse even more so. So he stopped at noon on the second day when he came to a peaceful spot beside a creek to let them rest for several hours. He built a fire, made some coffee, and roasted some beef jerky, and even grabbed an hour of sleep, knowing Buster would keep watch. When he woke up, he killed his fire and loaded the horses up again. He decided to ride the blue roan that Caleb had ridden, in order to give Buster a little more rest. But when he led Buster by his reins, the buckskin jerked at them and tossed and dragged his hooves until Will had to stop and climb back into Buster's saddle and lead the roan again. "I better take another look at you," Will told the petulant horse. "You sure you ain't a mare?" With harmony in the family again, he pushed them only about twelve miles farther that day and figured he'd arrive in Atoka the next day around noontime.

Since he had stopped to make camp much earlier than planned, he decided he would cook himself a proper supper, so he sliced some strips of bacon and mixed up his version of pan biscuits. And when he ate them, he fantasized about Louise Hill's fluffy biscuits. He figured he was going to have to reward Jim Little Eagle for the extra trouble of taking care of Reese Trainer. *I expect he'll be mighty glad to see me,* he thought. Jim ought to be pretty sick of Trainer by now. But there was always the hope that a jail wagon had already arrived there and left with the prisoner, relieving Jim of the obligation.

Starting early the next morning, his horses

were well rested, and he made good time. As was his usual habit when approaching Atoka from the West, he planned to stop at Jim Little Eagle's cabin just short of town. Most often, he arrived at Jim's at the end of the day, and on those occasions, he would make his camp there beside the creek. Today, it would be close to noontime, and if he was lucky, he might arrive before Jim and Mary had eaten the midday meal. It would probably depend on whether or not Reese Trainer was still in the Choctaw jail. In that case, Jim might be in town, delivering Trainer's dinner to him. In that case, he would eat at Lottie's, which was never a disappointment. It occurred to him that he was in an unusually lighthearted mood on this sunny morning, especially after the depressing ending to Caleb Hawkins's arrest. He put it out of his mind again when he caught sight of Jim's cabin through the branches of the trees along Muddy Boggy Creek.

When he pulled up into the yard, he figured he'd missed Jim because the Choctaw policeman's favorite horse, a gray gelding, was not in the small corral with the other horses. So he was surprised when both Jim and Mary walked out of the cabin to meet him. He was also puzzled by the expression of remorse on Jim's face and the look of worrisome dread on the face of Mary Light Walker. "Howdy Jim, Mary," he greeted them. Accustomed to a joyful welcome from

Mary and a friendly smile from Jim, he knew something was wrong. "One of you gonna tell me what's goin' on? Did the jail wagon not get here yet?"

Like a man standing before the judge, Jim Little Eagle confessed, "Jail wagon get here, only no prisoner to take back."

"What?" Will responded, not sure exactly what that meant, but certain it was nothing good. "What do you mean, Jim? Did something happen to Reese Trainer?"

"Something happen to Jim," Mary burst forth, unable to remain quiet when she knew how badly Jim hated to tell Will the prisoner escaped. "Will, it not Jim's fault. Other man there, Jim not know he there. He sneak up behind Jim when Jim open door to feed prisoner, just like you told him to."

"He hold gun in my back," Jim said then. "I don't know he even there." He went on in his broken English to tell Will about being shoved into the smokehouse while Reese stole his horse and escaped. It was Mary who eventually released Jim from his own jail. She waited for him to come home after going to feed Reese. When it became later and later and he didn't show up, she knew something was terribly wrong, so she went to look for him. When she went to the jail, she saw that the padlock had been put back on the latch, but it wasn't locked. She called his name and received a meek reply from inside the dark smokehouse. "I know you be mad," he said when he finished. "I let you down."

Will was mad, but not at Jim. He had hoped he would be done with Reese Trainer, and Trainer would be on his way to Fort Smith before he got back to Atoka. After a short pause to let Jim's report sink in, he said, "You've got nothin' to feel bad about. You just got caught in an unlucky situation. If it'd been me, and somebody stuck a gun in my back, I'da dropped my gun, too. Anybody would, if they had any sense a-tall. I feel real bad that I stuck you in that situation, and I'm glad you didn't get hurt. Sorry about your horse. You didn't notice any strangers in town that day?"

Jim shook his head. "No strangers."

"How 'bout the jail wagon?" Will asked. "When did it get here?"

"Next day after prisoner go," Jim answered. When Will asked who brought it, Jim said, "Ed Pine. He plenty mad. Turn around and start back, soon as horses rested."

Will couldn't suppress a grin when he pictured Deputy Ed Pine. "He'll get over it, I wouldn't worry about him. I don't suppose you know which way Trainer ran."

"No, plenty dark inside smokehouse," Jim replied.

"Reckon so," Will said, realizing what a dumb question he had asked. "I'll go on into town and ask around. See if anybody noticed any strangers or saw anything that might help me know where to start lookin' for Reese Trainer."

"We already eat dinner," Mary spoke up again. "I fix you something to eat."

"No, thanks anyway, Mary. I'll get something at Lottie's. If there was a stranger in town that day, there's a good chance they might have been in Lottie's Kitchen." He looked back at Jim. "You're welcome to come along with me if you want to." He said it just to let him know he wasn't mad at him, and he still welcomed his help.

"No," Jim replied. "I got some Choctaw business I need to take care of."

"Right, I'll talk to you later." Will doubted Jim had any Indian business he was going to take care of. He knew the Choctaw was embarrassed over being locked up in his own jail, and he wasn't comfortable in town just yet. He imagined he was worried as well about the report Ed Pine would submit to Marshal Dan Stone. Will was genuinely sorry it had happened to Jim and he planned to vouch for him when he returned to Fort Smith. "Too bad about that gray you like," he commented, knowing how much Jim liked that horse. "But I'm gonna leave this blue roan for you to ride. He's got a pretty good saddle on him, too."

Jim's eyes brightened a little in response, and he said, "I take good care of him for you."

"Not for me," Will told him. "The horse is yours. If you don't mind, I'd like to leave my packhorse with you while I'm in town, though. I'll take his packs off and you can just turn him out to graze with your horses. Is that all right?" Jim nodded, so Will took the packs off.

"I'll put them in my barn. You are true friend, Will Tanner," Jim said humbly.

"You'd do the same for me." He looked over at Mary Light Walker. "Wouldn't he, Mary?" She nodded slowly and smiled at him. Now he had to get onto Reese Trainer's trail, if at all possible. So he stepped up on the buckskin again and headed to town.

He was hungry, so he decided the first place he would go was Lottie's Kitchen. When he walked in the door, Lottie and Lou-Bell were standing at the kitchen door, talking. They both gaped at him with eyes wide open, as if they had been waiting for him to come in. To see his reaction to finding his prisoner escaped, he supposed. "Well, welcome back, Will," Lottie sang out. "Did you just now ride in?"

"Good afternoon, Lottie, Lou-Bell," he returned the greeting. "Yep, I just got back."

Lou-Bell wasn't patient to the point of waiting to see if he knew yet. "Have you been by the jail?"

"Yes, I have, and I've talked to Jim Little Eagle about Reese Trainer's escape, too. I was gonna ask you ladies if you've had any strangers come in while I was gone."

"Sure we did," Lou-Bell answered. "And we know the one that broke your prisoner outta jail. We woulda told Jim Little Eagle, but we ain't seen him since the night he got locked up."

"We were gonna tell Ed Pine when he came in, but he didn't even come in to eat. Stanley Coons, down at the stable, said he rested his horses and started back the way he came," Lottie said.

Will just stood there, looking from one of the women to the other, wondering how long the small talk was going to go on. "You reckon I could get something to eat? You do still sell food here, don't you?"

"All right, Mr. Know-It-All," Lou-Bell replied. "I'll fix you a plate and we'll just let you figure out who you need to chase for that jailbreak." Lottie followed him over to a table while Lou-Bell went to the kitchen to fix him a plate.

He couldn't help asking, "How do you know who broke Reese Trainer out of that smokehouse? Did you or anybody else see them when they jumped Jim?"

"No, didn't none of us see him do it," Lottie answered. "But we know who it had to be."

"Who?" Will asked, tired of the guessing game.

"Frank Trainer," Lottie answered.

That got Will's attention right away. He took a sip of the coffee Lou-Bell put on the table, never taking his eyes off Lottie. "*Frank* Trainer?" he asked, emphasizing the first name.

"That's right," Lou-Bell said. "Fellow we'd never seen before came in to eat supper. Said his name was Frank when we asked him. He was askin' about that place you and Jim Little Eagle burned down."

Lottie jumped in again. "He asked what happened to the man who was runnin' it."

"We told him that he was in the Choctaw jail," Lou-Bell finished for her. "Then when Jim Little Eagle came in to get Reese's supper plate, Frank got up and followed him outside."

"I told him he hadn't never told us his last name," Lottie said.

"Trainer," Lou-Bell inserted. "That's what he told her, Trainer. Ain't that right, Lottie?"

"God's truth, Will, he said his name was Trainer, and we never said Reese's last name was Trainer. I didn't even remember it was until Frank said it."

Will paused a minute to think about the double-barreled report just aimed at him by the two dueling women. He had to concede that still no one had seen this Frank Trainer ambush Jim Little Eagle. But if his name really was Frank Trainer, you had to believe he most likely did it. Will was no better off than he had been before he knew a second name. "If you don't eat that hash, it's gonna get cold," Lou-Bell said, interrupting his thoughts. He nodded and took a couple of big bites. The two women continued to watch him thinking and that didn't help his concentration.

"I'll decide what I'm gonna do after I finish my dinner," he finally announced, causing a nod of approval from Lottie and a shrug of the shoulders from Lou-Bell. But both women went about their business then and let him think. He was still without a clue as to the possible direction of their escape. He had 360 degrees to choose from. But even though logic reduced their route to Texas, Kansas, or to a hole in the Sans Bois or Arbuckle mountains, just to name a few, they could be anywhere, is what it amounted to. He was not at all comfortable with the thought that Reese Trainer had gotten away. Will had a reputation for never giving up on a felon, a reputation that had gotten him into trouble a few times, when he crossed over lines of his legal authority. He had just returned from an arrest in Texas that might or might not cause repercussions on the Texas side of the issue. It was just his nature. If he knew where the guilty party was, he went there and arrested him. He took another bite of a corn muffin and made a decision. *I'll just start scouting in a circle around Atoka, checking every place those two might have gone for help and supplies. Maybe I'll get lucky and stumble on something or somebody that can help.*

He finished his dinner and thanked the ladies

for their contribution in the tracking down of Reese and Frank Trainer. When Lottie asked when he would be back, he told her he wasn't sure, but he hoped it wouldn't be too long. As an afterthought, when he left Lottie's, he stopped in at the stable to see if Stanley Coons had had any dealings with this fellow Frank Trainer. But Stanley was of no help. Frank Trainer had not set foot in Stanley's place of business. Will had hoped he might have wanted to rest his horses up and feed them some grain in preparation for a long hard ride to someplace he might have carelessly mentioned. It was to no avail. Will finally decided to check Lem Stark's old place on the Blue River. If his rabbits were running to Texas, which was a good possibility, Tishomingo was a good place to buy supplies. And the new fellow on Blue River, Brady Thompson, might sell the fugitives a drink of whiskey to send them on their way.

CHAPTER 12

It was a short day's ride from Atoka to Tishomingo, but anxious as he was to get started, Will decided to leave Atoka that afternoon and make camp that night on Clear Boggy Creek, close to the saloon he and Jim Little Eagle had burned down. So he rode back to Jim's cabin and told him what he planned to do, then loaded up his packhorse again and said he'd see them whenever he started back to Fort Smith. He wasn't sure when that would be. He let Buster take a leisurely pace to Clear Boggy and when he got there, he rode up the creek a way until he found a spot with some grass growing near the water and plenty of wood for his fire.

In spite of all the discouraging news of the day, he spent a peaceful night and slept well until awakened by the first rays of a new day. He decided he would stop by Lem Stark's old place on Blue River before going into Tishomingo to replenish some of his basic supplies. It had been a while since he had paid a visit to Brady Thompson. Will had no interest in closing Brady down. He didn't do a great deal of business, and there was not much evidence that he was selling whiskey to the Chickasaw Indians. So Will decided not to hassle Brady until the Chickasaw police called for help to shut him down.

In the past there had been some dangerous people in the big log building he approached on this sunny morning, but that was when Lem Stark was operating there. It had a peaceful look about it this morning that would lead a stranger to believe it the perfect spot to live out the rest of his days. For Brady Thompson, it had been a peaceful morning. He was still sitting at a small table in the main room of the trading post, drinking coffee with Loafer Perkins, and telling Loafer about all the plans he now had for the store since the creation of his partnership with the Trainer brothers. Reese and Frank had left for Fort Worth the day before, and when they returned, they would be bringing a wagonload of whiskey with them. Brady's positive mood soured immediately after Loafer, who was seated facing the front door, uttered, "Uh-oh." Brady turned to see Deputy Marshal Will Tanner enter the store. Could he have possibly tracked Frank and Reese here from Atoka? They had assured him that no one could have. They even joked about starting out on a trail they hoped would lead them to Tishomingo, only to find it made a sharp change in direction. And they had to ask an Indian they met on the road how to get to Tishomingo. He was thankful now that they had left yesterday.

"Well, lookee here," Brady greeted Will in as cheerful a manner as he could manage. "Deputy

Will Tanner, what brings you out this way on an early mornin'?"

"Brady, Loafer," Will acknowledged them both. "I'm lookin' for a fellow that broke outta jail in Atoka, and the fellow who busted him out. Their names are Reese and Frank Trainer and I figured they mighta come this way."

Brady repeated the names as if hearing them for the first time. "No, ain't been nobody by those names been in here. What was they in jail for?"

"One of 'em was in jail for sellin' whiskey to the Indians and everybody else," Will replied. "The other one broke him outta jail. I expect you've heard about the one sellin' whiskey. He built a fancy saloon over near Atoka and didn't make any secret about his intention to make it a regular saloon and cathouse. It was like he dared the law to do anything about it." He added his last few remarks as cautionary reminders to Brady.

"That's right," Brady responded, "I believe I did hear about that feller. Burned his place to the ground, right?"

"That's the place," Will replied. "And you ain't seen 'em over this way a-tall?"

"No, sir. If I had I'd sure as hell tell you. Loafer will tell you that. Right, Loafer?"

"Yes, sir," Loafer answered, "he sure would." He got up from his chair and walked over to the window and set his cup down on a shelf there. "I swear," he remarked then, "I believe I'm gettin' absentminded as an old man. I left my blame bucket on the back of the corral. I better go get it or when I need it again, I won't remember where I left it." He went out the back of the building.

Brady chuckled. "You might think he was jokin', but he is gettin' kinda absentminded. How 'bout a cup of coffee? Sally just made a fresh pot and we ain't gonna drink it all up."

"I never turn down a cup of fresh coffee," Will said.

Brady chuckled again and yelled, "Sally! Bring Deputy Tanner a cup of that coffee."

Almost immediately, she appeared, carrying a large coffeepot and a cup. She filled the cup and handed it to Will, then she topped off Brady's cup. "Thank you," Will said to her, causing her to give him a look of surprise. She nodded and hurried back to the kitchen. Will didn't spend much time drinking his coffee because there was nothing more he expected to get from Brady, as far as information about Reese Trainer was concerned. When he drained his cup, he thanked Brady for the coffee and said he'd best be on his way. "I've got a lot of ground to cover and not much to go on," he said in leaving. Brady walked to the door with him and watched him as he rode up the path to the trail into Tishomingo.

Standing just inside the front door of the barn, Loafer watched the deputy marshal as well. And when Will disappeared on the trail to Tishomingo,

Loafer went back to the back door of the barn to find Tom Lame Horse still there. "I thought you'd gone," Loafer said to the old Indian. "You want some more firewater?"

"No more money," Lame Horse replied. He wanted to complain about the service. "I put bucket on corral post, like you say. I wait. You no come. Maybe next time I bang on bucket with stick."

"You do that, old man, and maybe no more firewater for you," Loafer said.

Will rode into the lower end of Tishomingo, by the stables, and surprised Tom Spotted Horse, the Chickasaw police chief. He was talking to Wilbur Greene, the owner of the stables, so Will guided Buster toward them. "Will Tanner," Wilbur greeted him. "What brings you to our little town?" Tom Spotted Horse acknowledged Will with no more than a nod.

"Howdy, Wilbur," Will said. "Just passin' through. I was on my way to see Tom," he lied. He had not planned to waste time with the belligerent Indian, even though it was a standard practice for a deputy marshal to contact the Indian police whenever he entered his territory. It was a courtesy that Will always practiced with the other Indian policemen. But not always with Tom because Tom considered all white men trespassers. "Just wanted to let you know I was in your town, so now you know. I'll be passin' right through, after I pick up some supplies at Dewey Sams's store. You got anything you need to talk to me about?"

"No, I take care of Tishomingo," Tom replied. "I don't need no help."

"Fine," Will said with enthusiasm. "That's good to hear. Well, I'll be movin' along. Good to see you again, Wilbur." He signaled Buster with a light tap from his heels and the buckskin departed the stables in an easy lope.

He rode up past the post office and the feed store and pulled up in front of Dewey Sams's General Merchandise to find Dewey and his brother, Jake, wrestling a heavy barrel to the ground from the back of a wagon. Seeing Will ride up, Jake cracked, "Uh-oh, try to lift a barrel off the wagon and the law shows up before you can get it inside. I swear, Deputy, there ain't no whiskey in this barrel. Please don't burn the store down." He had obviously heard about the burning of Reese Trainer's whiskey mill.

"Howdy, Will," Dewey greeted him. "Don't pay no attention to my brother. It ain't his fault all the brains were used up when he came along. You're back pretty soon. I didn't expect to see you again so soon."

"I didn't expect to be over again so soon, myself," Will said. "But we had a little jailbreak over in Atoka and I'm tryin' to see if I can find

198

out which way they ran. I used up a lot of those supplies I bought from you and I need to buy some more." He stepped down from the saddle. "Maybe I can give you a hand with that barrel."

"I think we got it," Dewey said. "Come on, Jake, let's just pull it right on off and set it on the ground." They did just that. Then they walked it to the store, turning it around and around until it was up against the boardwalk, and with Will's help, leaned it over until it fell on its side on the walk. After that, it was manageable to roll it into the store. Jake steered it into a corner, and they picked it up to stand straight up.

"That's where she stays," Dewey said. "I ain't movin' it again until it's empty."

"What's in the barrel?" Will asked.

"Dried apples," Jake answered. "I had to go to Durant to pick 'em up at the train station. We been waitin' for 'em for a month."

"Dried apples," Will repeated. "I'm gonna be your first customer for a little sack of 'em."

Dewey's wife, Melva, walked in from the back room at that moment. "Hello, Will. What are you gonna be the first customer for?"

"Dried apples," he said again.

"Oh, you got them!" she exclaimed to Jake, seeing him leaning with one hand on the barrel. "Well, what did you put 'em there for?" And she started looking around the room for a better place.

"Don't even start," Dewey warned. "You move 'em, it's gonna be by yourself."

"We'll talk about it later," she said, then quickly turned her attention to Will. "We don't usually see you for months and months, and here you are back already."

"That's right," Will said. "I didn't know I'd be back this way so soon, myself. I'm just passin' through town, and I've already gotten low on some of the supplies I bought here last time." He grinned and added, "And I was plum out of dried apples. I figured this was the place to get 'em."

"Well, tell me what else you need," Dewey said, "and maybe Jake'll get that barrel open while I'm roundin' it up." Will called out the items he was short on and Dewey retrieved each one until there was nothing else Will could think of. By that time, Jake had the barrel open and he and Melva each sampled a dried apple. "Maybe you'd like to sample one before you decide to buy any," Dewey offered.

"That's not a bad idea," Will responded, and picked a plump one out of the barrel. He chewed it up and swallowed it, and said, "I'll take two pounds of 'em."

"You ain't even asked how much they cost," Dewey said.

"I figure you'll be fair with me," Will replied. Then he gave Melva a little grin and said. " 'Cause if you ain't, I'll close you down for sellin' stuff to make apple cider with." It was good for a chuckle, then he let Dewey figure up his bill while Melva weighed out his apples. After he paid Dewey, he asked a question. "Have you, by any chance, seen a couple of fellows in the last few days come through town that you ain't seen around here before? I'm thinkin' they mighta stopped here to pick up supplies. One of 'em is ridin' a gray horse."

Dewey looked at Melva and said, "That sounds like those two fellows that were in here yesterday about this same time. They gave us a dang good order. Said they had a ways to go. They sounded like pretty decent men, didn't they, hon?" Melva nodded, her eyes getting bigger as she looked at Will. "Are they wanted by the law?"

"Yes," Will answered. "Did you see which way they went when they left here?"

"I didn't watch 'em leave. Did you, hon?" She shook her head. Dewey went on. "But one of 'em asked me how far it was from here to the Texas border."

That statement captured Will's interest at once. "And you say that was about this same time yesterday mornin'?" he asked.

Dewey said that it was and again looked to Melva for her confirmation. "I swear," he said, "those two fellows didn't seem like the typical saddle trash that comes through here. They sure had me fooled, and they had cash money to pay

201

for everything they ordered. What did they do?"

At this point, Will was in a hurry, so he gave them a brief version of what Reese and Frank Trainer were wanted for. All this was done while the four of them hurriedly gathered up Will's purchases and carried them out to his horses. "You can even add horse thief to the list of charges," Will said. "That gray one of 'em is ridin' was stolen from the Choctaw police chief after they broke out of jail." When he was packed up, the three of them stood back while he wheeled Buster away from the rail and rode away out the south end of town.

From Tishomingo, it was only a little over thirty miles to the Red River, and he knew it was wasted effort to ride down there at this point. So, as far as his authority to arrest them was concerned, it ended at the river. They were long ago free and clear of his jurisdiction. Still, he couldn't help riding the thirty miles just to make doubly sure they had not stopped for some reason. The Oklahoma boundary had not stopped him on numerous occasions before. He had just returned from Wichita Falls because he knew his target was just over the line in Texas. He had no idea where the two men he now chased were going. *I should just be glad they're riding out of my territory and hope they don't come back,* he thought. After a ride of about twenty miles, he came to a nice-sized stream, so he decided to rest

Buster and the packhorse. After he took care of his horses, he collected enough small limbs to build a fire. When it was burning well enough, he put his little coffeepot in the edge of it to bring it to a boil. When the coffee was ready, he looked in his packs to see where he had put his sack of dried apples, and when he found them, he sat down beside the stream to chomp on them while he decided whether to turn around or not.

After a while, Buster wandered over and nudged him in the back with his muzzle. Will reached around and stroked the buckskin's face. "Whadda you want? You tellin' me you're ready to get started? I know what you want." He reached in his sack and picked out a couple of the dried apples, then held them in his palm for the horse to take. "That's all you're gettin'. These have to last for a while." He picked out a couple more of the apples and gave them to the sorrel packhorse, then packed them away. "We ain't but ten miles from the Red," he said to Buster. "We might as well make damn sure those two got all the way outta the Nations." He knew the trail he was following ended when it connected to the wagon road to Sherman, Texas. So it was a good bet that was the road the two outlaws were headed for. He was hoping he might encounter someone along the road, before he reached the river, who might have seen the two men yesterday when they traveled the road. Otherwise, he could not be completely sure they had continued into Texas. The road to Sherman was the main road to Durant and Atoka, as well, if they had turned north instead of continuing south. Which would make no sense, he told himself. They were obviously fleeing the Oklahoma Territory and maybe they had a specific place in Texas that was like a home base for them. On the other hand, what if their intent was simply to get over the border and lie low for a while where he couldn't touch them. Then after he figured they were gone for good they could return to do their mischief. That option was what made Sherman look like a possibility to him. There was another small town called Denison just a few miles across the border, but Sherman had a hotel and a couple of saloons the last time he had ridden through. It would offer more to attract two scoundrels on the run.

When he reached the river, he pulled his horses to a stop on the Oklahoma side of it and sat there gazing across at Texas, still battling with his desire to continue the chase. He reached in his pocket and pulled out his lucky silver coin, the one with a head on both sides. "Tails, we turn around and go home," he told Buster. "Heads, we go on across." He very carefully flipped the coin, since he was sitting in the saddle, and he didn't want to lose his lucky piece. It was heads. "I guess we'll go on across," he said, "but we'll wait until mornin'." It was getting late, and his horses were tired. Since leaving Jim Little Eagle's cabin, he had traveled more than fifty miles. He had given the horses a couple of rests, but they were short ones. Even though it was only about fifteen miles to Sherman, it would be best to start out fresh in the morning. So he nudged Buster and walked the buckskin off the road and upstream to find a good camping spot.

CHAPTER 13

"Set down and have a drink with us, sweetheart," Frank Trainer invited when the bored-looking woman passed casually by their table. Tall and thin, with her hair piled up on top of her head like a plump pillow, she paused to look at the two men, who had shown no interest in her until that moment.

She favored Frank with a tired smile and asked, "Now, why would I wanna do that?"

" 'Cause you might learn something," Frank answered, then put his foot on the edge of an empty chair and pushed it back from the table. "Set down and have a drink."

She took another moment to consider the company, gazing at Frank, grinning at her like a hunter grinning at a fox about to step into his trap, and then at his brother, who was enjoying the show. "All right," she said, and sat down in the chair. Then she reached in the folds on the shoulders of her dress and pulled out a shot glass, which she put down on the table. Reese picked up the bottle and filled the glass. She tossed the whiskey back, then graced them with a smug grin.

"What's your name, honey?" Frank asked.

"They call me Princess," she answered.

"Why do they call you that?" Frank asked. "Are you a princess?"

"Come upstairs with me and you'll find out," she said. She had actually picked the name for herself because there was nothing really seductive about her real name, Jane Sedgefield. She sometimes imagined what her late husband would think of her calling herself Princess. Too bad whiskey had been the cause of his early death. Actually, it was more the bottle that contained the whiskey when it was smashed against the back of his head. At the time, she was hoping it might cure his urge to beat her when he was falling-down drunk. She couldn't deny the fact that it seemed to be the cure.

At first glance, she could tell that the two men were not the ordinary ranch hands who frequented the Red Rooster Saloon. When they first came in and went to the bar to get a bottle, she saw them talking to George Gilley, the owner of the saloon. When they took the bottle to a table, she went over to the bar to ask George who they were. He told her he didn't know who they were, but the one who paid for the bottle had a sizable roll of cash in his pocket. So she decided to see if there was room in that pocket for her. Saturday was usually a day when she picked up a little money from the farm hands, but they never had much to spend. "You boys look like you could be brothers," she remarked. "You might be able to take advantage of the family discount. What are your names?"

"You're a pretty good guesser," Frank answered. "We are brothers. I'm Frank and he's Reese, and I'm thinkin' you might be the lucky one to enjoy our company today."

Reese couldn't help being surprised by his brother's seemingly carefree attitude after just having fled from the Nations after their jailbreak. He experienced a feeling of relief as well when they crossed over the Red River, but it was Frank whose idea it was to spend a night in the Sherman Hotel and do a little celebrating at the Red Rooster Saloon. He was looking forward to taking over Brady Thompson's business on Blue River when they returned with that wagonload of whiskey. Frank talked him into one last visit to the Red Rooster before starting out for Fort Worth. So they were going to get a late start. Their horses were ready and standing at the rail. Princess kept glancing back and forth from one brother to the other, wondering if they were all talk or if there was going to be some business.

Seeing her puzzlement, Frank said, "I've never jumped in bed with a princess before, so why don't we go upstairs?"

"Both of you?" Princess asked, concerned about what they might have in mind. One of the other girls had suffered a bad beating recently when she entertained two cowboys in her room.

Frank hesitated for just a second before answering. "No, one at a time, Reese first, he's the youngest and we need to take care of the kids first. And he's had a rough time of it lately."

"You mean the old folks need a few more drinks of likker before they can get up their nerve," Reese japed. "But if you insist . . ."

Princess laughed and got up from her chair. She took Reese by the hand. "Come on, little boy, Princess is gonna take you to her palace." Reese let himself be pulled up out of his chair, and she led him up the stairs.

"Take your time," Frank called after them. "We got plenty of time." He poured himself another drink and put his feet up on the chair Princess had been sitting in and watched the early-Saturday-morning customers. One of them paused in the doorway to look the room over before walking over to talk to Gummy Taylor, the bartender. After a few minutes, the man thanked Gummy and came directly to him. "Now, what the hell?" Frank muttered, and dropped his hand to rest on the handle of his pistol.

"Are you and your friend ridin' a gray and a dun?" he asked.

"Maybe," Frank replied. "Why do you wanna know?"

"If that's your packhorse with 'em, a couple of your packs look like they busted open. Just thought you might wanna know."

"Busted open?" Frank responded. "There ain't no way. Somebody musta messed with 'em." He immediately got to his feet and started for the door. The Good Samaritan followed him outside. Frank went to the packhorse and looked on both sides of it. "You must be drunk," he said, and turned around to find himself staring at a drawn six-gun, aimed at him. "What the hell is this? A holdup in broad daylight, in the middle of the street? You are drunk."

"You're under arrest for breaking a prisoner out of jail and for stealing that gray horse. I'm gonna ask you to take your left hand and reach over to draw that pistol outta the holster, real slow, and drop it on the ground."

"Will Tanner." Frank pronounced the name softly and slowly. "So I finally get to meet you. Too bad we ain't in your territory, ain't it? I gotta give you credit, though. You're one stubborn son of a gun. But that badge of yours don't work here in Texas. So the best thing you can do is get on your horse and hightail it back to Oklahoma as fast as you can."

"If you're wantin' to sacrifice your life, then I'll be happy to accommodate you. This .44 in my hand works as well in Texas as it does in the Nations. I'll not waste time arguing with you, Trainer. Take the gun out and drop it on the ground or I'll shoot you down in the street. My boss will say, *Good job* either way."

"All right, damn it," Frank said, convinced Will would do what he threatened. "I'm takin' it out." He reached across very slowly with his left hand and grasped his pistol with only his thumb and forefinger. He lifted it up for Will to see before swinging his arm slowly around in front of him. Then he held it out as if to show Will he was dropping it. When he released it, however, his right hand was suddenly right under it to catch the weapon and cock it. He looked down, startled to see the hole in his shirt, and stood there for only a second before dropping to his knees.

Hadn't counted on that, Will thought. He had hoped to have Frank handcuffed to a post while he went back inside to find Reese. He had thought it was good luck when he was able to catch the two of them when they were not together. The bartender told him that the other fellow had gone upstairs with Princess, so he thought he would have time to secure Frank. Reese was bound to have heard the shot, so the question was, which way would he react? Come to look for his brother or run for his life? A small crowd of spectators was already beginning to gather. Will pulled his vest away to show his badge. "Nothin' more to see here, folks." He had no sooner said that when a young man wearing a deputy sheriff's badge ran up. "Good," Will said, "I can use your help." He showed his badge again briefly. "I'm a U.S. Deputy Marshal, and this man was wanted for breaking a man out of jail. I tried to arrest him, but he went for his gun. The other man's inside and I'm goin' in to look for him. Give me a hand and we'll just lay his body across the saddle of this dun. I'd appreciate it if you'd watch the body for me." He didn't mention that he was a deputy marshal from the Western District of Arkansas, and he didn't give the young deputy time to ask questions. He had to gamble one way or the other, with no time to think about it. So instead of running back in the front door, he ran around beside the building, in case Reese decided to escape through a window. There was a narrow porch all along the side of the saloon on the upstairs only. He didn't see anybody on the porch and none of the windows were open. So far, it appeared that Reese was still in the building, so Will decided an upstairs window was his best choice for entry.

In her room upstairs over the saloon, Princess was trying to persuade Reese to put his .44 back in the holster he had hung on the back of a chair. It had been several minutes since they had heard the single shot in the street in front of the saloon, and there had been no more to follow. "Put that thing away," she told him. "It makes me nervous. There wasn't but one shot and it was somebody out in the street. It ain't nothing for you and me to worry about. If we closed the town down every time somebody shoots a gun off, we wouldn't ever get anything done. We were just gettin' to know each other. Come on, Reese, relax. Here, give me the gun." Feeling kinda sheepish for his concern, he handed her the six-gun. She dropped it back in the holster on the chairback. Then on second thought, she took the gun belt and holster off the back of the chair and walked over to a chest of drawers, opened one of the drawers, and dropped it in. "There," she said. "Now there ain't nothin' to think about but me."

"There's one more thing."

Both Reese and Princess froze when they heard the voice behind them. So involved with each other, they had not heard the window when it was lifted, even though it had stuck briefly when only halfway up before Will forced it to continue upward. "Tanner!" Reese blurted, and started looking frantically around for his gun, forgetting in that moment where it actually was. Princess, uncertain what was happening, started to go to the chest of drawers, but Will stopped her. "Lady, you don't wanna make a bad mistake here. Best you stay away from that drawer." He pulled his vest aside to show her his badge. "This is U.S. Marshal business." Not sure what to do then, she backed away to a corner of the room.

Frantic with the situation he found himself in and scarcely able to believe it was actually happening, Reese sputtered in confusion until he thought to claim: "You can't make no arrest in Texas! You got no business here!" He made a move as if about to reach for the drawer where his gun was.

"That would be a bad mistake, Reese," Will calmly told him. "Frank made a mistake like that and he's layin' on his belly across the saddle on the horse you stole, waitin' to see if you're gonna go with him on his ride to hell. Now, I'm gonna tell you just exactly what I'm gonna do with you. If you choose to live, I'll take you all the way to Fort Smith and turn you over to the court for a trial. You give me no trouble, I'll treat you fairly. But if you choose to die, then I'll see that you get your wish. I've had all the trouble outta you that I plan to take. You give me more and I will kill you. I just wanna be sure you understand that." Reese just continued to stand there glaring at the man he hated above all the men he had ever known. "Do you understand that?" Will demanded.

"Yes, damn it, I understand," he roared back.

Will just stared at the belligerent man for a long moment before saying, "Let's see if you do. Turn around and put your hands behind your back." Reese didn't move. He just stood there and leered defiantly at Will. Then in the next instant, Will suddenly rapped him sharply beside his temple with the barrel of his six-gun, staggering him almost to the point of falling. "What did I tell you?" Will demanded. In compliance then,

Reese turned his back to Will. "Hands behind your back!" Will reminded him forcefully. Reese immediately complied and Will quickly handcuffed him before he had time to think about resisting. "Now, we'll walk downstairs and out the door." He looked at Princess, still huddled in shock in the corner. "Does he owe you any money for the time he spent with you?"

The question took her quite by surprise, and she had to gather her wits before she could think what to say. Then she recovered her senses enough to take advantage of his offer. "Yes, sir, he owes me five dollars for my time."

"That sounds a little bit high to me but reach in his pocket and see if you can find it."

"We never done nothin'," Reese complained. "We still got our clothes on."

"You heard her, you owe her for her visitin' time. Hurry up, lady, we're wastin' time here." She knew exactly which pocket of his vest he kept his money in, so she quickly reached in and pulled out a roll of bills. She looked quickly to see if Will was watching her, then peeled off five dollars and reluctantly returned the rest.

"You lyin' slut," Reese muttered as Will prodded him in the back to get him moving toward the door.

Knowing now that she was in no personal danger, she said, "Reese, honey, you know it was worth every penny to be with Princess at all.

Maybe next time you're in town I'll take you to my castle."

Well aware that he and Frank had given the deputy marshal plenty of reasons to have a special grudge against them, Reese made no attempt to refuse arrest. Already with blood running down the side of his face, his head was aching. He was marched through the saloon and out to the street, where the young deputy was standing by the horses. He watched as Will helped Reese up into his saddle, then tied his feet together under the horse's belly. "Don't want him to fall off and hurt himself," Will told the deputy. When Reese tried to tell the deputy that Will couldn't arrest him. Will cut him off short with a warning. "What did I tell you about startin' trouble?" It was enough to discourage Reese. The deputy sheriff held the horses while Will climbed aboard Buster. Then with the two packhorses on lead ropes tied to the saddles of Reese and Frank's horses, Will was ready to ride. When the deputy handed him the reins to Reese and Frank's horses, Will asked, "What is your name, Deputy?"

"Jeff Noland, sir," he answered.

"Jeff Noland," Will repeated, "I want to mention in my report how helpful you were on this arrest. Much obliged."

"Yes, sir, thank you, sir," Jeff replied. When the sheriff arrived back in town late that afternoon, and after hearing Jeff's report, it never occurred to him to ask in which direction Will rode out of town. He assumed south toward Dallas and Fort Worth. If the young deputy had thought about it at all, he might have been puzzled why Will rode north, toward Indian Territory.

Will's intention was to ride to Atoka to return Jim Little Eagle's gray gelding before he took his prisoner to Fort Smith. Atoka was sixty miles from Sherman, and since he was getting such a late start this morning, he decided to stop overnight at Durant, which was halfway. He was going to need more of almost everything he was carrying, as far as food was concerned, for the trip. So he planned to take care of that at Dixon Durant's general store in Durant, the town named for him. He made a stop to water and rest the horses after riding the fifteen miles to the Red River. He crossed over the river and stopped to rest the horses on the Oklahoma side of the river, however. This was just in case the Sherman sheriff returned to town and questioned the direction he had taken his prisoner out of town. He paid to take the ferry back across to Oklahoma because of all the horses he was leading, as well as to avoid any possibility of losing Frank Trainer's body in the river. The operator of the ferry, Bob Tucker, remembered Will from a previous crossing farther west of this one. Tucker explained that he relocated his ferry business here because there was more traffic on this road. "I see you're still in the business of huntin' people down," Tucker said as he gave Reese a looking-over. "Him, and the feller layin' across his saddle, took my ferry when they was goin' the other way." He nodded toward the body. "He don't look like he's enjoyin' the ride back."

"No, I reckon not," Will answered, but offered no details.

Once they were across, Will turned upstream and returned to the spot where he had camped the night before. After he helped Reese off his horse, he handcuffed his hands around a small tree while he took care of the horses, except the one carrying Frank's body. He led that one over in the trees a little way and dumped the corpse on the ground. Then he took the saddle off and let the horse go to water. After that, he made a fire on top of his ashes from that morning. When his fire was right, he put on some strips of jerky in his frying pan to warm up and made a pot of coffee. When it was ready, he poured two cups of coffee and set one of them beside the tree, along with the frying pan. "I need to warn you right now, this is one of the most dangerous times for a prisoner." That got Reese's attention. "I'm fixin' to unlock one of those cuffs, so you can drink that coffee and eat some of this jerky. It's a dangerous time because I've found after some years in this business, this is the time when a lot of prisoners decide they'll make a move to attack, and I have to shoot him. When a prisoner makes a move like that, it's awful tempting just to shoot him in the head. If you just wing him or put a bullet in his foot, he's just that much more trouble to transport."

He went ahead and unlocked one of the handcuffs. "What kin is that fellow to you? I know his name's Trainer, same as yours, but is he a brother, cousin, what?"

"He's my brother, least he was before you killed him."

"Yeah, well, that's too bad about that," Will replied. "I reckon he wasn't thinkin' too clearly. You'd say the same thing if you had seen what he tried to do when I told him to drop his gun. He played like he was gonna drop it from his left hand, but then he tried to catch it with his right. It was the dumbest thing I've ever seen, and me already holdin' my gun on him. Hell, he didn't give me no choice. I had to shoot him. Anyway, I thought you might wanna know how he came to get shot." He watched Reese carefully then when he drank his coffee and ate a couple of strips of the jerky. "Since he was your brother," Will said, "I'll let you dig a grave and bury him, if it'll make you feel any better. I've got a short-handle shovel on my packhorse you can use. But I ain't gonna tote his carcass all the way to Fort Smith. You wanna bury him?"

Reese didn't even hesitate. "Hell, no, I ain't gonna dig a grave."

Will nodded thoughtfully. "You two musta been real close," he remarked. "Well, we'll leave him where I left him and let the buzzards take care of it."

When the horses were rested, Will locked Reese around the tree again while he rinsed out his coffeepot and pan and packed them up. He walked into the trees and searched the body for anything of value that he might have missed before but found nothing but a ring with a ruby-colored piece of glass in the setting. So he showed it to Reese and put it in Reese's saddlebag, in case it had some sentimental value. When everything was ready, he got Reese in the saddle again and headed back to the road to Durant.

They pulled in beside Dixon Durant's store just before he was about to close. Will dismounted and tied Reese's horse securely to the hitching rail while just loosely wrapping the other reins over it. With Reese sitting in the saddle, his hands behind his back, his feet tied together, Will didn't think he could do much, but he stood in the open door while he listed his needs, anyway. "Will Tanner!" Leon Shipley greeted him when he heard the door open. "We ain't seen you in a coon's age."

"Howdy, Leon, I reckon it has been a while at

that. I'm gonna need some supplies, and if you don't mind, I'll stand here by the door while we do business. I'm ridin' with a fellow who doesn't like my company very much and I need to let him know I'm keepin' an eye on him."

"Right," Leon replied. "Just call 'em off and I'll fetch 'em." He walked over to the window to satisfy his curiosity. "I've seen that fellow before."

"Probably so," Will said. "He built that place over on Clear Boggy, the one that burnt down."

"Right," Leon said. "Did you have somethin' to do with that?"

"I reckon it was struck by lightnin'," Will said. "The Lord don't like folks sellin' firewater to the Choctaws."

"Right," Leon said once again. "I'll go get your stuff."

Will called out everything he could think of for the long trip back to Fort Smith. He paid for it with money he took out of Reese's pocket after Princess had taken her five dollars. He figured it only fair for Reese to pay the cost of his transport to jail. When he had completed his purchases, he and Leon carried them out to load on Will's packhorse. Will said so long to Leon and started the horses toward a spot beside a creek that he had camped on before.

CHAPTER 14

When they were ready to leave the next morning, Will put Reese on the horse his brother had ridden. He figured his Choctaw friend was going to be hot enough when he saw Reese, so there was no sense in fanning that flame by seeing him on his gray gelding. They arrived in Atoka in the early afternoon after having split the thirty-mile trip in half to rest the horses and eat a late breakfast of coffee, bacon, and fried apples. It finished Will's sack of dried apples, but he thought his prisoner deserved something special when he didn't want to go to the trouble of cooking something substantial. He told Reese he was going to get a big supper from Lottie's Kitchen to make up for it. Reese made no reply, but it was very obvious that his return to Atoka was making him very tense. "Kinda like comin' home, ain't it?" Will couldn't resist the taunt. It still made his blood boil when he thought about what Reese and his brother had done to Jim Little Eagle.

Seeing Stanley Coons out in front of his stables, Will pulled up and asked Stanley if he had seen Jim in town that day. "Not so far," Stanley said, gaping at Reese, his hands cuffed behind his back.

"I reckon we'll ride on out to Jim's place," Will said. "If you see him, tell him where we went."

"I expect he'll wanna scalp that one," Stanley said, nodding toward the scowling Reese Trainer as Will pulled away from the stable and headed for Jim's cabin on Muddy Boggy Creek.

Mary Light Walker was the one who saw them first. She was taking her wash off the clothesline when they turned onto the path to their cabin. She ran at once to tell Jim, who was working in the barn. He came out at once to meet them, a deep frown etched into his face. "Ho, Jim," Will called out as soon as he saw him. "I need your key to the jail."

"I see you got the man who lock me in my jail," Jim said.

It was plain to see that the Choctaw policeman was still carrying the guilt for having been the victim of Reese and Frank's jailbreak. Will did his best to ignore it. "If it's all right with you, I'll lock this one up for tonight only. And I'll start out for Fort Smith in the mornin'. I'll take care of him, get his supper from Lottie's, and be gone tomorrow. Is there anybody in the jail now?"

"No, nobody in jail," Jim answered. "Where is other man? The one who sneak up on me?"

"He's dead," Will answered. "I left him for the buzzards to eat near the Red River."

"My fault you have to catch this one two times," Jim started apologizing again.

"It wasn't your fault, Jim. It wasn't anybody's fault. Nobody knew the other man was his brother. I didn't know. If I had been in your place that night, what happened to you would have happened to me. I just want to lock him up in there tonight because I'd like to get a good night's sleep before I start a three-day ride with one eye open all the time." He wanted Jim to get over it. He was too valuable an ally in the Choctaw Nation, and he didn't want him to start pulling away because he got skunked one time.

Jim walked up to the gray gelding and took his head in his hands. The horse recognized his owner and nuzzled him with its muzzle. "I go watch this horse thief all night for you while you sleep. I sleep tomorrow," Jim said. "Mary fix you good supper."

"No, you don't have to do that. Nobody has to watch him. His brother's dead and there ain't nobody else that gives a damn if he's in that jail or not." He looked at Mary Light Walker then and said, "I always enjoy your cookin', Mary, but I have to go to Lottie's to make arrangements for some supper for my prisoner, so I might as well eat there, myself. I think I'll take a room in Mabry's roomin' house, if he's got one vacant. I'll put the horses in Stanley Coons's stable and get started early in the mornin'."

Jim nodded solemnly. Will wasn't sure if he had talked him out of guarding his jail or not. "Thank you, good friend, for bringing my horse back. I think you want black horse back now." He was referring to the blue roan that Caleb Hawkins had ridden.

"No, that horse was a gift from me. I want you to keep that horse," Will insisted. Right at this particular time, he didn't need another horse to deal with even had he wanted to take it back. After some more discussion back and forth, it was finally decided that Jim would go to the jail with him now to make sure Reese had water and an empty waste bucket. Then he would leave the key with Will.

When they got to the jail, Will pulled Reese off his horse and handcuffed him to the iron rod on the smokehouse door while he and Jim made sure his cell was ready for him. Jim took the water bucket to the pump and trough at the end of the street to fill it with fresh water. While he was gone, Reese made a plea to Will. "Have a heart, Tanner, you don't have to lock me up in that damn Injun's smokehouse. That black hole works on a man's mind. It ain't right to lock a man up in there. I'll give you my word, you can handcuff me to a tree, and I'll set up all night. I wouldn't shut a dog up in that hole. Just give me my blanket to put over me and I'll still be here in the mornin'."

"I wouldn't shut a dog up in there, myself, but we ain't talking about something you can trust, like a dog. My advice to you is to lay down on that cot in there, close your eyes, and go to sleep. You've already showed me what you'll do if you get the chance, and I don't give a prisoner a second chance to escape. If you and your brother hadn't pulled that trick on Jim, you woulda gotten a ride to Fort Smith in a jail wagon, with a cook to fix your meals. For the next two or three nights, after we leave here, you'll be sleepin' wrapped around a tree and you'll be homesick for this jail. So you'd best take advantage of that cot." His advice was taken with a scowl and a feeling of confidence that somewhere between here and Fort Smith, Will would get careless.

When Jim returned with the fresh water, the prisoner was released inside the dark enclosure and given a few minutes to locate the candle and matches before the door was closed and the lock put in place. "I'll let you eat your supper outside, like we did before," Will told him as the lock clicked shut. *It is a hell of a place to lock a man up in,* he thought as he led the horses away toward the stable. But it was the only place available to him to keep a prisoner.

Jim went with him to the stables, where they met Stanley Coons mucking out some stalls. "I'm glad to see you gettin' some stalls ready for my horses," Will japed. "Buster likes fresh hay in his stall."

Stanley laughed. "Is that so? I suppose he'd

like to have me sing him a lullaby to help him go to sleep, too."

"I don't know about that, Stanley," Will replied. "I've heard your voice and he might be too scared to close his eyes."

Coons chuckled again, then asked, "What can I do for you, Will?"

"I wanna leave 'em with you till the mornin'," Will said. "I'll be headin' out for Fort Smith early, so I'd like for you to give all of 'em a portion of oats tonight. I'll go ahead and leave you this one and the two packhorses. I'll bring the buckskin back in a little while. This bay packhorse belongs to the prisoner, and I need to take a look to see what he's carryin'." So they removed the pack saddles and Will opened all of Reese's goods. "Reckon it's a good thing I did," he commented to Jim, and held a Navy Colt .45 up for him to see. It had been in with a bag holding socks and underwear. Everything looked new, even a rain slicker and a blanket. Evidently his brother Frank had been carrying a large amount of money with him. Will had found a substantial amount of cash in the pockets of both Trainer brothers, and it was paying for all the expense of transporting Reese to Fort Smith, including supper at Lottie's and a room at Mabry's rooming house, if one was available.

Will put everything back in Reese's packs like he had found them, with the exception of the

Navy Colt. He opened the cylinder and removed all the cartridges. Coons took the three horses then and Will and Jim got on their horses and rode up the street to Mabry's rooming house. They found Doug sitting on the front porch and when they stopped at his walk, he got up to meet them. "Hello, Will, what can I do for ya? If you're comin' here to complain about Lottie's cookin'," he joked, "I ain't got nothin' to do with my wife's business." He laughed in appreciation of his wit. "How do, Jim?"

Jim nodded and Will chuckled when he replied, "No, it'd be pretty hard to find something to complain about with Lottie's cookin'. I'm lookin' to see if you've got a vacant room for the night."

"Hell, I thought you always slept on the ground with your horse," Doug said, still joking.

"I usually do. But tonight, I was hopin' to find a bed to get a good night's sleep on."

"Well, I can fix you right up with a bed," Doug said. "It's a small room next to the washroom, but there's a good bed in it. Oughta be just what you're lookin' for if you're just looking for one night. Come on, and I'll show it to ya."

"I'm sure it'll be all right," Will said. "I'll just bring my saddlebag and leave it in the room."

"I wait here," Jim Little Eagle said. Will had an idea Jim didn't feel comfortable walking through the white man's house.

The room was as Doug had described it, small, but neat and clean with one small window and a chest of drawers. Will walked in and dropped his saddlebag on the bed. "This'll do fine," he said, and walked back out in the hall. Doug locked the door and gave Will the key. "I'll be leavin' early in the mornin', so I'd best pay you now."

"It'll cost you a dollar for one night," Doug said. "It'd be cheaper if you were gonna rent it for a longer time. Then I'd give you a monthly rate."

"That's fine," Will said, and gave him a dollar. "I'll just leave the key on the chest of drawers when I leave in the mornin'." He paused, then japed, "Unless you rather I knocked on your door in the mornin' and returned the key to you." He knew that it would probably be a couple of hours before Doug got out of bed.

Doug laughed, knowing he was being japed. "On the chest of drawers will be fine." He walked Will back out to the front porch, where Jim was waiting. "When you come in tonight, you don't have to knock on the front door. You live here. Just come on in. I tell that to all my new renters. If I didn't, some jackass would stand out here on the porch knocking on the door till he woke somebody up."

"Is that a fact?" Will replied. He guessed that it must have happened once and woke him up. "Well, I won't be comin' in very late, anyway."

There was still over an hour before Lottie's

Kitchen would be open for supper, so Will rode back out to Jim's cabin with him to visit with him and Mary for a little while before he went to supper. Jim again offered to pick up Reese's supper for him, but Will told him he'd have to pay Lottie for the meal, and he was going to be there to eat, anyway. "If you wanna do me a favor, you can take the plate back tomorrow if it's still in the jail. If he finishes it tonight, I'll take the plate back."

"Evening, Will," Lottie greeted him when he walked in the door of her dining room, after leaving Buster at the stables. "I heard you were back, and you brought Reese Trainer with you. Doug said you're staying at the house tonight."

"That's all true," Will replied, "and I'm leavin' in the mornin' before you open up. So I'm hopin' tonight's supper will be something special for me to remember."

"You know I open this place up for breakfast at six o'clock, don't you?"

"Like I said, I'll be leavin' before you open up," he said with a grin. "I would like to buy one plate of supper for my prisoner, though."

"Doug said you only came back with Reese. What happened to Frank? Did he get away, or did you shoot him?"

"Unfortunately, Frank didn't wanna come back, so I had to leave him there," Will answered.

"You know, right here was where Frank dropped his last name," Lou-Bell joined the conversation. "What kin was he to Reese?" When Will said they were brothers, Lou-Bell said, "I knew it. They looked a lot alike, and they looked like they were close to the same age." Like Stanley and Doug, they wanted to know where Will had caught up with the two Trainer brothers. His answer to all of them was that they were trying to make it to Texas. In fact, he even told Coons that Frank's body was left on the Oklahoma side of the river. "Wow!" she exclaimed. "They almost made it, didn't they?"

"Almost," Will answered. "What are you ladies pushin' for supper tonight?" He was anxious to change the subject. Jim Little Eagle had not even asked where he had finally cornered the two brothers. Will figured Jim assumed the arrest was made in Oklahoma, and he was content to let him continue to believe that. He figured he was really going to be in hot water if Dan Stone found out he had gone into Texas to arrest Caleb Hawkins, just as he had when he arrested Caleb's older brother, Ward. Since Caleb decided to take his own life, Will saw no reason not to report that Caleb was arrested in Oklahoma, where the other members of his cattle rustling gang were killed. And the less he talked about it, the sooner it would be forgotten.

When he finished his supper of steak and

potatoes, he took the plate Lottie fixed up for Reese and a pint-sized jar of coffee and walked down to the jail with the meal. As he expected, Reese was more than ready for the food. So he told him, "You know the procedure if you wanna eat your supper outside on this crate. So the more you cooperate, the sooner you'll be sittin' out here in the fresh air eatin' steak and potatoes." After a short dose of the dark confines of the Choctaw jail, Reese was more than ready to cooperate in order to spend his suppertime outside his cage. After he handcuffed him to the door, Will waited for Reese to seat himself on the wooden crate, then he removed the top from the fruit jar and set it down where Reese could reach it. When he was all set, he placed the plate of food on his knees, one hand holding the plate, the other holding his Colt .44 six-gun aimed at Reese's face. When reminding him of the procedure for feeding him, Will had informed Reese that any sudden move on his part would result in the automatic squeezing of the trigger. Reese showed no inclination to test that theory, so he enjoyed a peaceful supper while Will watched with his back against the wall of the smokehouse.

The only strategy Reese attempted was slow motion, and this only to spend more time outside that jail. After a reasonable time and Reese had not finished half of his supper, Will told him he had fifteen minutes to finish and then he was going back inside. Reese protested, saying he had always been a slow eater. He couldn't help it. "Finish it now or take it inside with you but you're going back inside in fifteen minutes."

"All right, all right, damn it," Reese swore. "I'll eat it out here! It's so damn dark inside that hole, I might have it all over me and not know it." He finished with time to spare, but Will hustled him inside just the same. Once he was securely locked away for the night, Will told him he would see him at five in the morning and wished him a pleasant night. He then dropped the plate and fruit jar off at Lottie's and retired for the night.

Doug Mabry had not lied, it was a good bed, and Will woke up after a good night's rest right on the time he had set in his mind to wake up. It was a habit he had perfected over the years, with no logical reason for his success. He dressed quickly, grabbed his saddlebags, and went quietly out the door without arousing any of the other guests. He met Stanley Coons on his way to the stables, and the two of them saddled and packed up his horses. He thanked Stanley and led the horses down to the jail, pausing briefly when he detected a body standing in the shadows of the square smokehouse. About to draw his rifle from the saddle sling, he then realized it was Jim Little Eagle, waiting to help him load his prisoner. He came forward to meet Will, holding a sack outstretched toward him. "What's in the sack?" Will asked.

"Corn cakes," Jim answered. "Mary sent for your breakfast."

"Bless her heart," Will said. "You tell her this is gonna make my breakfast one helluva lot better and tell her how grateful I am to get 'em."

"Mary say you don't have to give any to prisoner if you don't want to."

Leaning right up against the door, Reese could hear them talking. "You oughta brought all them corn cakes to me for not shootin' you, you damn savage. If my brother hadn't stopped me, I'da shot you down that night. I wish now I had. Open the damn door and let me outta here!"

"He gonna shoot me, but brother tell him no, make too much noise," Jim explained to Will. "I think it better if you shoot him."

"I might do that," Will told him. "But my boss always wants me to give 'em a chance to behave first. So I'll give Mr. Trainer, here, a chance to be a good prisoner. Then if he ain't, that's when I'll shoot him." He unlocked the padlock and handed the key to Jim. "This is gonna be his first chance to prove he's gonna be a good prisoner. You stand there with your gun aimed right at his chest. If he comes out real slow, with his hands out in front of him, so I can put the handcuffs on him, then he's passed the first test. If he makes any move toward either one of us, then you can shoot him."

Jim nodded. "Only if he tries anything," Will reminded Jim. "All right, Reese, I'm openin' the door. Come on out."

"Hell, no!" Reese blurted. "That crazy Injun is just waitin' to shoot me!"

"Not if you behave yourself and come out nice and slow with your hands together, out in front of you. If you don't come out, we're both gonna start shootin' in the door. And I'm gettin' tired of waitin'."

"All right, all right, I'm comin' out, real slow, right now."

Will swung the door all the way open, and Reese's hands came out before him. Will quickly put the handcuffs on his wrists, then led him over to his horse. "I'm lettin' you start out this mornin' with your hands in front of you. If you don't give me any trouble, I'll let you ride that way from now on. If you give me a reason, I'll cuff your hands behind your back again and you can ride all the way to Fort Smith like that." He took the short piece of rope he had used on him before and tied his feet together again.

"Is that necessary?" Reese asked.

"Maybe not," Will answered him, "but I don't want you to decide to jump off that horse unless I tell you to. I reckon you'll just have to put up with it." He turned around to look at Jim then. "I reckon we're ready to ride, Jim. I appreciate all your help and be sure to tell Mary I'll enjoy those corn cakes. Don't know when I'll be back this way again, but I'll certainly contact you when I am." They shook hands and Will climbed up into the saddle, gave a little salute with his index finger against the brim of his hat, then led his horses out to the east. He crossed over the MKT train tracks and picked up a trail, very familiar to him, leading toward the Jack Fork Mountains. Buster seemed to know they were starting a long trip, so Will let the buckskin set the pace. Since the trail he followed was an old Indian trail, and one very narrow in places, he was leading the packhorses in single file on lead ropes behind Reese's horse. And Will held the reins of Reese's horse in his hand. He planned to stop for breakfast at one of his favorite camping spots, a deep spring not quite twenty miles from Atoka. The water was cool and clean and there was a meadow of good grass between two groves of trees. At the pace Buster had set, that was going to take close to four hours, so men and horses would be ready for a rest and something to eat.

When they arrived at the spring, there was evidence of other campfires there, but everyone had left their campsites tidy, just as Will would do when he moved on. He untied Reese's feet then stood back to give him room to dismount. "I'm gonna let you get a drink of water first, then I'm gonna park you by a tree while I take care of everything else. That's a pretty good deal, ain't it?" He pulled his rifle out of his saddle sling and holstered his six-gun. "Right over there," he said, and pointed with his rifle toward a mossy spot on the bank of the spring. Reese didn't hesitate, he went right to the spot and took a long drink from the cool water. When he was satisfied, he got to his feet and Will directed him to a tree large enough to hold him but small enough to give him room. "Straddle it," he said.

Reese complied but not without complaining. "I can't eat with my arms locked around this damn tree."

"I don't expect you to," Will said. "When I get something ready to eat, I'll let you eat." That served to appease Reese for the moment, while Will took care of the horses, then collected some wood for a fire. As always, he got his coffee working first, then cut some strips of bacon to fry in his pan. Instead of the hardtack he packed, he reached in the sack of corn cakes Jim Little Eagle had brought him. While Reese watched him like a dog begging at a campfire, Will took one of the cakes out and inspected it. Then he took a bite out of it and chewed it thoughtfully. Reese bit his lip in envy, fearing Will didn't intend to share the corn cakes. "I don't know," Will said. "They're pretty good, but I believe I'd prefer mine warmed up with a little of this bacon grease. How do you want yours?"

"In the grease, too," Reese replied at once, again like a hungry camp dog.

When Will had the breakfast ready, he split it on the two tin plates he carried on his packhorse. But before he served it, he took the short piece of rope that had held Reese's feet in the stirrups and tied them together again, this time around the tree. Then he unlocked the handcuffs to set his hands free. He gave Reese his plate and cup of coffee, then he sat down a few yards away, facing him, his rifle beside him and pointing toward Reese. Reese would get to know this routine every time they ate.

CHAPTER 15

After the horses were rested, they left the campsite beside the spring and continued following the old Indian trail that led toward the Jack Fork Mountains, an area of rugged pine-covered hills and mountains. Will planned another stop to rest the horses before completing a forty-mile day in the saddle. He would camp that night within the sight of Pine Mountain to the north. If Reese was planning to make an attempt for freedom, the isolated hills of the Jack Fork Mountains might be the place for it.

When they reached the spot where Will planned to camp for the night, he set the same routine as the two times before, with Reese anchored to a pine tree while Will took care of making the camp. "You musta made this trip a helluva lotta times," Reese commented, obviously trying to make light conversation. "You know every campsite you're gonna stop at before you ever get to it."

"That's right," Will replied, deciding to play along, thinking at the same time, *The sooner we get started, the sooner it'll be over with.* "The horses could go on a little farther than this, but there ain't a decent place to camp for another twenty miles after this."

"Well, I reckon, if I've gotta take the trip to Fort Smith, I'm glad I'm at least goin' with a deputy who knows the way. I bet you knew about this big open grassy patch in the middle of all these pine hills, too. Didn't ya?"

Will couldn't help a smile from forming. "Yeah, well, like I said, I've made this trip a helluva lotta times."

"I sure wouldn'ta known this stream was comin' outta the hill on the other side of the trail, if you hadn't cut off the trail and led us down here." Reese appeared to be marveled.

"Well, now you know it's here, if you're back this way again," Will said, wondering how far he was going to take this show before he made his move.

"You know, after I got to thinkin' about it," Reese started again, "I reckon I have done some pretty bad things. Maybe it'll be good for me to pay for what I've done. It's my fault my own brother got killed. I just want you to know I don't blame you for it. You just did what you had to do."

"Well, I've gotta say, that's mighty decent of you, Reese. Maybe I'll put in a good word to the judge for you."

"I appreciate it, Deputy, but I don't expect you to do that for me," Reese said most humbly. "But if it ain't askin' too much, you could do me one little favor. Are those all my packs you took off my packhorse?"

"Yep, that's all your stuff," Will answered. "I just take 'em off and put 'em back on the horse. I haven't loaded any of my stuff on your packs."

"I really need to wash my feet in that stream and put on some clean socks. Would it be askin' too much to unlock me from this tree just long enough to do that? I think I've got some clean socks in one of those packs. I bet I could find a pair right quick. Whaddaya say? I give you my word I won't take but a minute."

"I don't reckon that's askin' too much, if a fellow just wants to wash his feet," Will said. "I probably oughta wash mine." He propped his rifle against a tree, walked over, and unlocked the cuffs on Reese's wrists, then locked one of them again. "Just remember I'll be watchin' you."

Reese grinned broadly, then walked over to where his packs were put on the ground. "I'm pretty sure I've got some extra socks in here somewhere," he said as he went right to the sack that held them.

"I reckon I should carry more than one extra pair with me," Will continued their conversation. "I never seem to think about extra socks for some reason."

With his back still turned to Will, Reese got to his feet. When he turned to face him again, he was holding the Navy Colt .45 and aiming it at Will. "Now, this is where this damn dog and pony show ends, lawman," he growled.

"Another thing that would be smart," Will continued, "would be to take some extra underwear, especially in the wintertime."

"Are you blind?" Reese demanded, and held the gun out at arm's length, aimed at Will's chest. "Can you see this gun in my hand?"

"Yep, I believe it's a Navy Colt .45, ain't it?" Will responded.

"That's right, you damn fool, and it's fixin' to knock a hole in your chest."

"Nah, that's a pretty good gun, but it ain't worth a damn without some cartridges in it." When Will said that, Reese's eyes grew wide with shock. He pulled the trigger, cocked it, pulled the trigger again and again. Frantic to have been played for a fool, he threw the pistol at Will, who easily stepped aside to avoid it. "Here's what works," Will said, pulled his six-gun, and fired three quick shots, one on each side of Reese's feet, and one between his feet. "That last shot went in the ground between your feet. If I have to fire again, I'm gonna be aimin' at the same spot but a little higher up, just below hip-high." He brought his pistol up and sighted on the area. "Like you said"—he paused to remember—"What did you call it? Dog and pony show? Well, that's over. We're gonna play it by my rules from here on in." He paused again, then unable to resist it, said, "And I was just about at the point where I was thinkin' about turnin' you loose."

"All right, damn it, you win." Reese put his hands in the air and returned dutifully to his tree. Will locked his hands around it and returned to the preparation of their supper, which was to be the same as they had for breakfast, with the exception of hardtack instead of corn cakes. After supper, Will locked Reese's hands back around his tree again and told him his prisoners had found they could actually go to sleep if they straddled the tree with their legs. "Well, I'll guarantee you I can't sleep this way," Reese declared.

"Good," Will said. "You can watch the camp, and I'll get a little sleep tonight." He got Reese's blanket and draped it over him. Then he sat by the fire for a while, letting it burn down while he finished the little bit of coffee left in the pot. He heard nothing out of Reese for a long time, so he thought that he might possibly have gone to sleep. So he rolled up in his blanket with his pistol close beside him. After a long while, he drifted off to sleep.

When he woke up, it was not quite daylight yet. He looked at once toward the tree, but Reese was gone. Alert then, he grabbed his six-gun and rolled out of his blanket, expecting an attack from any direction, but there was none. Thinking he must still be asleep, he blinked his eyes frantically, trying to rid them of sleep. He rose slowly to one knee, still trying to see all around him in the darkness. It didn't make sense. If Reese escaped from the tree, why did he not attack him? He had sworn to kill him once before. What changed his mind? He stared again at the tall pine, swaying slightly with the breeze. It occurred to him then that there was no breeze where he knelt. So he raised his eyes up along the pine until he discovered the cause of the swaying. The large, dark form about twenty-five feet up the trunk had to be his prisoner.

He got up from his knee and walked over to the tree, where he saw Reese's boots lying on the ground. "Good mornin'," he said. "Did you sleep all right?"

"Go to hell," was the angry reply.

"It's gettin' about time to get started," Will told him. "I'll go ahead and get the horses packed and ready and you can come on down when you're ready." He walked all around the tree, looking at Reese's condition from every angle. As the first rays of morning broke through the pines, he could see what had occurred. Evidently Reese figured he could shinny up that pine until he bent it over to the ground because it wasn't a very large pine. He could understand why he had kicked his boots off. It definitely would have been difficult to shinny up that high with boots on. And as a result of that, he imagined Reese's socks must have caught hell from the bark on that pine tree.

It was Will's guess that when he got up to the

point where there were many more limbs, he couldn't get past them. They were bigger than they looked from the ground, and they were bunched, so he couldn't flatten them against the trunk. So he was stuck halfway back down, stopped by a small limb that he had been able to press close enough to the trunk to get past it, going up. Coming down was a different matter, for the limb had sprung back down and was too strong for him to break. Will wondered how long Reese had been hanging up there on that tree. He hoped all night.

When the horses were ready to go, Will went back to the tree. "Okay, Reese, I think we're ready to go. You can come on down now and we'll get started."

"Damn you! You can see I can't get down. You've gotta help me."

"What did you crawl up there for? To see the view? Can't you just come back down the way you went up?"

"No, I can't. I've been tryin' to get down and I can't get by this limb. You're gonna have to get me down."

"It'da been a whole lot easier if your hands weren't cuffed together. If you'da told me last night you wanted to climb that tree, I mighta unlocked your handcuffs so you coulda done it."

"Are you gonna get me down?"

"I'm thinkin' about leavin' you up there. Might

be the best place for you. That limb might break off if you jumped up and down on it. 'Course you'd still be locked around the trunk. I don't know, Reese, you sure got yourself in a spot." He was thoroughly enjoying the taunting of the man, but they were wasting time and he was anxious to be rid of him.

"I've been stompin' on the damn limb, tryin' to break it. It's too tough when I ain't got my boots on. You can't leave me here. It's your duty as a deputy marshal to transport me for trial."

Will took his hat off and scratched his head as if giving it some serious thought. "Well, when you put it that way, I reckon you're right. But I don't know but one way to get you down." He went to his packhorse and came back with his hand ax.

"Whoa!" Reese bellowed. "Whaddaya gonna do?"

"I'm gonna get you down."

"You're liable to kill me if you chop this tree down!"

"That's right," Will said. He paused as if to consider that, then he said, "It's a risk I'm willin' to take." He took a swing and sank his ax deep into the pine trunk. "This ain't gonna take as long as I thought. I've still got a good edge on this little ax. It wouldn't be no job at all with a good long-handle ax that you could take a full swing with, but this one will do the job."

"For Mercy's sake," Reese pleaded. "Can't you think of any other way?"

"I swear, will you quit complainin'?" Will scolded. "I'm the one doin' all the work here, swingin' this ax. All you have to do is ride her down." He kept swinging away with the ax until the tree was standing on only a couple of inches of trunk and starting to creak threateningly. "Uh-oh," Will said, "here comes the dangerous part. One more swing of this ax is gonna do the job, and I have to be careful that trunk don't buck back and hit me." He waited for Reese's answer to that but there was none. He looked up to see him hugging the tree and mumbling to himself. So Will took one last swing with the ax and jumped out of the way when the tree kicked back across the stump. He heard a long continuous yowl from Reese, all the way until the tree crashed to the ground.

He walked over to see how Reese had fared his ride down and discovered that he had been saved from a really hard impact with the ground when that portion of the trunk he was clinging to landed in a patch of blackberries and young pines. When Will got to him, he was hanging under the trunk, about five feet off the ground, caught in a cushion of thorny blackberry bushes. Will could see that he had not escaped some scrapes and bruises from the rebound when the tree crashed into the smaller trees and bounced back to its final position. With no intention of cutting him any slack in the taunting, Will asked, "It was a lot quicker comin' down than it was goin' up, wasn't it? You did find a nice patch of blackberries, though. Too bad they ain't ripe yet. We coulda picked a batch of 'em to eat for breakfast." He waited for Reese's comeback, but Reese was too miserable to speak. "Well, let's get you outta those briars." He made his way carefully through enough of the bushes to allow him to reach the handcuffs holding Reese to the tree. Then he reached over and unlocked the cuff on one wrist, releasing him from the tree and dropping him in the blackberry vines. "There you go," Will said cheerfully as he carefully backed out of the bushes. "Come on out."

Reese wasn't sure if it would be preferable for Will to just shoot him and put him out of his misery, for he came out of the blackberries with scratches on any exposed skin and rips in his clothes. That, added to the fact that he had not slept all night but hung in a tree instead, did not make for a good attitude toward sitting in a saddle all day. He put up no resistance when Will locked the cuffs again and got up into the saddle without being helped. He sat patiently while his feet were being tied together. They were not on the trail long before he fell over on his horse's neck and went to sleep. Will checked to see that he was not going to slide out of the saddle, and when it seemed he was secure, with his arms around his horse's neck, Will enjoyed a more peaceful ride to the next planned rest stop for the horses and breakfast for him and his prisoner.

He made his camp in a shallow ravine near the Sans Bois Mountains with a strong stream running down the center of it. It was the same stream that ran past Merle Teague's cabin, farther up in the mountains. Had he been traveling alone, he would have ordinarily stopped at Merle's cabin, but he chose not to take his prisoner there. *Besides,* he thought, *Merle should still have plenty of coffee from my last visit.* When he pictured the quaint little man in his mind, he had to chuckle to himself. "We could probably get some fresh deer meat if we had stopped at Merle's," he said aloud to Buster, knowing Reese couldn't hear him. His prisoner was astraddle another tree, fast asleep. Will wondered if Reese's ordeal with the pine tree was enough to kill all thoughts of escape before they reached Fort Smith. He also realized that it might have provided more fuel to throw on his desire for revenge at any cost. *Just have to wait and see,* he told himself, and started gathering wood for his fire.

By the time Will had fried the bacon and hardtack in the grease, Reese had recovered enough to want some coffee. And he had regained enough of his contempt for Will that he was able to complain again. "Don't you know how to cook anything but bacon and hardtack?"

"A few things," Will answered. "But when I'm travelin' like we are now, I just eat enough to keep the sides of my belly from rubbin' together. If you don't like what I cook, you surely don't have to eat it. The mistake you made was breakin' outta jail. You coulda been ridin' to Fort Smith in a wagon with a cook along to fix fancy food for you. You wouldn'ta been climbin' trees at night, either. Maybe next time you decide to break the law, you oughta request a different deputy to come after you."

Since Reese was afraid to go to sleep while he was up in a tree the night before, he had plenty of time to think. And one of the ideas he came up with, he was so proud of that he had to inform Will about it. "You may have the upper hand right now, Tanner, but if you had a grain of sense in your head, you'd turn me loose right now."

"Is that a fact?" Will replied, interested to hear what Reese could come up with.

"If you get me to Fort Smith, I'm gonna hire me a lawyer," Reese went on. "You made a mistake when you arrested me. You arrested me in Texas and you ain't legally authorized to arrest anybody in Texas. So they'd have to let me go, since I was illegally arrested. Then they'll arrest you for arrestin' somebody outside Injun Territory. If you was smart, you'd let me go."

"Well, that's a mighty interestin' theory you've come up with," Will responded. He couldn't believe that Reese really thought that was a possibility. And he did say, *If you get me to Fort Smith,* instead of, *When you get me to Fort Smith.* So that was warning enough for Will not to count on his ordeal with the tree to discourage any attempts to escape. "Maybe we'll end up in the same cell in prison," he said. " 'Cause there would still be that little matter of you sellin' whiskey in the Nations and breaking out of jail. And you know, you were legally arrested in Tishomingo for those offenses."

That stopped Reese for a few moments. In his enthusiasm for his idea to sue Will for false arrest, he forgot about that part of it. "You ain't got me to Fort Smith yet," he mumbled, barely loud enough for Will to hear it.

When the horses were rested, Will packed up again and they continued along on the old trail to Fort Smith. He planned to make his camp for the night at the little settlement of Milton. There was a good place to camp on Wolf Creek, which he had used before. About eight years ago, settlers had discovered the land around Wolf Creek and there were several farms in the area now. There was not what you might call a town there as yet. One small general mercantile store was basically it, with the addition of a blacksmith and a farrier. The store was almost constantly out of the basic items the farmers needed. So much so, that the town was often referred to as Needsville. Out of necessity, Buster had once had a shoe replaced there. The blacksmith and the farrier were one and the same, a husky man named Neil Pine. Will always remembered his name because of his fellow deputy Ed Pine. But Neil claimed that he had no relatives that were deputy marshals, and Ed said he knew of no blacksmiths among his relatives. Will also remembered that Neil Pine had done a first-rate job making Buster's new shoe. So good, in fact, that he had him replace the other three.

The trail they followed passed through Milton, then on to the creek east of the store. It was late afternoon when Will walked Buster toward the blacksmith shop, and Neil Pine was standing out front, waiting to see who was coming. When he saw who it was, his ruddy face lit up with a grin. "Will Tanner," he called out. "I shoulda recognized that buckskin. Them shoes ain't fell off yet?"

"Nope, they're still hangin' on," Will answered. "If I'm anywhere near here when they get so loose they start to rattle, I'll try to let you put on some new ones."

"You do that," Neil said. "You got time to stop for a drink of likker?" he asked with a great big grin. That was Neil's standard joke he liked to crack every time he saw Will, since Will was a deputy marshal and it was against the law to sell whiskey in the Nations.

"I'd take you up on that, but I've got a fellow with me who's needin' to rest his weary bones. So I'd best ride on and get us a camp set up."

Neil took another look at Reese and realized he was handcuffed, and his feet tied in the stirrups. So he took an even closer look. "He looks like you pulled him through a corn sheller."

"He fell in a blackberry patch," Will told him, "and he's kinda anxious to get to Fort Smith, so I'd best let him get some rest."

"Well, you take care of yourself," Neil said. "It's good to see you again."

"Same to you," Will said, and gave Buster a nudge.

When he got to the creek, he left the trail he had followed since picking it up back in the Jack Fork Mountains and guided the horses about a quarter of a mile upstream to a point where a lively stream joined Wolf Creek. The spot offered everything he needed for his camp: good water, grass for the horses, and wood for the fire. *Now, if we have a peaceful night,* he thought, *we'll have a short ride to Fort Smith.* They would have a ride of only a little over thirty-five miles, and if they made good time, he might be home for supper. He hadn't given that a thought until that moment, and a picture of Sophie's face appeared in his brain. It wasn't a smiling picture. *She'll warm up a little when I explain why I was gone so long,* he told himself. But for right now, he put that picture away and told himself to focus on Reese. If he let his mind get careless, Reese would kill him, given half a chance. With his mind firmly planted on Reese again, he dismounted and went to Reese's horse to hold the reins while he threw a leg over and slid out of the saddle. He untied his feet from the stirrups and stood back to give him room. "Whaddaya waitin' for?" Will asked, when Reese just sat there.

"Gimme a minute, will ya?" Reese answered. "I ain't feelin' so good. I think I broke something inside me when I rode that damn tree down." He held his hands over his chest. "Something ain't right."

Will's natural reaction was suspicion. Reese's chest was fine all afternoon, now there's something wrong inside it? He decided to play it cautious, and he'd have to see some proof. "Well, whatever it is, it ain't gonna help it by sittin' up there on that horse. You need to sit down on the ground."

"It'd help if you could gimme a hand," Reese implored. "It hurts when I try to pick my leg up."

"It won't hurt but a second if you do it fast," Will said. He felt certain Reese was going to try something. "Just jerk your leg out of that stirrup and throw it over. I'll catch you if you fall."

"Damn it," Reese protested. "You think I'm gonna try somethin'. I just hurt too bad to pull that leg up."

"What if I take hold of your leg and just push you off the blame horse?" Will asked. "And just dump you on the ground on the other side?" He was beginning to believe there really was something wrong with him, but he was convinced it was in his head.

"I don't know if that would work or not." Reese hesitated. "I don't think you could push me off like that."

"Well, I can't think of anything else. I ain't gonna chop a horse down to get you on the ground. Let's see if I can get you out of that saddle." He walked around to the right side of the horse and laid his rifle on the ground. Then he grabbed the reins with one hand to keep the horse from moving. With his other hand, he pulled Reese's boot out of the stirrup. "Can you feel me movin' your foot?"

"I can't feel nothin'," Reese said, sounding a little worried.

"All right, you ready?" Will asked. Reese said he guessed so, and Will tried to pick Reese's leg straight up, but it was too much with one hand. So he took both hands, his right one still grasping the reins, and put some force behind it. Suddenly, Reese's leg doubled up like a frog's leg, pulling Will off-balance to catch the full force of Reese's boot in his chest, while snatching the reins out of Will's hands. Will landed on the seat of his pants beside his rifle while Reese raced away on his horse. "Damn," Will swore calmly, picked up his rifle, and got to his feet. He put it to his shoulder and took dead aim. He figured Reese was one hundred yards when he pulled the trigger. He straightened up for an instant, then slid sideways off the horse. "Well," he said to Buster, "we got him off the horse."

He climbed on the buckskin and trotted across the meadow to the fallen man. He found him writhing in pain, a bullet in his left shoulder, and when Will dismounted and stood over him, he gasped, "You shot me."

"I sure did. I told you before we started this little trip together that if you tried any tricks like this, I'd shoot you. I thought you knew I was serious. I gotta admit, though, you had me goin' for a while there. Can you walk?"

"I ain't sure. I don't think so," Reese answered. "You shot me, man! I'm hurtin'. I need a doctor."

"Well, there ain't one any closer than Fort Smith, so you're just gonna have to make it till we get there tomorrow. I'll take a look at the wound back at the camp. First, I'm gonna have to get the camp set up. Then I'm gonna have to go find that horse you ran off with. If I don't, you're gonna have a rough walk to Fort Smith in the mornin'. You ready to walk back to camp now?"

"I can't walk, I'm bleedin', I'm hurtin'."

"Ain't no problem," Will said, "I'll take you

back." He took a rope from his saddle and wound it tightly around Reese's boots.

"What the . . ." Reese exclaimed.

"Hold on to your hat," Will said as he climbed up into the saddle. He wrapped a couple of turns around his saddle horn with the rope and started Buster back across the meadow to the accompaniment of Reese's yelps and curses.

When they reached the camp, Will freed Reese from his rope, and when Reese started to voice a complaint, Will cut him off. "Let's get one thing straight—this little caper today was your last chance. You've used up all the breaks I was willin' to give you. From now till we get to Fort Smith, you're gonna be treated like the dog you are."

CHAPTER 16

He rode the Appaloosa down the length of the main street of Atoka to get a feel for the town. He had never been to Atoka before, so he took note of the stores he rode past. At the end of the street, he turned the oddly marked horse around and walked it slowly back to the rooming house at the other end and the establishment beside it. The sign over the door, identified the building as Lottie's Kitchen. It was the only place he saw when he rode to the other end of the street and back, that offered food, so he dismounted and tied the Appaloosa loosely at the rail. He walked inside and paused to look the place over, a little surprised to find it so neat and clean. At the far end of the room, two women were standing, talking to a customer who was seated. They all stopped to look at him, a stranger to this town. He glanced at the table close to the door and saw the sign. Without hesitating, he unbuckled his gun belt and carefully rolled his gun and holster up in it, then placed it on the table. He purposely neglected to remove the vest-pocket pistol from inside his coat.

"Who in the world is that?" Lou-Bell muttered softly. "He looks like a preacher or an undertaker, maybe both."

"That's what you said about Frank Trainer when he came in here the first time," Lottie commented. "You said he looked like an undertaker, but this fellow looks more like the one the undertaker puts in the ground. At least he can read. I'll go meet him." Like Lou-Bell, she almost felt a chill when he walked in the door. "Good afternoon," she greeted him. "Welcome to Lottie's Kitchen. I'm Lottie. You can sit anywhere that suits you, and Lou-Bell will get you some coffee or water." He removed his hat and nodded politely to her. She couldn't help thinking, *I knew his hair would be solid black, just like everything he's wearing.* She also couldn't help asking, "Are you just passing through Atoka? I know you've never been in here before. I would have remembered you."

He gave her a patient smile, as if all women he met asked the same questions. "First time in Atoka," he said. "I'm trying to find a man I've got some business interests with."

This surprised Lottie. "You've got some business with someone here?" she asked, wondering what kind of business that might possibly be.

"He doesn't live here, but I was told that he often came here and that he had friends in this town. I travel quite a bit myself, so it's sometimes hard for us to make contact. So I thought as long as I was in this part of the territory, I'd see if he happened to be here." He had stopped again at Blue River, and Brady Thompson had told him that Will Tanner came to Atoka quite often.

Lottie could not restrain her curiosity any longer, so she asked, "Who is it that you're trying to find? If you don't mind me asking."

He favored her with another patient smile, as if she was playing her part as he intended her to. "Will Tanner," he said. "He's a deputy marshal out of Fort Smith."

"Will?" She reacted in surprise. "You're looking for Will Tanner?" She wondered what business Will had with a man who looked like he knew the devil personally.

"That's right, I'm looking for Will Tanner."

"Well, you just missed him by a couple of days. Will was here, but he took a prisoner to Fort Smith." She paused then when Lou-Bell brought his coffee to the table, looked at her, and said, "Mister . . ." She had to pause then to say, "I'm sorry, I didn't ask your name."

"Coffey," he said.

Lottie and Lou-Bell exchanged puzzled looks, then Lou-Bel said, "There's your coffee right there."

"My name is Jack Coffey," he said with no hint of emotion, "spelled C-o-f-f-e-y."

Lottie and Lou-Bell exchanged stares of embarrassment for a solid moment, then both women burst out laughing. Lottie was quick to apologize then. "I'm sorry, Mr. Coffey. Please excuse us for acting the fool." She turned to face Lou-Bell again. "As I started to say, Mr. Coffey is looking for Will Tanner."

"Will's gone to Fort Smith," Lou-Bell said.

"I know," Lottie said, "I told him that, and we never know when he'll pass through Atoka again. So, looks like you missed him." If he was disappointed to hear that, there was no evidence of it in his face. Except for the occasional hint of a patient smile when some response was called for, his expression remained lifeless. Lottie was prompted to ask, "Do you ever just throw your head back and laugh at something?"

He flashed the faint, patient smile briefly, since the question called for some response, and said, "Not that I can recall."

Lottie decided that light conversation was impossible with the somber stranger, and she was not likely to find out why he was looking for Will. So she gave up and asked, "You hit us when pork chops are the featured dinner. If you don't care for pork chops, you can have ham. What'll it be?"

"I'll risk the pork chops," he said.

"Good man," Lou-Bell said. "I admire a man who's fearless." Coffey gave her a patient smile. She went to the kitchen to fix him a plate.

He took his time eating dinner, disappointed that he had been that close to catching up with Will

Tanner, but not discouraged. It would have been nice if Tanner had still been here, and he could have gotten the job done soon enough to turn right around and go back to collect his money. He would now go to Fort Smith to track Tanner down. His first task, however, was to get a look at him to make sure he stalked the right man. It would have been much easier to identify him in this small town. But he knew he would eventually pick up his trail and that it would ultimately end with the same conclusion. Should he find him in the town of Fort Smith, he could still get the job done, but he would have to be careful to be sure there were no witnesses, since Tanner was a lawman. It might be difficult to prove the killing anything but murder if he was caught. It was of no real worry, however. Killing lawmen was just part of his profession.

In the kitchen, the discussion about the stranger was still the number one subject. Lou-Bell broke it off, however, when she said, "I better go see if Dead Man needs some more coffee."

Lottie giggled and warned, "You'd better quit callin' him that, or you're liable to slip and say it to his face." She had to admit that it was a good nickname for the somber man. They were still talking about him after he paid for his dinner and left. The joking about Dead Man began again at suppertime, when Sam Barnet came in to eat supper, his wife and son, Jimmy, having taken the train to Joplin to visit her parents. Since Sam was the station manager for the MKT Railroad, his family could ride the train free. Although he would never admit it to Edna, Sam always enjoyed eating at Lottie's when his wife was out of town. Always interested in hearing a funny story, Sam asked what the joke was about a dead man.

Lottie told him about the stranger who had come in hoping to find Will Tanner, that he looked like he just came out of a graveyard somewhere, and then how they laughed because of his name. "His name was Coffey, and when he said it, we thought he was asking for coffee, and Lou-Bell had just set it down in front of him. But he was just trying to tell us his name was Coffey." She and Lou-Bell laughed about it again.

Sam laughed with them, then said, "As long as he wasn't Jack Coffey."

"It was Jack Coffey," Lou-Bell said. "Ain't that right, Lottie?"

"That's what he said," Lottie answered, "Jack Coffey, even spelled it for us."

"Good Lord in heaven!" Sam exclaimed, and he was no longer laughing. "Are you tellin' me the truth? Jack Coffey was in here today? And he was lookin' for Will Tanner?" When they both assured him that he surely was, he asked, "Did he say anything about catchin' the train or waitin' for the train? Anything like that?" His immediate alarm captured their attention at once. When

Lottie asked who Jack Coffey was, Sam told her. "Train robber, bank robber, killer for hire, but in his later years, he specializes in murder. He's so good at it that he commands a pretty high price for his services. If he's movin' around in Indian Territory, lookin' for Will, then somebody's paid a high price to get rid of Will."

"And we told him where Will was going," Lou-Bell groaned.

Sam was capable of concern for Will, but his biggest fear was the railroad he worked for. "You're sure he didn't ask anything about when the evenin' train gets in, or anything at all about the railroad? He coulda just wanted to make sure there was no deputy marshal in town and he was plannin' to hop that train."

"He didn't mention the train," Lottie said. "He just talked about Will, and that him and Will had some business to talk over. Besides, he had a riding horse and a packhorse. He wasn't thinkin' about riding the train. He's been riding all over Indian Territory looking for Will."

"What the hell have we done?" Lou-Bell moaned. "If something happens to him because of my big mouth, I ain't never gonna be able to forgive myself."

"Sam, as soon as you get back to the telegraph office, you gotta send a wire to the U.S. Marshal in Fort Smith and tell him this Jack Coffey killer is trying to track Will. I'll pay you for it."

"I'll do it," Sam said, "and there won't be no charge for it. I'll go right now."

"Will said it would take him two and a half to three days to get there, and he's got a two-day head start on Jack Coffey, so you can finish your supper. Then do it as soon as you get back."

"You're right," Sam said. "He ain't even there yet." Still he choked his supper down as fast as he could and was soon out of there. The discovery of the true identity of the dark stranger was enough to close the damper on the usual high spirits at Lottie's Kitchen for the rest of the evening.

Like the mood at Lottie's Kitchen, the atmosphere at Will's camp on Wolf Creek was devoid of good spirits. Reese was not yet recovered from his trip across the meadow at the end of a rope. The back of his clothes already torn from his encounter with the blackberries, was now also stained green by the grass he was dragged across. Will made him take off his shirt, so he could take a look at the wound he put in the back of Reese's shoulder. He took the handcuffs off to let him take his shirt off without tearing it up. While Reese grunted and groaned with the effort to remove the garment, Will watched him and held his .44 on him, and promised that one slightly funny move would result in a matching hole in the other shoulder. When the shirt was off, he ordered Reese to get on his knees, facing the tree he picked out for him. "Gimme your hands," he said, and Reese dutifully extended his arms, one on each side of the tree while Will put the cuffs back on him. With Reese's hands locked around the tree again, Will, feeling no compassion for his prisoner after his last escape attempt, went around behind him. He reached down and grabbed Reese's ankles and yanked his knees out from under him, so that Reese landed flat on his belly. Not wasting any time, Will was immediately on top of his legs, pinning him down while he coiled his rope around his ankles. Then he pulled the rope around a tree behind him, stretching Reese out flat on his stomach.

When he was finished, he stood over his prisoner and said, "Now I'm gonna be able to work on that wound with no trouble from you."

Lying helpless and afraid, Reese still tried to maintain a defiant manner. He knew the tricks he thought to pull by pretending to be repentant and cooperative were of no value now. "You know you're crazy, don't you, Tanner? Whaddaya fixin' to do to me?"

"Tell you the truth, now that I see you lyin' there, stretched out so helpless, I'm thinkin' you're in a good position to take a good whippin' with the knotted end of my rope. You know, I owe you something for that kick in the chest you gave me, back when I was tryin' to be nice to you. Then maybe I might pack some sand in that bullet hole you've got in your shoulder. You know you pulled that little trick of yours before I even got a chance to make camp. So I think I'll leave you on your belly while I do that now. It'll give me a little time to decide how I'm gonna work on you."

"That ain't gonna be so good for you, when I tell the judge what you did to me," he threatened.

"You're talkin' like you think you're gonna make it to Fort Smith," Will taunted. "You know, there's a good possibility you might die from that wound. You just rest easy there while I go find that horse you tried to steal. I hadn't thought about that; that makes two horses you stole. I'll have to remember to put that in my report." He climbed back into the saddle and wheeled Buster away to lope across the meadow again and into the woods on the other side.

He found the horse grazing in a small patch of grass on the other side of a ring of trees. It waited patiently while Will pulled Buster up beside it and took the reins. When he got back to his campsite, he glanced over to make sure Reese was still flat on the ground, before taking care of the horses. That done, he went about making his campfire. Once it was going good, he walked down to the edge of the creek to fill his coffeepot. When that was set just right in the edge of his fire, he looked through his packs until he found the old sheet he carried to make bandages from. Remembering then the small tin basin he had seen in Reese's packs, he looked again until he found it. He had a use for it now, so he took it to the creek and filled it with water. Then he returned and placed it on two sizable limbs in the fire to warm.

All set then, he used the old sheet to carry the hot basin over to the helpless man. He had never treated a prisoner so badly before, and although he had purposefully punished Reese, he was tired of giving him a rough time. "Whaddaya gonna do?" Reese asked fearfully, prepared for the worst.

"I'm gonna clean that wound a little bit, if I can. Then I'll put a bandage on it, if I can tie one that'll stay on. If I can, then you can put your shirt back on and I'll give you something to eat."

"Damn you!" Reese spat, thinking Will was being sarcastic. He tried to wriggle around any way he could in a useless effort to get away from Will's hands. Stretched out like he was, however, it was impossible to keep Will from having his way.

Ignoring his patient's efforts to resist, Will tore off a piece of the sheet and soaked it in the hot water. Then he cleaned all the dirt and dried blood away from the bullet hole. "That bullet is in there pretty deep. It looks like the muscle is already tryin' to close over it. I ain't got nothin' but a skinnin' knife to go after it and I don't think you could stand that, even if I could get the bullet

271

out. You'll have to wait till the doctor at the jail can go after it. So I'm cleanin' it up as best I can, then I'll bandage it and maybe you can keep it clean. So hold still."

Reese's whole body tensed up, waiting for the deep thrust of Will's skinning knife that he was certain was coming. After a few minutes when he felt nothing but the piece of warm wet cloth around the edges of the wound, he was at first confused, then he relaxed, scarcely able to believe he was alive.

After several different attempts to tie a bandage on that would stay for any length of time, Will finally came up with one that used up the whole sheet almost, with ties around Reese's chest, over his shoulder, and around his neck. Finished, he announced, "It ain't pretty, but it'll stay put if you don't get rough with it." Reese didn't know what to say, so he didn't. Will untied his rope from Reese's feet and told him to get on his knees. When he did, Will unlocked the handcuffs, stood back a couple of steps, and held his six-gun on him while he managed to get his shirt back on. Then he locked him to the tree again while he went to cook supper.

There was not much said between the two for the rest of the evening, and when it was time to turn in, Reese spent a quiet night with his hands still locked around the tree, falling asleep while sitting up for short periods, then lying sideways on his good shoulder some of the time. He thought to complain, but he knew the contest was over and he had lost. They started out early the next morning, and after one stop to rest the horses, they crossed over the Poteau River a few miles south of its confluence with the Arkansas River at Belle Point. They entered the bustling town of Fort Smith in the early afternoon and Will led his prisoner straight to the U.S. courthouse and the jail in the basement.

Will marched a thoroughly defeated Reese Trainer into the booking office of the jail and turned him over to a uniformed guard working the desk. Through the open door of his tiny office, Sid Randolph saw who it was and came out to greet him. "Will, whatcha got there?"

"Howdy, Sid," Will returned. "We've got Reese Trainer on charges of operating an illegal whiskey mill in the Nations, resisting arrest, jail breaking, and horse stealin'. I'll get Dan Stone to send you the paperwork. I don't have any. He's gonna need to have Doc Peters take a look at a bullet wound in his shoulder. The bullet's still in it."

Sid took a look at Reese and said, "He looks like you dragged him all the way back from Indian Territory."

"Just partway," Will said. "He's in pretty good shape otherwise. He's hungry, though, didn't like my cookin' much."

"Well, he's a little too late for dinner, but we'll

get him in to see Doc Peters, so he won't miss supper." He paused a second, then said, "And, Will, Dan Stone sent a message over here to tell you to come to his office before you go anywhere else. Said it's important."

Will nodded. "Everything's important to Dan, ain't it? I've got some horses outside that I need to take care of. I'll go to see Dan as soon as I take care of them. If you happen to talk to him before I get there, tell him I'm on my way." He took one last look at Reese Trainer, then turned and walked out the door. He was only casually curious about the message from his boss to come report to him before going anywhere else. Stone most likely wanted a full report on the cattle rustling he was sent out there to investigate.

From the jail, he went directly to the stables, where he found Vern Tuttle repairing a broken sideboard in one of the stalls, the result of a stallion that didn't want to be saddled. "Will Tanner, how you doin', boy?"

"Can't complain, Vern. How 'bout yourself?"

"I'm gettin' older, but I ain't gettin' no smarter. You ain't in no trouble, are you? Dan Stone sent somebody over here early this mornin' to tell me he wanted to see you, if you came in here. Said to come to his office before you went anywhere else."

"He did?" Will replied, curious now. "Maybe I am in trouble. He sent the same message to Sid

Randolph." He thought about it for a moment, then decided that possibly that young deputy in Sherman, Jeff Somebody, might have been smarter than he thought and reported him for making that arrest and killing Frank Trainer in Texas. *But, hell,* he thought, *he didn't even know my name.* Maybe it was a report from Wichita Falls, but that was unlikely. He couldn't imagine Fanny Hawkins contacting the law. "I expect I'd best leave these horses with you and go see my boss." Tuttle helped him unsaddle the horses and put his packs away to be taken care of later. Will told him which horses belonged to the court and Vern knew to take extra good care of Buster and Will's sorrel packhorse. When they were done, Will took his rifle and saddlebags and walked back to the courthouse and Marshal Daniel Stone's office.

"Will, come on in," Dan said when he saw Will through the open door. "Glad you got my message."

"Yes, sir, I got it," Will replied. "I was comin' to see you, anyway. I just got back in town and I had to drop a prisoner off at the jail. I reckon you want my report, I woulda wrote it all down, but it turned out to be more to do than what you sent me over there for." He started out with the delay in getting out to take care of the rustling complaints because of Jim Little Eagle's problem with Reese Trainer. "He's the prisoner I dropped off at the jail." He explained why he was gone a little longer because of Trainer's escape from the Choctaw jail. Then he assured Dan that the cattle rustling had been stopped at least for the time being. "Like we thought, it was the Hawkins son. I was bringin' him back, but he hanged himself." Bit by bit, Will reported everything that had happened on this latest trip to the Nations. Of course, there were some details that were omitted, but they all happened in Texas, so were not worthy of reporting.

Stone made notes as Will related facts and names, to forward in a formal report to the people he reported to. His oral report took more than an hour to relate most of the details. When they were finished with his report, Stone said, "Now, I need to pass on to you a wire I got first thing this morning. The stationmaster in Atoka wired me that Jack Coffey came through there yesterday, looking for you."

"Who's Jack Coffey?" Will asked. He thought he had heard the name before, but he didn't remember in connection to what.

"He might be the highest-priced professional killer in the country," Stone answered. "And somebody must want you dead bad enough to pay his price."

The name that popped into Will's head right away was Fanny Hawkins. She certainly had reason to want him dead. He was totally responsible for the death of all four of her sons, and with the audacity to ride right into her headquarters to snatch them away. "If this fellow is so famous for murderin' folks, why doesn't somebody arrest him?"

"Because there has never been any real evidence to tie him to any of his victims. That's one reason why he's so high priced. There's plenty of evidence that he has killed, because some of his killings have been duels and not punishable by law. But the cases that drive the law crazy are the times when the victim was shot by a single rifle shot at long distance. And they know Jack Coffey was in the area, know that he did it, but there wasn't any evidence or witnesses." He paused to let Will think about that before saying, "Damn it, Will, you've got to lay low for a while. Keep a sharp eye out."

" 'Preciate the warnin'," Will said. "I'll try to do that. But if he was in Atoka yesterday lookin' for me, then he ain't likely to show up here today or tomorrow, unless he's got one of those flyin' horses. I wouldn't think he'd come to Fort Smith after me, anyway. It'd be a whole lot easier to just wait for me out on a trail somewhere. Hell, even a low-price killer can get you when you ain't in any town."

CHAPTER 17

As usual, Leonard Dickens and Ron Sample were occupying the two rocking chairs on the front porch of Ruth Bennett's boardinghouse while waiting for Margaret, Ruth's cook, to signal that supper was ready. Leonard's comments on how fast the city of Fort Smith was getting crowded with new people arriving every day was interrupted when Ron pointed toward town and said, "Look who's comin' here. Is that Will?"

Leonard turned to look at once. "Sure looks like him. Reckon we oughta go tell Sophie and Ruth?"

"Nah," Ron replied, a wicked grin spreading across his face. "Let 'em find out when he gets here. We don't wanna ruin his surprise."

"This is gonna be good," Leonard predicted. They both turned around to sit straight in their chairs. Leonard was the first to welcome Will when he opened the gate. "Well, howdy, Will. You was gone for quite a spell this time."

"Evenin', boys," Will returned the greeting. "Yeah, reckon I was at that. It's sure good to get back home. I hope I'm in time to let Margaret know she'll have one more mouth to feed. I ain't had nothin' since breakfast, and that wasn't anything but bacon and hardtack."

"Well, we're glad to see you made it back all right," Ron said. "Supper oughta be ready any minute now."

Will walked into the house and Ron and Leonard got up and walked in behind him. He walked on through the parlor and down the hall to the kitchen. "Will!" Margaret uttered, startled.

"Didn't mean to surprise you," Will said. "I just wanted to let you know I was home. I know you haven't planned for me, and if you're running short of food, I can get by with some biscuits and coffee."

"Nonsense," she remarked. "There's plenty for everybody." She looked at Ron and Leonard standing behind him in the hallway and said, "I didn't ring the dinner bell yet. It'll be a little while yet."

"Please, Margaret, don't make supper late for me. You don't have to cook more food." He was concerned that his unannounced appearance had disrupted her schedule.

"I'm not cookin' more. It's just that this roast is takin' longer to get done than I thought. It's bigger than we usually get, anyway." She looked at Will and smiled. "Maybe we knew you might be home tonight."

Their conversation in the hallway was overheard upstairs and they were suddenly joined by Ruth Bennett. Everything got quiet. "Will," she acknowledged. "I see you're back."

"Yes, ma'am, like the bad penny always turns up, I reckon. Have you been gettin' along all right?" He felt odd talking to her since he and Sophie were married. It seemed they were no longer friends. "I'd like to clean up a little bit before supper. Is Sophie upstairs in our room?"

"You look like you could use a little cleanup," Ruth replied. "Yes, Sophie's in her room. Why don't you dump your saddlebags and rifle in your old room? Sophie's feeling a little under the weather and she's resting now. Maybe she'll be out later."

He realized that the air in the hallway seemed to have suddenly become frigid, and he felt compelled to say, "I got back as quick as I could." He turned back to face Margaret. "Have I got time to clean up before supper?"

"Yes, you do," Margaret answered, with complete compassion for him. "And if you're late, I'll save a plate for you."

"Then I'd better get goin'," he said, and walked past Ruth, Ron, and Leonard in the hallway. "Excuse me," he offered as he made his way to the stairs, taking care not to hit anyone with his saddlebags or rifle.

Upstairs, he went quietly down the hall to his and Sophie's room, thinking Ruth probably didn't even tell her he was home. If she was asleep, though, he didn't want to wake her. So, he turned the knob very slowly to peek inside, but the door was locked. He was about to tap lightly on the door but decided maybe he'd better let her rest. So he went down to the end of the hall to the room he used to rent before they were married. He went inside, dropped his saddlebags on the bed, and propped his rifle in the corner. Only then, did it occur to him that he had to get into their room to get a clean shirt. He had a pair of clean socks in his saddlebags but no clean underwear. "Damn," he muttered, thinking this a fine way to return to his bride. Then he thought to look in the chest of drawers to see if he had left an old shirt by chance. Perhaps he left a torn shirt there when they moved in together. *Bottom drawer's the best bet,* he thought, so he pulled it open. The drawer was almost filled with heavy winter shirts. He opened the drawer above it and found it contained extra socks. He had never owned many clothes, but he realized the chest was filled with all the various clothing articles he wore in the different seasons of the year. He stood staring at his shaving mug and brush on top of the chest for a moment before the fact slammed hard against his brain. *She had moved him out of the wedding bed!* He was staggered almost as hard as when he was shot. At a total loss, he didn't know what to do. He was not of a nature to walk back up the hall and kick the door open and have it out with her once and for all. If she was unhappy and thought now that she had made a mistake, then he would not stand in her way. Maybe this might be a good thing, then, he speculated. *Good for both of us to see how we feel when I'm around for a while.* Dan Stone thought it might be a good idea for him to stay close to Fort Smith for a while. "We'll just see what happens," he murmured. With that, he picked out a clean shirt, some clean underwear and socks, and took his shaving kit down to the washroom.

A lot cleaner and clean-shaven, he was a little late getting to the supper table, but there were two empty chairs, so he assumed Sophie would be joining them. "Well, hello, stranger," Margaret greeted him when he sat down, and served him a choice slice of the roast before she set the platter down before Ruth at the end of the table. After a couple of minutes, Will decided he had had enough of whatever the game was called that Ruth and Sophie were playing. So, he asked, "Is Sophie coming down to supper?"

"No," Ruth answered him.

"Why not?" Will asked.

"She's not feeling well. I'm going to take her supper upstairs to her," Ruth said. "Margaret," she called out, "is Sophie's plate ready?"

"Yes, ma'am," Margaret called back to her. "I'm bringing it right now."

Ruth pushed her chair back, but Will was on his feet first. He met Margaret at the kitchen door, carrying a tray with a plate and a glass of water on it. "Give me that damn tray," he said.

"Yes, sir," Margaret replied with a great big grin across her face. She handed it to him, then gave Ruth a helpless shrug.

"Hoo-boy!" Ron Sample exclaimed, and winked at a grinning Leonard Dickens. Ruth seemed stunned by the sudden insurrection.

Will took the stairs two steps at a time, stormed down the hall, prepared to kick the door open but found it standing ajar. "Come in, Will," she said softly. Now he was confused. Still, he was tired of this game of nonsense she and her mother appeared to be playing, and he intended to tell her so. "You brought my supper to me, how sweet of you." She was sitting on the bed, with her legs folded Indian style, and fully dressed.

"Yeah, here's your supper," he said, and placed the tray on her thighs. "Listen, I've had all the nonsense I intend to take. You and your mother are playin' some kinda silly game and I refuse to play it. I've been gone a long time, but I got home as soon as I could. And you lock yourself up here in this room, don't even welcome me home. You moved me out of the room. Now, damn it, I'm your husband. This marriage is between you and me, and your mother ain't got a say in it at all. So if anybody gets moved out, it'll be her. But if you want me moved out of your room, you can have it that way. I'll move out of the whole damn house." He reached down and picked the tray up again. "If you want this supper, you can come downstairs and sit at the table with the grown-ups." He turned around and walked out with the tray. She had never seen evidence of a temper in him before. She decided that to be a good sign. She got off the bed and went downstairs to join the others, all of whom were beaming, with the exception of her mother and her husband.

There was no more discussion between the two after supper. Sophie helped Margaret with the cleanup of the kitchen and dining room. Then she took a bath and retired to her room again. Will joined Ron and Leonard on the porch, while they smoked their pipes and tried to get him to talk about where he had been and what he had done. His usual answer was that he was investigating some complaints and making some arrests with little more detail than that. When he was ready for bed, he went to his old room and crawled into a bed he was well familiar with, so he was asleep almost immediately. He awoke once in the middle of the night when Sophie crawled into bed beside him.

When he woke up the next morning, she was still sleeping soundly, so he rolled out of the bed very carefully to keep from waking her. He put his clothes on, then picked up his boots and carried them to the top of the stairs, where he sat down and pulled them on. He could hear Margaret getting her stove ready, so he went out the back door to commune with Mother Nature, then went in the kitchen to keep Margaret company. "Well, good morning, Mr. Tanner," she greeted him cheerfully. "Did you sleep well?"

"Yes, ma'am, I did," he answered. "I figured it was because of that fine supper I had last night."

"I expect just about anything would taste pretty good to you after you've been riding all over Indian Territory, living on bacon and hardtack and coffee. Speaking of which, that pot's just starting to boil. I'll have you a cup of coffee in a jiffy." She didn't have to ask him if his situation with his wife was any better than it was last night. The answer was in his peaceful manner. "Are you going to be riding off on another assignment real soon?"

"I never know that from week to week," he replied. "It always depends on what happens in the district, either Arkansas or Indian Territory. But my boss told me yesterday he wanted me to stay in town for a few days at least. I've just gotta go into the office and do some kinda paperwork, I reckon."

"Well, that'll be good for Sophie to know." Margaret laughed, still thinking about the night just passed. "But if I know you, hanging around the office is just another kind of hanging."

"I reckon you know me pretty well," he said.

"That coffee sounds like it's gettin' about right, don't it?"

"Yep," she agreed, and pulled the pot over toward the edge of the stove. When it settled down a little, she got two cups and poured it. This was how Sophie found them, standing in the kitchen, drinking coffee.

Still in her robe, she walked over and put her arms around Will's arm and hugged it. "Were you down here trying to steal my husband, Margaret?"

"No, but if I was about twenty years younger, I mighta considered it," Margaret said. "He just told me that his boss wanted him to go right back out this morning, but he told him he was gonna spend a few days at home with his wife."

"Did you tell Dan Stone that?" Sophie asked.

"I can't lie to you, darlin', that's exactly what I told him." He winked at Margaret. "But he said I'd have to come to the office every day and help around there."

"Well, bless your heart," Sophie said. "You're both lying, but I forgive you." She looked up at him then and asked, "Are you really just going to the office today?"

"Yep, that's right, for a few days, is what he said."

"Are you going to eat breakfast here before you go?" she asked because he normally left long before breakfast at the boardinghouse. Usually, only Margaret got a glimpse of him as he sneaked down the back steps when she was just building the fire in her stove.

"I might as well," he answered. "I'm not headin' out anywhere, and Dan doesn't get to the office that early. So, if I go now, I'll just be sittin' on the courthouse steps, waiting for Dan to come to work. I thought about goin' by the stable to check on Buster, but I know Vern will take good care of him. Sittin' with you two women ain't all that great, but it's a little better than sittin' on the courthouse steps," he japed, which earned him a punch on the shoulder from Sophie. Their innocent joking was a welcome sign to Margaret.

When Margaret put her big pan of biscuits in the oven, Sophie volunteered to take her mother's coffee to her. It was a practice that Ruth had begun several months before Will and Sophie's wedding, due to the "sickly feeling" she had in the morning. It was one of the reasons Sophie had announced to Will before the wedding that she did not want to go to his ranch in Texas. She said it was an obvious sign that her mother was getting too weak to manage Bennett House. Will had agreed with her reason to stay in Fort Smith, even though Ruth Bennett still looked pretty strong to him. He suspected it was Ruth's plan for an early retirement, but he didn't care because he was content to continue working for Dan Stone. He was more comfortable sitting in a saddle than he was in a rocking chair, shooting the breeze with Ron and Leonard. When Sophie took the coffee back to her mother's bedroom, Will went back upstairs to get his saddlebags and rifle, so he could go right out the door when he finished eating breakfast.

Leonard Dickens was the first of the other boarders to come down to breakfast. Like Sophie, he was surprised to see Will at the table. "Well, I see somebody told you Margaret serves breakfast every mornin', so you didn't get out early to eat hay with your horse."

"I just decided to hang around to see if you had the gall to come to breakfast this mornin' after all you ate for supper last night," Will countered. "Ruth needs to up your rent."

When he finished breakfast, he complimented Margaret on the biscuits, which she fully expected because he always did. He picked up his saddlebags and rifle and Sophie walked with him to the front door. After she sent him off to the office with a wifely kiss on the cheek, she returned to a chorus of smiles and admiring glances. "What are you all gaping at? You knew I wasn't gonna take a chance on losing him."

During the next couple of days, Will stuck to the same routine with Dan Stone trying to find something to keep Will busy. They pulled a chair up on the front side of Ormand Anders's desk for Will to use. Ormand was Stone's clerk and Will could tell that he wasn't any happier with the arrangement than he was. They searched through all the files they had on wanted criminals in the Western District of Arkansas. There was no photograph or artist sketch of Jack Coffey, nothing to give him any marks or scars of identification. It didn't take long for Stone to realize that Will was already like a wild animal in a cage, and he was willing to risk an encounter with Jack Coffey rather than remain in that office. A telegram from the sheriff of Clarksville, Arkansas, over in Johnson County, offered a reprieve for the caged lion. It would only be some relief for a day, but it might help lighten up some of the tension. He called Will into his office.

"I'm gonna send you on a little train ride, Will. Sheriff Marvin Leach over in Clarksville wired me this morning. He's got a man in jail that killed a woman over there, and I need to have you pick him up. You need to take the morning train out of here. It leaves at seven-thirty. Clarksville ain't but about fifty-five miles east of here, so you oughta get there pretty quick. You'll pick this fellow up at the jail and bring him back on the afternoon train that gets here around six o'clock. So you'll be home for supper. His name's Rayford Pickens. Ormand will give you the paperwork today, so you can go straight to the railroad station in the morning. Any questions?" Will didn't have any, and he said he was thankful for the assignment. Dan chuckled and said, "I know you are. I'll notify Sid Randolph, and he'll most likely have a couple of guards meet you at the train, and you can turn him over to them. If he doesn't, just walk the prisoner over to the jail and turn him over to Sid."

It was a welcome assignment for Will, out of that office for a day and getting paid for taking a train ride. Fifty-five miles, he would be paid six cents per mile to make the trip, and since he would be bringing a prisoner back, he'd be paid ten cents per mile for the return mileage as well, plus any incidental expenses he might have to pay. Even after it was all added up, and Dan took his 25 percent, there would be a little bit to put in his pocket.

When he got back to Bennett House that afternoon, Sophie met him with a cup of coffee, knowing that was what he wanted. He didn't express the thought, but he couldn't help thinking of what a difference it was from a couple of days ago when he came home. He told her he was leaving the next morning to pick up a prisoner to transport back for trial. Then turned her frown upside down when he said he would be home for supper. Another evening passed pleasantly, and Sophie was up early the next morning to make sure he ate a good breakfast before he went to catch his train.

The Little Rock and Fort Smith Railroad had begun reliable train service right after the Civil War ended, and the morning train pulled out right on time at seven-thirty. Clarksville, Arkansas was its first stop, and it pulled in there at a little before ten. Will couldn't help marveling over the short amount of time it took to cover the fifty-five miles. The same distance would have been a long day's ride on Buster, with a couple of rest stops thrown in. He stepped off the train in Clarksville and hesitated before walking off the platform, in case someone was on their way to meet him. After a few minutes and no one with any interest toward him, he walked over to the ticket window and asked which way the jail was. He was told which way to turn on the main street, so he said, "Much obliged," and started to leave but decided to ask, "Is the afternoon train back to Fort Smith on time?"

"I ain't heard any different," the ticket agent said, "but it's a little too early to know."

"Right," Will said, and started walking toward the main street about thirty yards away. When he walked between two buildings and came out on the main thoroughfare, he found that he had walked between the barbershop and a feed store. He looked to his right and saw the sheriff's office and jail right across from the Friendly Saloon, just as the man had said. So he walked down that way. He walked into the sheriff's office to find the sheriff sitting at his desk, leaning back in a swivel chair with his feet propped on the desk, drinking a cup of coffee. On the other side of the desk, a young man wearing a deputy sheriff's badge was sitting in a straight-back chair, leaning back against the wall, the chair resting on its two back legs.

"Can I help you?" the sheriff asked casually, without changing his position, or sounding like he wanted to help him.

"I'm Deputy Marshal Will Tanner. I just got here from Fort Smith to transport the prisoner you wired about—a Mr. Rayford Pickens."

"Ha!" the deputy blurted. "He ain't a mister nobody, that low-down hound."

Ignoring his deputy's comment, Sheriff Leach said, "Right, Deputy Tanner, did you bring the authorization papers for me, so I'll know you're really Deputy Tanner?"

Will handed him the envelope Ormand Anders had prepared for him. Leach sat up in his chair then and looked at the papers. "All right," he said. "Looks like he's yours. You wanna see him?" When Will said he would, Leach said, "Jim, take the man back to see his prisoner." He led him to a cell where Will saw a bruised and bloody Rayford Pickens lying on his cot.

"Get your butt up offa that bed, Rayford!" Deputy Jim Turner ordered. "We got the government man here to take you to your hangin'." When Rayford didn't move right away, Turner threatened, "Don't make me come in there after you." Slowly, with great effort, it appeared, Rayford rolled over to let his feet fall on the floor. Then he pushed himself up until he was sitting on the cot. "You better get movin'," Turner threatened. "I'm fixin' to come in there and walk up and down your sorry ass with my walkin' stick."

"Let him alone," Will snapped, and the look on his face told Jim Turner he meant right now. Then to the prisoner, he asked, "Can you walk?"

"Yes, sir, I think so," he answered.

"Get up off the cot and walk over here to me," Will said. Rayford slowly managed to get up on his feet, then carefully placing his feet, he stepped over to the bars in front of Will. After a few moments, Will looked back at Turner. "When did you arrest him?"

"Yesterday, about noon. That happened to him before I arrested him," the deputy said, referring to the obvious wounds on the prisoner's face.

"Yesterday, huh?" Will responded. "This is fresh blood, fresh cuts on his face. If you locked him up yesterday, why has he got all this fresh blood all over his face?"

"Hell, I don't know," Turner answered. "Maybe he fell down."

Back to Rayford, Will said, "If I take you outta here, you're gonna have to walk to the train. Can you do that?"

"I'll sure as hell walk outta here, if it's the last thing I do," Rayford muttered painfully.

"All right, you can go on back and sit down," Will told him. Then he walked past Jim Turner and went to confront the sheriff. "That man's just had the crap beat outta him and he can barely walk. He's a bloody mess and I have to walk him to the train and take him back without scarin' the hell outta all the passengers on that train. I want a bucket of water and a washrag to clean him up a little."

In defense of his deputy, Sheriff Leach thought he should say, "Jim mighta been a little rough on him when he locked him up."

"That's fresh blood all over his face," Will countered. "That ain't dried blood from yesterday. You coulda saved your town some money when you hired that deputy and bought a bulldog instead."

"Now, hold on there, Deputy Tanner, you don't know what that piece of scum did. He murdered the wife of one of our citizens!"

"Then he oughta been arrested," Will replied, "and he oughta stand before a judge to decide his punishment. You and me, and your deputy ain't supposed to do the punishin'. Our job is to see that he does stand and face the prosecution."

"Maybe we have been a little rough on him, but we all knew that lady he murdered, and I reckon the whole town wanted to hang Rayford for killin' her. You're right, it ain't our job to do the punishin'. I'll get some clean water and a washrag, and we'll clean him up as best we can, so you can take him on the train. But I'm countin' on Judge Parker to hang him."

"I expect he will, if Rayford did what you say he did," Will said. "I'm catchin' the four o'clock train back to Fort Smith. After he's cleaned up some, can I trust you to make sure he don't get bloodied up again before I can get him on the train?"

"You have my word," Leach said, "and I won't let Jim near him. All right?"

"I 'preciate it, Sheriff. I'll do the cleanup if you'll get me the water and the washrag. I don't know the prisoner or the lady he murdered, so I don't have anything to settle with him. I just don't want him to scare folks on the train."

CHAPTER 18

It was past noon by the time Will had cleaned his prisoner up as well as he could. At least, Rayford didn't look like the battering of his face had happened in the last five minutes. Bored with watching Will work on Rayford, Jim Turner announced that he was going to dinner. "I reckon it is about time to eat dinner," Will said to Leach. "Don't let me hold you up if you're waitin' to go, yourself. Will Jim bring Rayford's dinner back with him?"

"Ah no," Leach hedged. "We ain't made no arrangements to feed him, since we figured you folks would take care of him after I wired your boss."

Will paused. "You mean you ain't fed him nothin' since you arrested him?"

"Like I said, we figured you'd be here first thing this mornin' and you'd take care of all that stuff."

Will didn't respond right away. He took the time to lecture himself on the importance of keeping a good line of communication between the town sheriffs and the U.S. Marshals Service. When he spoke, he kept it casual. "I'm gonna want to eat something, myself. Where's a good place to get something?"

"Well, if you want somethin' fancy, the hotel's

the place. But if you just want a quick dinner that don't cost a lot, Friendly Saloon, right across the street, is where I eat. Tom Futch owns that place, and he's got him a good cook. If you don't mind the company, I'll go with you. Mabel said she was gonna cook up a pork roast today."

"That sounds to my likin'," Will said. "You wanna wait till your deputy gets back?"

"Nah, I'll just lock it up. Jim goes to eat with a gal he's been seein', and sometimes he don't get back till late."

Leach locked the door to the office, and they walked across the street to the Friendly Saloon. When they walked inside, a man Will figured was Tom Futch, the owner, waved to them and called out, "Mabel's been waitin' for you to come in, Sheriff. She said she cooked today's roast just because you like it." A couple of customers at different tables yelled that they thought Mabel made it for them as Leach and Will passed by them. Judging by the number of people who were eating dinner in the saloon, Will figured Mabel must be good, indeed. "Who's this you got with you, Sheriff?" Futch asked.

"Tom Futch, this is U.S. Deputy Marshal Will Tanner," Leach said. "He's in town to pick up Rayford Pickens and take him to trial in Fort Smith. I told him he couldn't get no better food than right here, so don't disappoint me." Will nodded a howdy and Futch nodded in return.

"Looks like you've got a lot of folks that agree with you on Mabel's cookin'," Will said, talking a little louder because of the noise in the crowded saloon. One table in particular on the far side of the room may have been the loudest. It was occupied by three men, and they seemed to be enjoying themselves more than all the rest of the crowd combined. One of the reasons could be the whiskey bottle sitting in the middle of their table, Will figured. Typical, he thought—when you're drunk enough, every comment made is hilarious. And the one who was laughing the loudest and the most often appeared to be sitting up taller in his chair than his two companions.

Noticing that Will was distracted by the three men, Leach informed him, "That one doin' most of the laughing is Long Bob Butler. It was his wife, Jolene, that your man, Rayford Pickens, murdered."

"What?" Will questioned, thinking he hadn't heard Leach right. He looked at Leach and the sheriff nodded slowly. "He's got a funny way of mournin' her death. Are you sure you arrested the right person?"

"Yeah, there ain't no doubt about it. Jolene's own sister was a witness. She saw Rayford when he stabbed his knife in her belly." He shook his head slowly. "It's a terrible thing. Everybody thought the world of that poor little girl. Some folks said they thought Long Bob was extra hard on Jolene, but she always stuck with him, no matter what he got into." He shook his head again. "And he gets into some wild things, but everybody knows ol' Long Bob is just a fun-lovin' fellow."

Will was amazed by what Leach had just told him. He wondered how an apparent weakling like Rayford would hazard riling the temper of someone like Long Bob Butler. Evidently the poor soul was lacking in some brain cells. The discussion of the insane mourning of Long Bob Butler was interrupted by the arrival of two heaping plates of roast pork. Will was glad to drop the subject. He was happy to discover that everything Leach had said about Mabel's cooking was accurate. He could find nothing to criticize other than it caused him to eat too much. When they had finished and were sitting there soaking more coffee into the meal just devoured, Will ordered another plate of food and a cup of coffee to take with him for the prisoner. "I'll bring the dishes back," he told Tom Futch.

It was obvious that Leach was not at all sympathetic with Will's decision, but he said nothing. Will took the food straight back to Rayford, who could scarcely believe Will had done it. "You've got plenty of time to finish it, and I wanna make sure you've got enough strength to walk to the depot." Rayford took the tray back to his cot, where he sat down and attacked the plate, taking slurps of coffee in between bites. Will just shook his head, then announced, "Three-thirty, be ready to walk outta here at three-thirty."

"Yes, sir," Rayford answered meekly, his mouth full of food. Will was reminded of a starving orphan out of a children's storybook.

"I've got a little time to kill," he told Marvin Leach when he went back in the office. "I'm gonna take a walk around town. I've never been in Clarksville before. It's a right lively-lookin' town."

"Good idea," Leach replied. "If you see anybody breakin' the law, arrest 'em," he japed. Then when Will was about to go out the door, Leach asked, "You reckon they'll expect me to come over to Fort Smith when they have that trial for Rayford?"

"I expect they might," Will told him. "You made the arrest, didn't you?"

"No, I didn't. Jim did. He was right next door at the barbershop when he heard some screamin' and cussin' comin' outta the back of the feed store. That's where Rayford and Jolene's sister, Loretta, worked. Well, turns out Rayford was sweet on Jolene and he decided to take advantage of her in the back of the feed store. I reckon Jolene weren't feelin' the same about him, so he tried to force his way on her. She fought him, and he stabbed her with a knife he used to cut sacks with. Too bad for Rayford that Long Bob come along right then, lookin' for his wife. And Loretta saw the whole thing. So now, you got the whole picture, and if the court wants a witness, then Loretta is the one they oughta want. I didn't witness anything."

"I think maybe you're right about that," Will agreed. "What's Loretta's last name?"

"Carson," Leach answered, "Loretta Carson. Will you be workin' on that trial?"

"I doubt it," Will said. "It was unusual that I was sent over this way to pick up the prisoner. I work mostly in the Nations." He glanced up at the clock on the wall behind Leach's desk. "I reckon if I'm gonna stretch my legs a little, I'd best get at it." Outside, he headed back toward the train depot, for he remembered when he had left the depot, he had walked through an alley between a barbershop and a feed store. He had only glanced at the feed store, but he remembered it had an unusual name, and now he couldn't recall it. When he came to the alley, he saw the sign, GALLOWAY'S FEED STORE, so he walked inside. The town was sizable, so there might be more than one feed store, but he doubted it.

There was no one in the front of the store, so he walked through an open door that led to the back, where there were rows of racks stacked with burlap sacks, a corncrib, and various barrels and containers. In a corner of the building, a man was talking to a young woman sitting at a sewing machine. The man turned around when the young woman pointed to Will. "Yes, sir, can I help you, sir?"

"I'd appreciate it, if you could," Will answered. He walked on inside and the man walked to meet him halfway. "Are you the owner?"

"Yes, sir, I'm the owner," he replied. "John Galloway. What can I do for you?"

Will opened his coat to reveal his badge. "My name's Will Tanner. I'm a U.S. Deputy Marshal, and I'm in town today to pick up Rayford Pickens, to transport him back to Fort Smith for trial. Do you mind if I ask you a few questions about that murder?"

"No, not at all," Galloway responded. "I'll tell you what I know, which isn't much, since I was gone to dinner when that awful thing happened. Rayford worked here in the back of the store for me, and he was always a good worker. I just couldn't believe it when I heard what he did to that poor little girl. When I came back, Jolene was lyin' dead across Loretta's lap. Loretta's her sister. She works for me. Jolene came to see her, and I reckon Rayford musta had a hankerin' for her somethin' awful, and when she wasn't havin' none of it, I reckon he went outta his mind and killed her. There was blood all over the place back there, but most of it was Rayford's 'cause Jolene's husband was lookin' for her. And when he saw what had happened, he liked to've killed Rayford. I think he woulda beat that boy to death if Jim Turner hadn't come in here to arrest Rayford."

"Is that Loretta back there at the sewin' machine?" Will asked.

"Yes, sir, that's Loretta. She's shook up pretty bad. I told her to take a few days off till after Jolene's funeral, but she acts like she's afraid to be home alone. I told her that Rayford was locked up and there ain't no way he can hurt her."

"All right if I talk to her for a minute? Just me and her?"

Galloway looked uncertain, but he wasn't sure he could tell the deputy marshal to leave the poor girl alone. "I reckon it'd be all right."

"All I need is a couple of minutes," Will said, and went to the back corner of the building. "How you doin', Loretta? My name's Will Tanner. I'm a U.S. Deputy Marshal and I've come to take Rayford Pickens back to Fort Smith to stand trial. Is what Mr. Galloway just told me about what happened to Jolene the whole truth? That Rayford tried to attack her and when she wouldn't give in to him, he stabbed her?"

Already shivering with fright, Loretta hung her head and started wringing her hands. "Is that what really happened?" She gave a few quick nods of her head but would still not look at him. "Loretta, look at me." As if in pain, she slowly raised her head to look at him. "Loretta, did Long Bob Butler threaten you, if you said he killed your sister?" She suddenly looked terrified and started to draw away from him. "Don't be afraid," he said as gently as he could manage. "This is just between you and me. Did he say he would hurt you if you said it was him who killed your sister?" Still, she was too terrified to answer him. He was convinced that he was right. "I'll tell you what I think," he said then. "I think Long Bob Butler took your sister's life with that knife. You don't have to say anything, just nod your head if I'm right." There was no response from her for several long seconds, and then she nodded slowly. "I've only talked to Rayford a little bit," he continued, "but he didn't strike me as the kind of young man who would react violently. He seems to me like the opposite of a fighter."

She raised her head and looked at him, and suddenly big tears formed in her eyes and rolled down her cheeks. "That's not true," she said. "Rayford tried to protect Jolene when Long Bob hit her with his fist. Rayford jumped in between them, and Bob got so mad he beat Rayford to the floor. When Jolene tried to pull him away from Rayford, he picked that knife up from the bench and plunged it into her belly, over and over." She sobbed openly then. "And I didn't do anything to help them." She let it all out. "Bob put his hand around my neck and lifted me off my feet. He swore he would kill me if I didn't say Rayford stabbed Jolene. He knows I live alone ever since he married Jolene. He said he'd come visit me one night, if I didn't say it was Rayford."

Will had to stop and think for a minute. He had learned a whole lot more than he had anticipated. His hunch had been right about Long Bob Butler, and now that he was sure he knew the complete story, he had to take more action than just transporting Rayford back to the Fort Smith lockup. He was suddenly concerned with the safety of Rayford and Loretta over the arrest of Long Bob Butler. He made a quick decision. He hoped it was the right one. He looked the young girl in the eye and said, "All right, here's what we're gonna do. You say you live alone?" She nodded, confused by his sudden change in manner. "I want you to go home and pack a suitcase with whatever you need for a few days away from home. Don't say anything to anybody about what you're doin'. Can you slip outta here, if I take Galloway up front?"

"I can go right out the back door," she said, still confused.

"Good. I'm goin' to take you to Fort Smith with me on the four o'clock train. When we get to Fort Smith, I'll take you to the house where my wife and I live, where you'll be safe. We'll tell the court the truth about your sister's murder. Then I'll see about settlin' up with Long Bob

Butler." He could see her eyes getting bigger and bigger and he knew that she had begun to think of avenging her sister in spite of her fear. "Rayford and I are leavin' on that four o'clock train, and I'm plannin' on bein' at the train depot at three-thirty. So, you've gotta be there at three-thirty, if you want to go with us. Don't worry about your ticket. I'll take care of that. Have we got a deal?"

"Yes, sir," she answered, nodding her head with determination. "I'll be there."

"All right," I'll see you then." He turned and walked back to join John Galloway, who was still standing in the open doorway. Will offered his hand and when Galloway shook it, Will continued to grip it while continuing to walk toward the front door, forcing Galloway to accompany him. At the front door, he released his hand and thanked him for his cooperation, then wished him a good day.

He glanced at the clock on the wall of the feed store as he walked out. There was still time to kill before he took Rayford out of the jail. With time to think, he naturally began to second-guess his decisions over the last half hour. Dan Stone might question his jumping to conclusions about the true guilt in this case. But Dan was a fair man and wanted true justice done, so Will was sure he would understand why he had done his own investigation instead of just picking up the package he was sent there to get. On the other hand, he was not so sure of the reception he would get when he showed up with a young girl at Bennett House. Sophie and her mother might not admire him for his act of chivalry on behalf of Loretta Carson. *I wonder if I'll ever enjoy a peaceful period in my married life longer than a couple of days,* he thought. *I think I need a drink.* He crossed the street and walked back to the Friendly Saloon. He was surprised to find there were still a lot of people inside. With dinnertime over, the drinkers and card players had taken over. He noticed that Long Bob Butler was still in full force mourning the loss of his young wife. Will had kinda wanted to get another look at Butler before he left. And he was halfway serious when he thought about making an arrest right then, and go back to Fort Smith with the accused, the witness, and the guilty party, all in one bundle. He chuckled to himself when he thought they might be a little too much to handle on a train. No, he told himself, he wanted to return to Fort Smith to make his case and get a federal warrant before coming back to make the arrest.

The bartender interrupted his thoughts then, so he ordered a shot of rye whiskey. Instead of tossing the whole shot back, he took it in two swallows because he wanted to taste the whiskey and feel the burn a little. Then he put the glass back upside down and reached into his pocket for a quarter. Before he pulled his hand out of his pocket, a quarter bounced across the bar and onto the floor. The bartender reached down and picked it up and Will turned around to see Long Bob Butler standing behind him with a grin that was more smirk than smile. "I wanted to buy a drink for the deputy marshal who came to take that sorry coward that killed my wife off to the gallows," Butler blurted, his words slurring from alcohol consumption.

"I see you're still in mournin' for the loss of your wife," Will said.

"Hell, yeah," Butler blurted. "Wouldn't you be? I'da beat that little sissy into a puddle, if Jim Turner hadn't showed up."

"Shouldn'ta been too hard," Will commented. "He's about half your size."

"Hell, everybody's about half his size," the bartender offered with a chuckle. Then he quickly added, "I can't blame you, though, anybody who does that to a helpless little woman like Jolene was, deserves to get beat to death."

"I agree with that," Will said, looking Long Bob in the eye. "Anybody who takes it out on a helpless little woman is a low-down dog, and a coward, to boot."

"I hope to hell they hang him," Butler declared. "I want him to get what's comin' to him."

"Well, I've got a train to catch, me and Rayford, so I'd best get goin'. Thanks for the drink of likker."

"You ever back this way, I'll buy you another 'un," Butler replied.

"I'm pretty sure I'll be back, and I'm gonna remind you of that drink."

When he got back to the jail, he was happy to see there were no new visible marks on his prisoner. He got the key and opened the cell door. "Hold out your hands, Rayford," he said. "I'm afraid you're gonna have to wear these handcuffs, since I'm pickin' you up on an arrest warrant. It's standard procedure." Rayford didn't object. Will didn't tell him the procedure was for Sheriff Leach's benefit. He walked Rayford back through the office, where Leach and his deputy were sitting in the same positions Will found them in when he arrived in town that morning, Leach with his feet on the desk, Turner sitting in a chair leaning against the wall. "Thank you for your cooperation, Sheriff," Will said. "We'll get along now and get out of your way."

"No trouble at all, Will," Leach responded. "Glad we could help you."

Will and Rayford walked up the street to the barbershop and went through the alley beside the feed store. Rayford walked along in front of Will, his head down, obviously feeling the shame of being marched out of town by a deputy marshal. When they walked up on the platform, Rayford raised his head long enough to keep from stumbling on the steps. When he did, he stopped abruptly, causing Will to bump into him, startled by the sight of Loretta Carson standing on the platform, a battered suitcase at her feet. Will gave him a little nudge to get him started again. "It's Loretta," Rayford blurted. "She's the one who said I did it."

"Yeah, she's going with us," Will said. "Just go on over where she is." He walked Rayford over to her. "Glad to see you made it," he said to her.

"I've been here since three o'clock," she said. "I was afraid the train might get here early."

"You two wait right here while I go over and get you a ticket," Will said. He walked away and left them to talk.

When he walked up to the ticket window, the agent was eyeballing the two young people who were evidently with him. "Is that man with you in handcuffs?" he asked. "Is he dangerous?"

"Does he look dangerous?" Will couldn't help replying. "No, he's anything but dangerous. I've got a ticket for him. I need to buy another one to Fort Smith for the young lady with him."

When he got the ticket, he went back in time to hear Loretta telling Rayford that she had decided to tell the truth in court. When Will walked up, Rayford asked, "Does this mean you don't think I killed Jolene?"

"I never did, to tell you the truth," Will answered. "Once we get on the train, I'll take those cuffs off. Unfortunately, the charges

311

were made against you and a request to my headquarters to send a deputy to transport you to court was sent out. Because of that, I have to take you to the jail at the courthouse. It's better than leaving you with Leach and Turner, and I don't know how much I can do to make it easier while you are locked up. I'm hopin' my boss can get your trial on Judge Parker's docket ahead of some of the others."

"Mister, I just thank God for sendin' you to get me," Rayford said. "They was gonna kill me, Deputy Turner especially. He said he was gonna let Long Bob come in to see me when Sheriff Leach wasn't there. I couldn't tell nobody I didn't kill Jolene because Long Bob said he would kill Loretta if she didn't say I done it."

"We're doin' the right thing now," Loretta told him. "I'm gonna tell the judge who killed my sister, then Deputy Tanner can go arrest him."

"That's what I'm plannin' on," Will said.

CHAPTER 19

The train arrived close to schedule and when they boarded, the conductor was even more concerned about the odd threesome than the ticket agent had been. Will removed Rayford's handcuffs, which helped a little, but still the passengers were staring at the armed officer, the timid little woman, and the young man who looked as if he might have been run over by the train. Not wishing to make passengers or conductor uncomfortable, Will suggested that the conductor might consider letting them ride in the mail car. "We can't allow passengers in the mail car," the conductor was adamant in refusing. "We have to protect the U.S. mail."

"What better protection could you have than a U.S. Deputy Marshal guarding your mail?" Will asked.

"That is a point," the conductor said. He smiled then and decided to allow it. So they rode the fifty-five miles to Fort Smith sitting on bags of mail. They made good time and arrived a little before six o'clock.

"Step lively," Will said, and picked up Loretta's suitcase, "and maybe we can get you checked into the jail in time to get some supper." Luckily, Sid Randolph was behind the desk when the trio walked in.

"Will, what in the world . . ."

Will slapped some papers on the desk. "Here's the warrant for Rayford Pickens, and this is Mr. Pickens, himself."

Sid took a look at the battered face and asked, "What did you do, drag him behind your horse?"

"No," Will answered. "I brought him on the train from Clarksville."

"On the train, or behind the train?" Sid went on.

"Sid, I've got a special case here. I'm bringin' in an innocent man."

"Wish I had a dollar for every time I've heard that one," Sid replied while taking a curious look at the timid little woman standing by the door. He finally permitted Will to explain the special situation and, trusting Will, he accepted it. "I won't put him in the basement with the general population. I'll put him in one of the individual holding cells till your boss tells us what to do with him. I can get him something from the kitchen so he won't starve tonight."

"Thanks, Sid. I knew I could count on you. He's already been through enough hell, for somebody who didn't commit a crime."

"What are you gonna do with the little lady?" Sid was curious to know.

"I'm takin' her home with me," Will said.

Sid shook his head slowly as if trying to picture it. "That oughta tickle your new bride."

"I expect it might," Will agreed, "but I don't know what else to do with her." Sid wished him luck and Will hurried back to the door to pick up Loretta's suitcase. "It ain't half a mile from here to the boardin'house. If we make it quick, we might get there before supper's cleaned up."

"That was mighty tasty corn puddin'," Ron Sample declared as he pulled his rocking chair closer to the edge of the porch, so he could more easily spit tobacco juice over the railing.

Coming out the door behind him, Leonard Dickens replied, "It sure was. I wish Margaret would fix that more often. I could eat that every day." He pulled his chair over closer to Ron's and was about to sit down when someone on the street caught his eye. He paused to wait for them to come into focus. "Forever more . . ." He slowly dragged out. "That's Will comin' there." Ron turned in his chair and craned his neck in an effort to see for himself. "And it looks like a woman with him."

"What's that he's totin'?" Ron wondered.

"Looks like a suitcase," Leonard answered. "She looks like a young woman, too. I wonder what that's about." He looked at Ron and grinned. "Hot damn!" he exclaimed. "That boy sure makes it interestin' around here when he's back in town." Ron met his grin with one of his own and both of them were eager to witness the reception Will would get from Sophie and Ruth. The two older men were both on their feet to greet Will and Loretta when they reached the front steps. "Evenin', Will," Leonard said.

Will looked down at Loretta. "This is Leonard Dickens and Ron Sample," he said. "They live on the front porch. Boys, say howdy to Loretta Carson."

"How do, ma'am? Pleased to make your acquaintance," Ron greeted her eloquently.

"Me, too, ma'am," Leonard said.

"Pleased to meet you," Loretta was barely able to respond before Will hurried her through the door.

He led her through the parlor, where he set her suitcase down at the foot of the stairs, then into the dining room where the women were clearing the supper dishes. Spotting him first, Sophie beamed a broad smile of welcome. Seconds later, it froze on her face when Loretta came into the room behind him. "Will?" Sophie uttered, that being all she could think to say. He hesitated before introducing Loretta because he was aware that he was assuming he could rent his old room to someone without first seeking Ruth Bennett's permission.

All three women of Bennett House seemed held in a state of astonishment until Margaret asked, "Who is this young lady you've brought home with you?"

Feeling as if he might be risking the possibility of both Loretta and himself being kicked out of the boardinghouse by an angry mother and daughter, he said, "Ladies, I'd like you to meet Loretta Carson. I was thinkin' she might stay in my old room for a little while until her court case comes up." His statement caused Sophie and her mother to look at each other with expressions of disbelief, while Margaret couldn't suppress a grin, eager to hear the story behind it. Before any of them could comment, Will hurried to explain, emphasizing the threat upon Loretta's life, if she had remained alone in Clarksville. He also stressed the fact that she had witnessed the slaying of her sister, and that her testimony in court would save two lives, hers and that of the innocent Rayford Pickens.

After she heard his reasons for Loretta's appearance at her house, even Ruth could not fault him for bringing the young girl home with him. "Well, of course she can stay here," she said. "We'll have to put clean sheets on that bed and make sure the room is clean." Her statement brought grunts of approval from the hallway, where Ron and Leonard stood listening.

"Thank you, ma'am," Loretta spoke then. "I can clean the room up and put the sheets on."

"Have you two had any supper?" Margaret asked. Will told her that they had not had any opportunity to get anything to eat, so she promptly started for the kitchen. "You're in luck. I made corn pudding tonight and there's some left over. It's still warm. If it isn't, I'll put it back in the oven for a few minutes. There's ham left and beans. I'll fix you up a couple of plates."

"What do you want to drink with your supper?" Sophie asked Loretta. She answered that a glass of water would be fine. "I know what Will wants," Sophie said. "I'll make a small pot of coffee while the stove is still hot." She gave him a playful look and said, "I ought not make him any coffee. Coming home with a pretty young girl with him."

Loretta's reception was better than what Will had hoped for and all the women wanted to pitch in to help her feel welcome. Loretta, for her part, was so grateful that she wanted to help with the kitchen and the housework to help pay for her keep. Will couldn't have been more pleased and prouder of the women for their compassion.

At breakfast the next morning, the rest of Ruth's boarders met Loretta, but they were not told the circumstances that caused her sudden appearance at the house. Will had to caution Ron and Leonard about the need for secrecy regarding her presence there. They both felt honored to be included in the few who knew her real story. He was not overly concerned as long as they didn't discuss it with the other boarders. They never left the house, themselves, so were not likely to tell anyone outside the house.

He didn't linger long at the breakfast table because he wanted to stop by the jail on his way to the office to check on Rayford. As Sid Randolph had promised, Rayford was in a holding cell. Sid wasn't there, but the guard at the admittance desk told Will where it was and that he could go on back to see him. When Will asked for a key, the guard told him the cell wasn't locked. When Will walked into the cell, he found a different Rayford Pickens. He still had the cuts and bruises, but there was something missing in his face, and Will decided it was that look of desolation that was there when he first saw him in the Clarksville jail. He was glad to see Will and asked if Loretta was all right. Will told him Loretta was very happy where she was and he was on his way to give his boss a full report on what actually took place at the scene of the murder. Rayford told him he was being treated well, so Will said he would check on him after the court decided what they were going to do as far as Long Bob Butler was concerned.

Will hesitated momentarily when he walked out of the jail, trying to decide if he wanted one more cup of coffee before going to Dan Stone's office. The Courthouse Café was on the opposite corner from the courthouse, and he had bought coffee there before. Ormand Anders, Dan's clerk, always made a big pot of coffee at the office. The trouble was it wasn't very strong. Will took a step toward the café, then changed his mind. *I'll drink some more of Ormand's swamp water,* he thought. *I drink too much coffee, anyway.* He stepped back on the walk and continued toward the back entrance to the courthouse.

"Who's that fellow walkin' outta the jail now? He looks like he's got somethin' important on his mind."

"Most likely goin' up to the U.S. Marshals' office," the waiter said.

"I bet you don't know his name."

"I told you," the waiter insisted. "I know the name of every one of them deputies and the guards that work in the jail over there. That feller right there is easy. That's Will Tanner. He spends most of his time over in Injun Territory."

"Hell, I bet you're makin' that up. You don't know every last deputy that rides outta here."

"Hell, I don't. That's Will Tanner and he rides a buckskin horse," the waiter insisted. "You don't believe me? I'll bet you five dollars that's Will Tanner and I'll go with you to ask him when he comes outta the courthouse."

"You know what? I believe you," the man said. "I've wasted enough time just settin' around gabbin' with you." He got up from his table by the window, placed fifty cents beside his plate, and walked out the door.

"Yeah, well, come on back when you wanna know the rest of the deputies' names." the waiter mumbled under his breath.

Outside the café, he untied his horse from the rail and led it across the street to the rail near the rear door of the courthouse. If possible, he wanted a closer look at the man the waiter identified as Will Tanner. And if the circumstances happened to be just right, he was ready to approach him right now. He went up the steps to the first floor, where the courtroom and various offices were located, and found himself in a corridor that circled the courtroom. So he walked slowly down the corridor, reading the names on the doors as he passed each one. A door opened down toward the end of the corridor, and two men came out. One of them was the man the waiter identified as Will Tanner. The man stopped when they turned his way and started walking toward him. He pressed his back against the wall to let them pass.

Dan Stone was talking nonstop as he and Will approached the man dressed in black. Since there was no office past his at the end of the corridor, Dan paused to ask him whom he was looking for. "Nobody," he answered. "I'm lookin' for the door out."

"You won't find it down that way," Stone told him. "Go the same way we're going and just keep going straight till you get to the double doors. You'll see the outside steps."

"Much obliged," he said, and let them go ahead of him. Stone resumed his talking to Will, who paid no attention to the man dressed in all black. The strange-looking man was tempted to approach Will while he was right in front of him in the corridor, but he wanted no one else around when he did. But there might not be an opportunity to catch Tanner alone, so he decided to chance it. As soon as he made his decision, he heard a door open behind him in the corridor and several men walked out. He decided it was not a good time, so he quickly made his way to the double doors and went to his horse. He knew Will would have to come out of the courthouse sometime, so he would just wait him out.

The meeting Will and Dan Stone were hurrying to when they encountered the odd man in black in the corridor, was a hastily arranged talk with Judge Isaac Parker in his office. The "Hanging Judge," as he was known since being appointed to the Western District of Arkansas, was as fair as he was strict. And when he was presented with the facts of the Rayford Pickens case, he was inclined to believe the deputy marshal's report on the special circumstances. He was not anxious to hang an innocent man. "We have a witness to the killing of Jolene Carson Butler," Stone kept stressing, "Loretta Carson, the victim's sister, and whose life was threatened by the killer, Long Bob

Butler. I want a warrant for the arrest of Long Bob Butler." Stone had also planned to push for the immediate release of Rayford Pickens from custody, but Will advised him to keep Rayford where he was until Long Bob was arrested.

When the meeting was over, Will and Stone returned to Stone's office with a warrant for the arrest of one George Robert Butler, also known as Long Bob Butler. They decided it best to send a jail wagon with Will because Long Bob would not likely go peacefully and would be too much to handle on the train. Stone sent for Ed Pine to again act as a posseman for Will. Ed was still complaining about taking a jail wagon down to Atoka, only to find no one to transport back to Fort Smith when he got there. He would have received ten cents per mile for the return trip. But since he came back with no prisoner, he received nothing for his mileage back. "Don't look at me," Will japed. "Reese Trainer was in that jail when I left there. Besides, you got six cents a mile for going over there. It ain't the money that counts. You're in it for the glory. Right?"

"Yeah, right," Ed replied. "I'll tell you one thing, though. I'm gettin' Barney Tatum to cook on this job. Charlie Tate went with me to Atoka and he's gettin' too old to cook. I thought I was gonna starve to death before we got back here."

"You just didn't catch him on a good week," Will said, mostly for Dan Stone's benefit. Charlie

Tate was Fletcher Pride's regular cook, and Fletcher Pride was the man responsible for Will's offer of a job as a deputy marshal. "But whatever you want is all right with me, so why don't you tell Barney to get his wagon stocked up for three days. Day and a half up, and a day and a half back, is that about what you figure?"

"Yeah, it'd be pushin' it to make that trip in one day," Ed agreed. " 'Course, it might take us three days to track him down."

"In that case, Barney will have to restock in Clarksville," Will said, chuckling.

They agreed to meet at the stable at five in the morning to head out for Clarksville. Dan Stone wished them good luck and told Will to hold up a minute when he and Ed started out the door. Ed went on ahead, anxious to find Barney Tatum. "Will," Dan began, "we've been so wound up in this business with that arrest you're goin' on in the mornin', but there's still this issue with that hired killer, Jack Coffey. I hope to hell you're keeping your eyes open."

"I am, Boss," Will replied. "But I don't think a professional, like this fellow Coffey is supposed to be, is gonna take a risk in a city the size of Fort Smith. Too many people that might witness it. I think he'll be waitin' for me to show up down in the Nations again, where we've lost deputies before who just disappeared. That's when I'll really be on my toes."

"You be on your toes here, too," Stone said.

"I will, Boss." Will left his office and went directly to the stable to check on his horse. When he went down the outside steps to the street, he casually noticed the odd-looking man, dressed in black, he and Dan had bumped into earlier that morning. *Still hasn't found who he's looking for, I reckon,* Will thought. When he got to the stable, he saw Vern Tuttle in the corral with some of the horses, and Buster was one of them. Buster nickered hello when he saw Will walk up to the rails and he trotted over to greet him. That got Vern's attention and he turned to see Will at the corner of the corral. He walked over. "Ed Pine was here two seconds ago. Said you and him was headin' out early in the mornin'."

"That's right," Will answered. "I just came by to see if Buster wanted to go with me."

"He wants to go, all right. He's fit as a fiddle. I don't think he likes to miss his exercise."

"Is that right, boy?" Will asked, stroking the buckskin's face and neck. "Well, I'm gonna take you on a little trip in the mornin'. You just don't give Vern any trouble till then, understand?" Back to Vern then, he asked, "Did Ed tell you we're gonna saddle up at about the time you open up in the mornin'?" Vern verified that. "All right, I'll see you bright and early—early, anyway."

He turned and started out for Bennett House, noticing the man in black again, this time leaning up against the wall in front of the Courthouse Café. While not appearing to be looking his way, Will noticed the man was wearing a gun belt beneath the black coat. He had to laugh at himself for even letting Dan Stone's words of warning about a professional killer cause him to take second looks at freakish-looking men like this one. If this clown was a hired killer, he couldn't be more obvious. He'd stand out in any crowd. Turning his thoughts toward dinner and seeing how Sophie was getting along with the new boarder, he turned onto Garrison Avenue. Walking past the hotel, he paused when he got to the lamppost at the corner, just to satisfy his curiosity. Bending over, he pretended to be checking the heel of his boot while he glanced back at the way he had just come. He suddenly came around the corner, the same man in black. "The son of a gun is followin' me," he mumbled to himself. It could be a coincidence, but he decided to make sure. He picked up his pace a little and headed for the Morning Glory Saloon, which was on his way home.

Lucy Tyler saw him first when he walked in, and she sang out a welcome. "Will Tanner, I thought you wasn't ever comin' back to see your old friends since you got married on us."

"Howdy, Lucy, I've just been out of town most of the time since the weddin'," he told her.

She laughed and commented, "That don't sound

like a very good way to start out your married life. What does your bride say about that?"

"She says she's glad I don't hang around the house that much," he answered.

"Now you're lyin' to me. Ain't that right, Gus?"

"I expect it is," Gus Johnson, the bartender, answered, with a wide grin on his face. "Ol' Will had to go outta town to get some rest. Ain't that more like it, Will?"

"I'll never tell," Will came back at him. He was not inclined to talk about his bride or their relationship in the neighborhood saloon.

"You lookin' for a drink of likker?" Gus asked.

"No, but I'd buy a cup of coffee, if Mammy has any on the stove back there. I just thought I'd stop in and say howdy, since it's been a while."

"Well, we appreciate that, don't we, Lucy?" Gus said. "Mammy's always got a pot of coffee on the stove, and there won't be no charge for it."

"Well, that's mighty neighborly of you folks," Will said, just as the front door opened and the man in black stepped inside. "I'm gonna go make some room for that cup of coffee," Will told Gus, preferring not to chance gunfire in the saloon. "I'll be right back." He turned and headed for the back door before Gus had time to comment.

As soon as Will disappeared out the back door, the strange-looking man walked up to the bar. And when Gus asked his pleasure, the man asked, "That was Will Tanner, weren't it?"

Puzzled by the man's behavior, Gus answered, "Yep, that was Will Tanner. What can I get you?"

"Where was he goin'?"

"To the outhouse, I reckon," Gus answered, baffled by the man's questions. "Don't everybody now and then?"

"That's a fact," the man said, and headed for the back door as well.

"Damn!" Gus swore. "Hey! It ain't a two-seater!" But the man was already out the door. He turned to look at Lucy, who was standing there holding a cup of coffee for Will. "We're doin' more business in the outhouse than we are in here today."

CHAPTER 20

He hurried out the back door, his eyes glued to the little outhouse some fifty feet from the back steps. "Hold it right there!" Will commanded from behind him. "Get your hands up in the air," he ordered as he stepped out from behind a low shed in the back of the saloon. "Keep 'em up there," Will ordered again as he moved up behind him. Then Will reached around and pulled a revolver out of his holster. He took one look at the cheap revolver, surprised because he expected a better gun on a professional killer. Most of his work was done at long range with a high-powered rifle, he supposed. "You can put 'em down now and tell me how much I'm worth to Fanny Hawkins."

"I don't know no Fanny Hawkins," he replied, his voice trembling just a bit.

"Jack Coffey?"

"Sir?"

"Your name," Will replied. "Jack Coffey?"

"No, sir. My name's Wiley Carson. I don't know no Jack Coffey."

Will realized then after getting a close look at him that he was a much younger man than he first appeared. Will dropped his Colt .44 back in his holster, but held on to Wiley Carson's cheap revolver, just in case the weird young man had some wild plan in mind. To get a better look at the man who had been stalking him, he reached over and pulled the big black hat off Wiley's head. He was young, indeed, maybe sixteen or seventeen. "Why have you been followin' me, Wiley?"

"I wanted to see if you would tell me what you did with my sister," Wiley answered.

"I didn't do anything with your sister. Why do you think I did?" The young man had obviously gotten him confused with somebody else.

"They told me you took her on the train with you and Rayford Pickens."

A candle suddenly lit in Will's mind. It should have dawned on him sooner and would have had he not set his brain to working on Jack Coffey, thanks to Dan Stone. "What's your sister's name?"

"Loretta Carson," Wiley said. "They told me at the depot that you arrested her with Rayford Pickens and put 'em on the train to Fort Smith. I wanted to tell you that Loretta didn't have no part in that killin'. She loved Jolene. She wouldn'ta ever done nothin' to hurt her sister. Long Bob Butler is who you oughta be arrestin'. He's the one who beat Jolene up all the time."

Will handed Wiley's gun back to him. "I owe you an apology, Wiley, but you should have just asked me when you saw me in the courthouse.

Loretta's not under arrest, she's a witness against Long Bob Butler. I brought her to Fort Smith to keep Butler from threatenin' her. I'll take you to see her. That's where I was headed when I thought you were tailin' me. Why are you wearin' those big, black, baggy clothes, anyway?"

"I'm in mournin' for my sister," Wiley said. "This was my daddy's funeral suit. I just never grew into it. But I wanted to show some respect for Jolene."

"I'm sure Jolene is aware of it and appreciates it," Will told him. "I was just fixin' to have a cup of coffee, but I expect it's gettin' pretty cold by now. Let's go back inside for a minute, then we'll go see Loretta. You want some coffee?"

"Yes, sir," he answered simply. Will had an idea Wiley didn't have much to spend on food, or anything else.

They went back inside and Will introduced Wiley to Lucy and Gus and ordered another cup of coffee for Wiley. He was purposely rather vague on exactly why Wiley was visiting his sister here. Will paid for the coffee, since he had offered a cup to a third party.

When Will brought Wiley home with him to Bennett House, his mother-in-law was visibly upset until he told her he would pay for Wiley's dinner. Ruth's usual coolness warmed considerably when she witnessed the tearful reunion of brother and sister. When Sophie had a chance to pull Will aside from the joyful event, she half seriously asked him if he intended to continue bringing stray souls home with him. "I'm gonna stop letting you leave town, if this keeps up," she japed. And he thought that was as good a time as any to let her know that he was leaving town at about five the next morning for a trip of about three days.

"To do what?" she asked, no longer joking.

"Nothin' much," he said. "Ed Pine and I are gonna take a wagon up to Clarksville with a warrant to pick up a fellow. Just routine stuff."

"Clarksville," she repeated. "Has this got anything to do with the man who killed Loretta's sister?"

"Well, yeah, just routine stuff, though, nothin' to worry about," he said. "Stuff we do every day. And Ed will be with me. Nothing to worry your head about."

She gave him a look of disappointment; one he was getting accustomed to seeing. "Go on in and eat your dinner. I'm gonna be mad at you for a while. If you're lucky, I may be over it by bedtime."

There was naturally a big discussion during the afternoon about what to do with Wiley. He worked on a farm near Clarksville at a job that he liked very much. The owner of the farm was getting on in years and he needed Wiley to do most of the heavy work. He had approved of Wiley's wish to visit his sister but wanted him back as soon as he was ready to return. Wiley said he had his bedroll, and he would just sleep under a tree somewhere while he was in Fort Smith. Ruth had no vacant rooms, since Loretta was now occupying Will's old room. The problem was solved when Margaret suggested that Loretta could double up with her in her room, and Wiley could stay in Loretta's room for the day or so he was going to be there. "She might as well sleep in my room. She's with me, helping me in the kitchen all the time, anyway."

Will slipped out of bed before five the next morning. He dressed quietly so as not to waken Sophie, then went down the back stairs and picked up his rifle and saddlebags at the foot of the steps where he had left them when he went to bed. When he went out the back door and passed under the kitchen window, he waved to Margaret, who was just getting her fire in the stove started. "She'll be rollin' out biscuits to bake," he muttered. "Wish I had a couple of hot ones right now." He and Ed planned to stop for breakfast only when it was time to rest the horses.

He got to the stables at the same time Barney Tatum drove up in his wagon. His wagon was not the typical jail wagon. It was his own creation, a combination jail wagon/chuck wagon, with room for up to four prisoners in the front of the wagon, and his cooking pantry on the back. It saved the trouble of taking two wagons to transport prisoners. Ed showed up shortly after Will and Barney, and they saddled their horses while Barney loaded the packhorse and tied it on a line behind his wagon. "I really don't know why we're startin' out so early," Ed Pine remarked. "We ain't plannin' to try to make it there in one day."

"I don't spend as much time in Arkansas as you do," Will said to Ed. "But if I remember correctly that little settlement where we have to cross the river is about thirty or thirty-five miles from here. That's enough for Barney's horses in one day, and we'd have to cross the river there. So why don't we stay there tonight? We can make one stop, halfway, for breakfast while we rest the horses."

"That sounds as good as any," Ed said. "Okay with you, Barney?"

"Whatever you fellows want," Barney answered. So agreed, they pulled out of Fort Smith near the banks of the Arkansas River, until the river turned sharply northward while they continued to follow the wagon road almost directly east. They would not contact the mighty river again until having to cross it when it turned back to the south and they struck the little settlement there. It was half past five o'clock, according to Barney Tatum's railroad watch, when they actually left the city limits of Fort Smith. Most of the town's citizens were still asleep in their beds. So there was no one to see the departure of the jail wagon and the two horsemen, except the one lone man near the bend in the river, who watched with interest this early-morning expedition. After a few minutes, he climbed aboard the waiting Appaloosa and followed along behind.

Three hours on the road found them at the crossing of a wide stream, obviously fed by the river now north of them. "This looks like the spot to me," Ed declared, and Will and Barney agreed. They decided the best place looked like a grassy strip between the trees on the other side of the creek, so they crossed over. Barney pulled his wagon down close to the water and unhitched the team. Will and Ed took care of their horses as well. Back just short of a curve in the road, the man on the Appaloosa pulled the horse to a stop. In the trees, close to the creek, it was difficult to see the party he followed. So he wheeled the Appaloosa to the north, leaving the road to circle around and intercept the creek farther north. Then he rode back down the creek until reaching a point where he could watch the party of lawmen without being seen, himself. Like them, he took advantage of the creek to water his horse, but he didn't risk building a fire to make coffee or to cook anything, lest they spot the smoke. He settled for some beef jerky for his breakfast. From his position only about one hundred yards from their fire, he could easily fulfill his contract to kill Will Tanner. The 1874 Sharps Big Fifty single-loader rifle he carried strapped on his packhorse could knock a buffalo down at a distance of several hundred yards and had been known on one occasion to kill an Indian at a distance of fifteen hundred–plus yards. He hesitated to take the shot now because of the confusion it would cause with the other two men, and the trouble he might have collecting the articles of proof he needed to take back to Fanny Hawkins. He was a patient man, so he was content to follow the three men, convinced that the opportunity would come when he could catch Tanner apart from his companions.

It amused him to think how he came to identify Will Tanner. Maybe he should share some of his contract money with the odd-looking young man, dressed in the baggy black clothes, he japed to himself. Or maybe he should pay the waiter, instead. He was the one who identified Tanner for the idiot in the oversized clothes. His decision to eat at that restaurant on the corner was going to result in collecting his fee sooner than he had anticipated.

Meanwhile, with no hint they were being stalked, Will and Ed waited for the coffee to boil while Barney mixed up some pan biscuits to eat with the bacon he was frying. He soon had a quick breakfast for them to eat at their leisure while the horses were resting. When Will was inspired to release the coffee he had consumed, he got up from where he was sitting with his back to a tree, to walk away from the camp. Standing between two laurel bushes, he felt a twinge in the nerves in his back. He attributed the feeling to the chill of the morning, since he could not be aware of the Sharps buffalo rifle drawing a bead between his shoulder blades. One hundred yards away, Jack Coffey uttered, "Bam. Good-bye, Deputy Tanner." He strapped the rifle back on his packhorse and waited patiently for the lawmen to call an end to their rest stop and get under way again. With no idea where they were going, he knew he was going to have to put a limit on how far he would follow and how long he could remain patient. He decided that he would wait until they stopped for the night. And if he couldn't catch Tanner when he was alone, he'd kill all three of them if he had to in order to collect the evidence he needed to ensure his reward of five hundred dollars.

Barney killed his fire and hitched up his horses, while Will and Ed saddled up. They pulled out on the road again, planning to camp for the night by the Arkansas River near the little settlement. Behind them, Jack Coffey rode along the bank of the creek until he came back to the road. He held the Appaloosa there in the trees until the party of three disappeared in the distance, then he rode out onto the road and followed them.

"We oughta get to Clarksville by noon tomorrow, wouldn't you say, Will?" Barney asked when Will pulled Buster up beside the wagon seat.

"I expect so," Will answered. "It ain't but about twenty miles from that little town to Clarksville, accordin' to the map on Dan Stone's wall."

"We'da been there an hour ago, if we'd took the train to arrest this jasper," Ed commented.

"Maybe so," Barney replied, "but you woulda missed my company and my cookin'."

"He'da been a handful to handle on the train," Will reminded them. "He's a big sucker and he ain't been housebroke, accordin' to what Sheriff Leach told me. Even with two of us, I figured it would be a constant battle to control him, especially with other folks in there with him."

After a ride of about the same distance as the first leg of their journey, they caught sight of the few buildings that made up the little settlement and the Arkansas River just beyond it. The main building was a large log structure with a sign on the front that proclaimed it to be Stover's Store. It looked to be a trading post, built back a little way from the bank of the river, to accommodate the possibility of flooding, it appeared. There was a stable farther up the bank, and a blacksmith. Beyond that, there were three cabins in a row. "Stover's," Barney repeated the name. "I wonder if Mr. Stover might have somethin' in there to drink, somethin' a little stronger than coffee, maybe."

"I don't know," Ed replied. "Maybe we oughta go over there after supper and find out."

"Damn good idea," Barney said. "Let's go get our camp set up."

They drove upriver about forty yards from the store and set up their camp on the riverbank. When the horses were taken care of, Barney threw some ham in the pot of beans he had soaked all day. They were ready to be cooked. "I'm gonna roll out some biscuits to go with 'em, but I ain't got no oven, so I'll have to fry 'em in the pan."

"Listen to him, Will," Ed said. "He's already makin' excuses and he ain't even set his pot on the fire yet. Maybe we'd best walk up to that store and get us somethin' to eat."

"Shoot," Barney came back. "You give me a good oven to work with and I'd have you cussin' your mama's cookin'."

"I can see you two are feelin' your oats after ridin' all day," Will commented. "I'll stay here and watch the camp while you go see if Mr. Stover's sellin' anything to drink."

"Well, that's mighty sportin' of you, Will, but it

ain't really fair, is it?" Ed suggested. "Why don't we flip for it, odd man out?"

"I'll tell you what," Will countered, "I'll just flip a coin. Heads I stay here, tails I don't. Then, if it lands tails up, one of you can flip it to see if you go or stay. All right?" He didn't wait for their answer, reached in his pocket for his lucky silver coin. "Heads, I stay here," he reminded them. He flipped it, caught it, and showed them the side that was up. "It's heads, I stay here."

"I reckon you just ain't lucky," Barney said. "Maybe there ain't nothin' in that store to drink, anyhow, and me and Ed'll be right back. But I hope he's got some smokin' tobacca because I'm runnin' low."

"You can get it in Clarksville if he doesn't," Will said. "That's a good-sized town."

Barney didn't waste any time cleaning up his pot and pan in the river after supper was finished. Ed gave him a hard time because Barney was married, and Ed japed him about being under his wife's thumb. "Man, I'm glad I ain't got a wife, like you two boys. Have to ride six hours out in the woods before you ain't too scared to go get a drink of likker."

"Hell, Will's the one," Barney japed. "No longer'n you been married, how'd you get your wife to let you go this long?"

"I didn't tell her I wouldn't be home for

supper," Will joked. Their childish banter carried a long way down the quiet river, so much so, that Will was reminding himself why he preferred to work alone. He had become addicted to the quiet of the hills and rivers.

There was another who agreed with him on that subject. Jack Coffey, at another cold camp, two hundred yards downriver, was again too close to build a fire. He tied his horse to a tree limb and made his way along the riverbank until he could see the camp. He took out his field glass and scanned it. Then he fixed on Will Tanner for a long time, until he realized the other two men with him were saying something to him. And then, they left, both of them, and walked toward the store. *They left Tanner alone!* Coffey nodded his thanks to them. He had known he would very likely get the opportunity he needed. He would wait until the two men went into the store, then he could take the shot and get some form of proof, his badge, for sure, and maybe an ear to show that he was dead. He would deal with that after he killed him, but for now, he needed to be ready to strike as soon as Tanner's companions disappeared. He started to go to his packhorse to get the Sharps, then hesitated. He was counting on making a quick departure as soon as the deed was done, so he needed to be closer to him to get to his body fast, with his horses close. The Winchester would be better at the closer distance and provide continuous fire if it became necessary.

He pulled the Winchester '73 from his saddle sling and checked the load. He had not unsaddled his horses yet, somehow sensing he might need to leave there in a hurry. So he untied the Appaloosa's reins and led the horses closer along the riverbank until he found the spot he liked and left them there. He was no more than fifty yards from their camp, a can't-miss range for the rifle. Now there was nothing to do but wait for the shot.

Coffey's target was moving quite a bit as Will was busy getting his bedroll positioned where he wanted it. He picked up his saddle and carried it over to place it by his bedroll. He smiled when he thought of the coin toss and he reached in his pocket and pulled his lucky silver coin out to look at the identical head on both sides of it. With a little chuckle, he flipped it high in the air, and when it came down, he misjudged it, causing it to land on the tip of his finger and bounce forward. He quickly bent forward to catch it just before it hit the ground and heard the snap of the bullet as it passed directly over his bent back. Confused for a fraction of a second but then certain when he heard the report of the Winchester almost immediately after. Without having to think about it, he went down flat on the ground and lay still. With no idea where the shot was fired from, only that it went right over his back, his first thought was to find cover. The name Jack Coffey came to mind instantly, so he knew he was not the chance target of some two-bit bushwhacker. He was a contract killing, by a man who was supposedly a master at his craft. There was no second shot, so he figured that Coffey wasn't sure if he had hit him or not, and he was waiting to see if he moved. And Will was sure that, if he tried to crawl to the edge of the bank, he wouldn't be so lucky on the next shot. His best chance was to remain absolutely still and try to gradually move his right arm down far enough to reach the .44 in his holster. As he lay there, his cheek flat against the ground, he was sure Coffey could clearly see his legs, but he wasn't sure about anything from his thighs on up. The ground was rough and uneven there, so there was a chance his legs were all Coffey could see, although not much of one.

Coffey waited, undecided. He was sure of his accuracy with his weapons, and he had held the front sight dead on the middle of Will's back, right between his shoulder blades. He pulled the trigger and almost instantly Will went down. He could see his victim's legs, and they had not twitched or moved an inch, and it had been several minutes since he took the shot. It would be better if he could see Will's upper body, but the slope of the ground prevented that. He began to worry about the time now. He didn't want to fire another shot unless it was absolutely necessary. Thinking about the two men who went to the store, he thought they might be curious when hearing one shot fired, but not curious enough to investigate. On the other hand, two or more shots might bring them rushing out of the store to find the cause. *I've wasted enough time,* he thought. *If he's still breathing, I'll cut his throat.* Still cautious, however, he left his cover and moved quickly toward the body.

Inside the store, Ed and Barney paused when they heard the shot. When there were no more, Lonnie Stover said, "Most likely some of them boys squirrel huntin'. They hunt up and down this river all the time."

"Maybe so," Ed Pine said, "but that sounded to me like a Winchester rifle. Who hunts squirrels with a Winchester rifle?"

"Or a Henry," Barney offered. "It kinda sounded like one or the other."

"Maybe we oughta take a look," Ed decided.

Down near the edge of the bank, Jack Coffey walked carefully, so as not to break a twig or rustle a leaf, in case Will was playing possum. Still the body did not move. Directly in line with the way Will was lying now, Coffey could see his face flat against the ground. He drew the skinning knife from his belt and took a step toward the body when the front door of Stover's Store opened, and Ed and Barney came out on

344

the porch. "Hey!" Ed shouted, "What the hell?" Coffey dropped his knife, turned at once, and started firing his rifle as fast as he could, sending Ed and Barney to dive for cover under the porch. Coffey turned back to Will then in time to catch a .44 slug in the chest and a second one in his side. He went down, his rifle aimed at Will as he pulled the trigger only to find he had not extracted the spent cartridge.

"He's down!" Ed exclaimed. "Will got him! But Will ain't on his feet yet. Come on!" He crawled out from under the porch, but Barney stayed where he was. Ed stopped to look back at him. "Are you hit?" There were quite a few shots thrown at them from Coffey's rifle.

"No, I ain't hit," Barney replied. "I'll stay right here till you make sure that feller is dead. That's your job. I'm the cook. I ain't supposed to get shot at. I don't know why I ran out here in the first place."

"I swear," Ed replied, unable to think of any comment. He yelled out then and started running back to the camp, "Will! You okay?"

"Yeah, I'm all right," Will answered. On his feet now, he went over to get a closer look at the man who had sought to kill him. "Jack Coffey," he announced when Ed got there.

"Jack Coffey?" Ed repeated. "Do you know this fellow?"

"Not exactly," Will answered. "We just met for

the first time today. I know who he is, though."
He went on to tell Ed who Jack Coffey was and
that he had been hired to kill him.

"Well, I'll be . . ." Ed started. "And you knew
this joker was stalkin' you the whole time?" He
was a little upset that Will had not seen fit to
warn him. "Who hired him? Do you know?"

"Not for sure," Will answered, "but I suspect
it mighta been Fanny Hawkins. And I reckon I
can't blame her too much. I put a lotta hurt on
that old witch. I tried to arrest her sons, but they
just wouldn't have it that way." They both turned
when Barney came down to join them.

"You all right?" Will asked.

"I bumped my head pretty good when I went
under the porch," he replied. "I thought at first
I'd got hit with one of them bullets that was flyin'
around that porch. Who's he?" he asked, pointing
at the body. Will explained again and when he
was finished, Barney asked, "Why didn't you tell
us about it?"

"I didn't wanna worry you," Will answered.

"Next time, I druther you tell me. I druther
worry a little bit," Barney said. *Or stay home,* he
thought.

"I'm gonna walk down the river a ways,"
Will told them, "back the way he came from.
He musta left his horse back there somewhere."
He left Ed to relieve Coffey of his gun belt and
anything of value he had on him. He didn't

walk far before he came to the Appaloosa and a dun packhorse. He couldn't help admiring the Appaloosa. He stepped up into the saddle and rode the horse back to his camp. "I reckon we can just worry about arrestin' Long Bob Butler now." He grinned at Barney. "Did you and Ed find anything you wanted in that store?"

"He's got some kinda stuff he's sellin' in fruit jars," Ed answered. "I took a taste of it. It had a pretty good burn to it. Might be kerosene, but it tasted a little like corn whiskey. I reckon it'd do to celebrate the end of Jack Coffey."

CHAPTER 21

As they had figured, they pulled into Clarksville close to noontime, attracting a lot of curious eyes as the combination jail wagon and chuck wagon rolled down the middle of the street, led by two mounted deputy marshals. In his customary location this time of day, Sheriff Marvin Leach leaned back in his desk chair, his feet propped on his desk, his coffee cup in his hand. Propped against the wall in the straight-back chair, Deputy Sheriff Jim Turner caught a glimpse of something he was curious enough to lower the front legs of his chair back to the floor to get up to see. When he went to the window, he remarked, "We got company." And when Leach asked who, he said, "That deputy marshal, Will Tanner, and he ain't alone. He's got another one with him, a deputy or a posseman, and a jail wagon."

That was enough to capture Leach's interest. "A jail wagon? Is there anybody in it?"

"Nope, just an empty wagon," Turner replied. He remained at the window until Will and Ed tied their horses at the hitching rail, then returned to his chair when they started up the two steps.

"Deputy Tanner," the sheriff greeted him. "What brings you back to Clarksville?"

"Sheriff," Will acknowledged. "This is Deputy

Marshal Ed Pine. Ed, say howdy to Sheriff Leach and Deputy Turner." Ed acknowledged with a nod of his head in each man's direction. Back to Leach then, Will said, "I've got a warrant for the arrest of George Robert Butler that we're in town to serve."

"Long Bob?" Jim Turner exclaimed. "You wanna arrest Long Bob? For what?"

"The murder of his wife, Jolene Carson Butler, and for threatening the life of her sister, Loretta Carson. It's all right here," he said, and placed the warrant on the sheriff's desk.

Leach picked up the paper and briefly glanced at it before laying it back on his desk. "Ain't you gettin' things a little bass-ackwards there, Tanner? You took the guilty man who killed Jolene Butler into custody the last time you was here."

"That's a fact," Will replied. "I took the accused man into custody, where he still is. I also took the key witness to the murder into custody."

"I heard you took Loretta Carson on the train with you. I was wonderin' why you arrested her."

"I didn't arrest her," Will corrected him. "I took her into protective custody."

"What for?" Jim Turner asked. "Protect her from what? She's a witness, and you got the man who did the killin' in jail. So she ain't in no danger."

"I understand why you think that, but after

further investigation, we found that Rayford Pickens is not guilty of any crime, so we're here today to take the guilty man in custody, the man on that warrant, George Robert Butler." Will was trying to sound as official as he could make it, when the "investigation" really amounted to Loretta changing her story and he believed it.

The sheriff was plainly stunned. "You think Long Bob killed that little gal he was married to. I swear, if he did, he oughta be hanged for sure. He's loud and he's rough, and he's been in more'n one fight, but I never heard of him takin' it out on a woman." He paused to think about it for a moment before asking, "Well, what do you want from me?"

"Nothing except you can tell us where we can find him," Will said. "We'll do the rest. But I had to notify you about what we're doin', since you're the sheriff."

"Him and Jolene lived in a room at the back of Sally Belcher's roomin' house," Leach said. "I reckon he still lives there."

"We might as well look there first," Will said to Ed. "Then we'll search the whole town, startin' with the saloons." He figured they were the most likely. "Barney can pull his wagon around behind the jail while we search. That all right with you, Sheriff?"

"Sure, that's all right with me," Leach replied.

When Will and Ed went back outside to help

Barney pick a spot for his wagon, in case it ended up as their temporary base for a while, Jim watched until they pulled around back. He looked at Leach then and said, "You know, Long Bob might be over at the Friendly Saloon. I'm gonna step over there real quick. I might be able to save those deputies a lotta time." He didn't wait for Leach to comment and was out the door while Leach was still thinking about it.

Jim wasted no time crossing the street, but instead of going in the front door of the saloon, he walked around the side to the back door. Inside, he walked as quietly as he could manage up the hallway, past the kitchen, to the back door of the saloon. He could hear Long Bob's booming voice even before he opened the door. When he pushed the door halfway open, he checked to see where Tom Futch was, and didn't see him anywhere. *Good,* he thought, and looked for Long Bob. He wasn't hard to find. Sitting at a table playing cards, he was laughing loud and often. Using the half-open door for concealment, Jim waved his arm up and down until he caught Long Bob's eye. When he did, he motioned for Long Bob to come to him. When he finally realized what Jim was trying to do, Long Bob got up from the table, said he'd be right back, and walked to the back door. "What the hell are you doin'?" he asked before Jim grabbed his arm and pulled him into the hall. "What the hell's ailin' you?" Long Bob insisted.

"You need to get your long butt outta here," Jim told him. "There's two deputy marshals just come to town with a jail wagon and they're lookin' for you."

"Lookin' for me?" Long Bob blurted. "Why are they lookin' for me?"

"You know why," Jim said. "It's that damn Tanner. I knew when he took Loretta Carson with him on that train that he didn't believe her when she said it was Rayford."

"I shoulda just wrung her neck that day. Where is that damn marshal? The best thing to do is to just call him out right now, and we'll settle it for good."

"No, that ain't the best thing," Jim insisted. "He ain't gonna face up to you in the street. There's two of 'em—three, if you count the feller drivin' the jail wagon. They'll just shoot you down if you don't give yourself up. You'd best get your horse and get outta Clarksville. Go down to the shack and lay low for a while. I'll tell 'em you left town for good."

Long Bob was beginning to see that Jim was right, he'd best make himself scarce, but he didn't want to ride down to the river and stay in that lonely cabin. "There ain't no supplies in that cabin," he complained. "There ain't nothin' to eat in the cabin. I can't stay there."

Jim knew that to be a fact. "I'll ride down there tonight and bring you some stuff you can cook.

You just hang in there and I'll get you some stuff tonight."

"Bring me one of them gals from Annie Mae's," Long Bob japed.

"Yeah, that's what got you into trouble in the first place. You couldn't stay outta that place," Jim scolded. "You ain't got time to fool around. Get on outta here now. Don't worry, I'll get down there tonight."

"I left some money on the table," Long Bob said. "I ain't leavin' that."

"I'll get it. You just get goin'." Jim gave him a push toward the back door.

Long Bob grinned at him. "I owe you, partner."

"Damn right you do. Now get outta here before I arrest you." He watched to make sure Long Bob went out the back door. Then he pushed the door to the saloon open and walked in. He went over to the table where Long Bob had been playing cards. "I'm lookin' for Long Bob Butler," he told the three players still at the table. "Somebody said he was playin' cards with you fellers."

"He was, he was settin' right there," one of the men said. "But he just got up and walked out the back door over there. We figured he had to go to the outhouse, but he ain't come back yet."

"I just came in that way," Jim said. "He ain't back there." He took off his hat and swept Long Bob's money into it. "If he comes back, tell him he can pick up his money at the sheriff's office."

"Right, we'll tell him, Deputy," the man said.

Jim pocketed the money plopped his hat back on his head and walked over in front of the bar. "I'm lookin' for Long Bob Butler," he announced loudly. "Anybody seen him?"

No one volunteered to tell him that Long Bob was just in the saloon minutes before, although everyone knew he was. Finally, the bartender said, "He was in here a little while ago, Jim, but I don't know where he went."

When Jim walked out the front door of the Friendly Saloon, he met Will coming across the street. "I just checked in there," Jim said. "I thought that might be the first place to look. He was there, sure enough, but he'd already gone."

Will hesitated before deciding whether to take the young deputy sheriff's word or not. He had a feeling that Jim really wanted to keep him from checking the saloon. "Well, thanks, Deputy, we appreciate the help. I'm gonna go in, anyway. I wanna ask the bartender some questions."

Jim shrugged as if unconcerned. "Want me to go back in with you?"

"No, that ain't necessary," Will said. "I just wanna ask questions about Long Bob's usual habits, when he usually comes in, things like that. Just routine questions. I'll see you back at the sheriff's office." He turned then and continued toward the Friendly Saloon.

Inside the saloon, the noise automatically

quieted down when he walked in. Most of the regulars remembered him because they were there when he had come to Clarksville to pick up Rayford Pickens. He walked over to the bar to talk to the bartender. "I'm sorry, I don't remember if you told me your name when I was here before."

"It's Alvin," he answered, "Alvin Jones."

"All right, Alvin, my name's Will Tanner. I understand Long Bob Butler was in here a little while ago." Alvin nodded, so Will continued. "Was he in here a long time today, or just a few minutes?"

"He came in like he usually does, a little before noon, has a few drinks, plays some cards."

"So he was here a pretty good while today?" Alvin nodded. "But he left all of a sudden?"

"That's right," Alvin said. "Them three fellers over there was playin' cards with him, and they said he just got up all of a sudden and went out the door in the back. Left his money on the table, didn't say squat. They figured he had a sudden call to visit the outhouse, but he never came back. They already told all that to Jim Turner."

"Yeah, that's what Jim told me," Will said. "So Long Bob was playin' cards for a pretty good while. Then he jumped up and left. Maybe he saw Deputy Turner come in the front door, and that's when he decided he'd better leave out the back door."

"Only thing is, Jim Turner didn't come in the front door," Alvin said. "He came in the door in the back, same one Long Bob went out."

Will grinned. "It's a wonder they didn't bump into each other."

Alvin scratched his head when he thought about it. "Yeah, it is, ain't it? Long Bob musta popped in the kitchen when Jim went by."

"I'll bet that's what happened," Will declared. "I wish Long Bob had stayed in the hall. Woulda made this job a lot easier. Much obliged, Alvin. I think I'll go out the back way." He headed for the door in the back of the room.

In the hall, he walked to an open door not quite halfway down to the outside door. He stuck his head inside and saw Mabel, her back to him, leaning over a pot on the stove. "I'll have more stew out there in a minute," she said without turning around.

"I declare, lady, you do have good hearin'," Will said. "Are you still bakin' those prize biscuits?"

That got her attention right away, and she turned around to see who made the remark. She remembered him at once as the nice young man who said her biscuits were the best in the whole state of Arkansas. "So you're back in town, are ya? Are you eatin' with us today?"

"Not today," he answered, "but I'm gonna make it a point to get in here before I leave town to get some of those biscuits."

"You be sure that you do," she told him.

"Right now, I'm tryin' to catch up with Long Bob Butler. I think he mighta stopped in here to visit you a little while ago."

"Long Bob in here?" she replied. "I expect I mighta noticed that. I ain't quite young enough to attract Long Bob's notice. And if I was, I wouldn't want it."

"I hear you," Will said, laughing. "I'll be seein' you later."

He walked out of the saloon with a picture he had formed in his mind that he realized could be totally wrong. But it was a picture that made sense to him because he had a definite feeling of mistrust when it came to Deputy Jim Turner. He walked back across the street and went around behind the sheriff's office and jail where Ed and Barney had set up a temporary camp. In addition to his and Ed's two horses, they had Barney's team and his packhorse, plus Jack Coffey's Appaloosa and packhorse. As Ed put it, "We're gonna be too busy protectin' our herd of horses to try to find Long Bob Butler, especially since we took on that Appaloosa."

Will told Ed what he had been doing in the saloon. He told him of his suspicions regarding Jim Turner. "I don't know if he's got something workin' with Long Bob or not, but it seems to me like he's too anxious to get involved with our business. I may be totally wrong, but I don't think we're gonna find Long Bob in this town tonight. We'll go check his room out at the roomin' house, but we ain't gonna find him there. I think I wanna get on Jim Turner's tail tonight, and he's more likely to lead us to Long Bob Butler." He knew that the brutal way Jim roughed Rayford Pickens up when he was in jail, influenced his opinion of the young deputy sheriff. But he still held suspicions of a conspiracy between Jim and Long Bob to pin Jolene's death on the hapless young man who had come to Jolene's defense.

"We're all set up here for tonight," Ed said, and suggested, "Why don't we go over to that roomin' house and make sure he ain't in there?"

"We might as well," Will replied. "Then I wanna find out where Jim Turner sleeps." He paused then to say, "I'm just sayin' what I think is best, but I wanna know what you think, too. So jump in any time you think of something better."

"Sounds to me like you're on the right track, so far," Ed told him. "This is your show as far as I'm concerned. I just came along as a posseman. You're in charge." He grinned then and added, "Then, if you screw it all up, I'll say I told you so."

Will chuckled and commented, "You might get that chance. Come on, let's go take a look at Long Bob's room."

Leaving Barney to watch the camp, the two deputy marshals went down a side street to a large two-story house with a wide front porch that, according to Sheriff Leach's directions, was Sally Belcher's rooming house. Just in case, Will went in the front door, while Ed went around the house to the back door. Walking inside the parlor, Will saw no one, but he could hear the sounds of someone cleaning up after dinner in the dining room. He started to go to the dining room but noticed a little bell on a stand near the front door. So he picked it up and rang it, guessing that was what it was there for. The cleanup noise in the dining room stopped, and after a few seconds, a plump little gray-haired woman appeared in the doorway. "Can I help you?" she asked.

"Yes, ma'am," Will said as he showed his badge. "I'm Deputy Marshal Will Tanner. Are you Miz Sally Belcher?"

"I am," she stated.

"Miz Belcher, I have a court order to find George Robert Butler, and I understand he rents a room here in your house. Do you know if he's here?"

"No, I mean, yeah, I know he ain't here. Least he wasn't here for dinner, but that ain't unusual. Since his wife was killed, he eats at the Friendly Saloon more'n he eats here."

"Well, I need to take a look in his room. Can I ask you to show me which one is his and have you unlock it for me?" She looked a little uncertain and hesitated to respond, so he said, "I'd like for you to go with me, so you can see that I won't take anything."

"All right, let me get my keys," Sally said.

She left him in the hallway while she went into her room and returned with a key to Long Bob's room. Will followed her down the long hallway to the back door and out on a porch to find Ed Pine waiting there. When Sally reacted in surprise, Will said, "This is Deputy Marshal Ed Pine. Ed, say howdy to Miz Belcher." Ed complied, and Sally went to the door of a single attachment to the main house.

When she opened the door, she said, "Long Bob don't need this big room no more since Jolene ain't here to cook for him." She took a look inside and said, "And it sure looks like it could use a good cleanin'."

Will could see why she might be concerned. Basically, the room was a bedroom large enough to have a small cookstove at one end of it with a table and chairs. It was obvious she could ask more rent for this room. And the room was a mess, with a woman's clothes strewn on the floor as well as some of Long Bob's. But there was no sign of a hasty packing of anything like Will would have expected to find. In fact, there was a set of saddlebags lying in the corner. A new thought suddenly struck him. "Miz Belcher," he asked, "has Jim Turner got a room here?"

She nodded and said, "Jim's room is upstairs. You wanna see it, too?"

"No, ma'am," Will replied. "I was just curious.

Matter of fact, I think we're through here. Right, Ed?" Ed said yes, so Will thanked Sally for her cooperation and said he hoped they hadn't caused her too much trouble. "We'll just go right out the back door," Will said, while she was locking Long Bob's door.

"It weren't no trouble," Sally said as she went back into the main house.

Outside, as they walked around the house, Will was looking toward the woods on the other side of a garden patch behind the boardinghouse. He was picking out a spot to watch the house from, if things continued to fall in place as they had begun to do so far. For his theory to be proven correct, there were other pieces that had to fall in place, and they began with Jim Turner and what he did with the rest of that day. On the way back to their camp behind the jail, Will explained to Ed what he planned to do. Ed was concerned that Will was taking on too much of the arrest by himself, and he thought the two of them should plan to arrest Long Bob Butler. "From everything I've heard about this jasper, some of it from you, Long Bob is one helluva handful to take on."

"I agree," Will replied. "That's why I plan to tail Jim Turner just to find out where Long Bob is hidin' out. Once we find that out, you and I will go get him. That make more sense?"

"That makes more sense," Ed concurred.

CHAPTER 22

When they got back to their camp, they found Sheriff Leach talking to Barney over a cup of coffee. "Well, I see you ain't walkin' Long Bob between ya, so I reckon he weren't home."

"That's a fact," Will replied. "I reckon the next thing we need to do is see if his horse is gone. Does he keep a horse in the stable down the street there? Or has he got someplace else where he keeps it? There wasn't a stable or a barn behind that boardin'house."

"He kept his horse at Murphy's stable, big ol' bay geldin' he called Devil," Leach answered.

"What does Long Bob do for a livin'?" Ed asked. "He spends a helluva lotta time in the saloon, rents a big room with a kitchen at the boardin'house, and he keeps his horse at the stable. Where does he get money for all that?"

Leach laughed at his curiosity. "Well, he ain't got no steady job. I can tell you that. He claims he wins his money gamblin' over in Little Rock. If you watch him playin' cards very long, you don't figure that's very likely. I don't worry my head about it. Wherever he gets it, it ain't here in Clarksville, so it ain't my problem."

"I see what you mean, Sheriff, and I hope we can finish up our little business and get out of your way before too much longer," Will told him. "I'm just gonna take a little walk down to that stable."

"Ain't no hurry," Leach replied. "Your partner, here, makes a pretty good cup of coffee. You boys just stay as long as you like. Jim's in the office. Want me to send him down to Murphy's to check on Long Bob's horse?"

"No, I can do it," Will said. "I need to stretch my legs a little." He started right away before Leach could insist on sending his deputy. Ed fell in step with him and walked as far as the front of the building. "You keep an eye on Deputy Jim Turner," Will said. "We need to know if he leaves to go anywhere."

"Right," Ed said. "I was fixin' to tell you that I was gonna do just that."

Will found Frank Murphy pumping water into the trough in the corral. "Mr. Murphy," Will called to him from the corral gate.

Murphy turned to see who called, and when he saw Will, he pumped a couple more times, then came over to the gate. "You're the deputy marshal that came to pick up that poor Pickens boy, ain't you?"

"That's right," Will answered. "Will Tanner."

"Well, have they hung him yet?" Murphy asked.

"No, as a matter of fact, they haven't," Will replied, curious as to the stable owner's feelings on the subject. "He hasn't gone to trial yet. You think they oughta hang him for killin' that young lady?"

"Hell, no!" Murphy exclaimed. "I've dealt with that miserable soul ever since he started workin' in Galloway's Feed Store, and I know for a fact that boy ain't got it in him to hurt a flea, much less kill a woman. He ain't as bright as a horse turd, but he's as honest as the day is long and he was worth every penny of what ol' John Galloway was payin' him when it came to workin'."

Will was taken totally by surprise by Murphy's unsolicited testimony for Rayford Pickens. He couldn't help smiling at the frank opinion offered by Murphy. "Your first name's Frank, ain't it, Mr. Murphy?" Murphy said it was and Will said, "I think I know why. If Rayford Pickens needed a character witness at his trial, I believe I'd call you."

"I don't know about that," Murphy said. "I'm just callin' a spade a spade."

"What would you think if I told you Rayford Pickens ain't goin' on trial for killin' anybody. And right now, he's sittin' in a holdin' cell, away from the general prison population, with the door not even locked, eatin' three meals a day, being held as a witness. And another witness is in protection from the man she's gonna testify against for the murder of Jolene Carson Butler.

And that man is the man I'm lookin' for today. So tell me, Frank Murphy, which one of these horses belongs to Long Bob Butler?"

Murphy looked stunned. "Are you tellin' me the God's honest truth?"

"I am," Will replied. "Is his horse here?"

"No, he came in here and took that big bay of his just a little while ago," Murphy answered. "Said he had to take a little trip and he might not be back tonight." He shook his head slowly, then looked at Will and smiled. "That's the best news I coulda heard today." Then he adopted a serious expression. "But you be careful, young feller. They don't come no meaner than Long Bob." He shook his head again. "Lord! I hope you catch that devil."

"Did you notice which road he took out of town?" Will asked.

"Yeah, he took the south road to Spadra," Murphy said. "He was headin' down to the river, I reckon. Ain't no tellin' where he was goin' down that way."

"All right, well, much obliged, Mr. Murphy." He offered his hand and Murphy shook it.

"You be real careful with that devil," Murphy cautioned again. "He's strong as an ox."

When Will got back to the jail, he told them that Murphy said Long Bob had saddled his horse and left town. He wanted Leach to think that he and Ed were not holding back any information from him. "He say which way he rode out?" Leach asked.

"No," Will answered. "That mighta helped a little, wouldn't it?" He glanced at Ed and winked. "I reckon there ain't much we can do but start scoutin' around tomorrow to see if we can pick up any sign."

"That don't sound too promisin', does it?" Leach asked. "That boy's a wild one. I wouldn't expect to see him in these parts any time soon, if he knows the law is after him."

"I'm afraid you may be right," Will said. "Mighta been a waste of time comin' up here." He reached over and gave Ed a playful punch on the shoulder. "But I reckon there ain't much we can do about it tonight, so we might as well eat a good supper and give Barney the night off, too."

"Now you're talkin'," Ed said, playing his part. Then he directed a question to the sheriff. "Do you and Jim eat supper across the street at the saloon?"

"Most of the time we do," Leach answered. "And that's where I'm plannin' to eat tonight. Jim told me before he went in the office that he thought he might take supper back at Sally Belcher's place tonight. Said she wanted to have all the boarders come to supper tonight 'cause she's got some things she wants to change."

"Uh-oh," Ed cracked. "Sounds like she's wantin' Jim to take his boots off when he jumps in the bed." It got a halfhearted chuckle. "What about you, Barney?" Ed went on. "You wanna eat at the saloon with the rest of us?"

"No, thanks," Barney said at once. "I go to supper in a saloon and before I know it, I'll be mixin' it with shots of rye whiskey. I need to stay here and keep an eye on the camp."

"Suit yourself," Ed continued. "Will and I'll go eat with the sheriff."

The rest of the afternoon was passed off shooting the breeze with every subject Will and Ed could think to ask about. So they had a pretty thorough picture of Clarksville's history by the time Jim came out of the office and told Leach that he was going to supper. That was signal enough for the rest of them to do the same. Leach locked the office door and they started to cross the street when Will suddenly stopped. "Damn, I don't know what's wrong with me. I plum forgot to take Buster's saddle off of him. You two go on, don't wait for me. I'll catch up." He didn't wait for any reply but turned around and ran back behind the jail where Barney was waiting, holding the buckskin's reins. Will climbed up into the saddle and turned Buster toward the other end of the jail and waited for a signal from Barney.

"Go!" Barney barked when he saw Ed and the sheriff go inside the front door of the saloon, and Buster jumped out from the corner of the jail at a lope.

Having already picked out the spot he was going to stake out, Will rode down the side street until reaching a point where he could guide Buster through the woods behind Sally Belcher's boardinghouse. Before he got to the end of the woods, he dismounted and tied Buster to a tree limb. Then he moved up closer to the edge of the trees with now only a small garden patch between the woods and the back of the house. As he suspected, Jim's saddled horse was tied at the back steps of the house, so he took a knee and waited. In a short while, Jim came down the steps, carrying two sacks that Will guessed held something Long Bob could cook, bacon maybe, or jerky, anything he could eat. Jim tied the sacks on the front of his saddle and went back inside Long Bob's room. When he came back, he was carrying a long bundle wrapped in a blanket. He laid that behind his saddle where his saddlebags usually rode. *So far, you're doing everything right,* Will thought. *Now just lead me to him.* As if he heard him, Jim climbed up into the saddle and rode around the house to take the side road back to the main street. Will ran back and jumped on his horse. No longer worried about being seen by someone in the house, he rode around the garden patch and went out the same way Jim did.

He held the buckskin back when he reached the main street to be sure he didn't give himself away. He watched as Jim took the south road out of town, the same road Frank Murphy said Long Bob took. Murphy said it was the road to Spadra, a little town on the north bank of the Arkansas River that was there before Clarksville developed. The task for Will now was to follow Jim without getting too close. Will wasn't sure, but he thought it was a ride of only three or four miles to Spadra. So he became extra cautious lest he ride around one of the many curves in the road and suddenly find himself in the middle of a little town with nowhere to hide. He was approaching a sharp curve at the moment, so he slowed Buster down to make sure he didn't do what had just occurred to him. If he had not come almost to a dead stop before rounding the curve, he most likely would have missed the small path leading off to the east of the road, and the clear hoofprint at the beginning of it.

"Damn," he swore for his carelessness, and nudged Buster to plunge through some laurel bushes that were growing over the path. Once the buckskin forged through the bushes, the path was a little more visible. It was obvious, however, that it had not been used for quite some time. He dismounted to take a closer look at the hoofprints on the path to make sure they were recent before he continued to follow it. In the saddle again, he was even more cautious. It would be really hard to explain his presence there, and it was pretty tight quarters to have a gunfight. His intent was just as he had told Ed, to find where Long Bob was holed up, so the two of them could arrest him. There was also one more thing to be considered—Jim Turner's involvement in Long Bob's escape. To make things right, Will needed to arrest Jim for aiding and abetting. *We'll worry about Long Bob first,* he told himself.

The ground continued to slope down toward the river as he followed the path through woods so thick, it was difficult to see more than ten yards ahead of him. Finally, he reined Buster to a halt at a point where the path suddenly descended sharply to the river. Below him, close to a wide bend in the river, he saw a rough shack. Behind the shack, Will guessed to be a fishing shack, he saw the two horses. That was all he needed to see. He knew where Long Bob was hiding. As far as Deputy Jim Turner, it would be best to keep them apart in two separate arrests. It was tempting to try to move on them now, but every advantage was in their favor. Will would likely end up dead, and Ed still wouldn't know where Long Bob was. He backed the buckskin up, then turned him around and figured he and Ed would be back later that night.

When he returned to Clarksville, he found Barney waiting for him. Ed and Leach had not returned from the saloon and Barney had made some biscuits and ham for him, as well as a pot of coffee. Will quickly pulled the saddle off his horse and sat down by the fire with Barney. He was just finishing his supper when Ed and the sheriff returned. "Well, we was wonderin' what in the world happened to you," Ed sang out upon seeing Will there. "You missed a fine supper."

"I came back to pull Buster's saddle off, and he was actin' kinda strange, like he was favorin' one of his front legs. I checked his hoof, and he had a little sliver of rock wedged in it. I pulled it out. It wasn't anything really, but then I saw Barney sittin' over here lookin' lonesome, so I took pity on him and ate some of the grub he cooked up."

"Ed's right," Leach said, "you missed a good supper. Mabel asked why you didn't come to eat. Said she baked some biscuits for you."

"Dang, if I'd known that, I'da gone over there," Will said.

"If I'da known it, I mighta gone with him," Barney said.

Sheriff Leach went back into the office. He told them that he usually stayed an hour or two after supper to make sure the town quieted down before he retired to the little house he lived in on the same street Sally's house was on. "That's when there ain't nobody in the cells, like tonight. If we got prisoners, either me or Jim will sleep in the office."

The only one who didn't talk about his supper when he showed up at the office a little later, was Jim Turner. When the sheriff asked him if he enjoyed his dinner, Jim just said it was okay. He didn't tell him about the scraps of food he had eaten. All he could find in Long Bob's room was some jerky, a jar of pickled peaches, a couple of cans of sardines, and some crackers. He did find coffee and a bottle of whiskey, which received more of their attention. Since that was all he could find for food, it was easy to get drunk instead. Long Bob complained, but Jim told him he couldn't very well load up a packhorse. "I'll get you somethin' you can cook tomorrow when I ain't got two deputy marshals hangin' around," he had promised Long Bob when he left him. "Get off your big lazy butt and go catch some fish." There were a couple of fishing poles lying across the open ceiling joists. They had used the cabin before, but they had no idea whom it belonged to. No one was ever there. They had never worried about the owners. As Long Bob said, possession was nine-tenths of the law.

When Jim came back from the stable, after leaving his horse with Frank Murphy, Will decided that was the go-ahead sign. He saddled Buster once again. If the big buckskin minded, he didn't show any evidence of it. The test was going to be whether or not Will, in the dark, could find the little path that led to the cabin. He and Ed led their horses quietly away from the jail right after the sheriff decided he had stayed late enough and said good night. Will led the way down the Spadra road at a considerably faster pace than when he had tailed Jim. Consequently, they reached the tiny path sooner than he expected. And he would have passed it by had he not broken a sizable branch of an oak tree a couple of yards short of it. "Damn," Ed swore softly as he followed him through the bushes. "How'd you ever find this? You sure we're on the right path?"

Will didn't answer. He just kept going until reaching the point where he first saw the cabin. He pulled up then and waited for Ed to come up beside him. "Yonder it is," he said, and pointed. Ed had to look twice before he really saw the outline of the crude shack sitting close to the bank of the river. After staring at the dark cabin for a few minutes, they detected a tiny glow of a fire through the one window. Since Ed had never seen Long Bob, Will felt it necessary to tell him their best bet would be to surprise him and try to cuff him before he knew what hit him. "If we go in with guns drawn and tell him he's under arrest, he's just gonna go wild, and believe me, he's a handful. We would be real lucky if he's drank himself to sleep. I expect we'd be in our rights if we just shot him when he resists arrest, but I'd kinda like to see him face the hanging judge." He let Ed consider that, then he asked, "All right?" Ed said it was. "Well, let's see if we can sneak up to that shack and get a look in the window."

They left their horses halfway down the slope and, holding handcuffs and a coil of rope, walked the rest of the way down to the cabin. The bay horse named Devil enquired softly and Buster answered, but there was no indication that the party inside the cabin had heard. With his six-gun in hand ready to fire, Will edged up to one side of the window. He pulled his hat off his head, then exposed one eye to peek inside. He saw the long outline of Long Bob's body stretched out against one side of the tiny shack, sound asleep. There was no mystery as to why Long Bob hadn't heard the horses. Will signaled to Ed. He held up his handcuffs and pointed to himself, then he handed Ed the coil of rope and pointed to his feet. Ed nodded that he understood.

They moved as quietly as possible to the door and discovered that there had been a padlock on it at one time, but the entire hasp had been torn off. Will very slowly tried the door and discovered there was nothing holding it shut from the inside. So he opened it all the way and stepped inside. Ed followed right behind him. They stood for a brief minute, their guns drawn, ready for his reaction, but there was none. The only response was an unconscious puff of air from Long Bob's lips, followed by a soft string of snoring. Will looked at Ed and mouthed, *Ready?* Ed nodded, and with his rope ready, he knelt by Long Bob's feet. Will took hold of the big man's shoulder and

Long Bob twitched slightly. Will gently patted the shoulder, then slowly pulled him over on his stomach. Sleeping too soundly to know what was going on, Long Bob offered no resistance when Will pulled his hands together behind his back and locked the cuffs on his wrists while Ed quickly bound his feet together. In the span of a few seconds, it was done.

Still struggling to come out of his drunken slumber, Long Bob gradually realized why he couldn't seem to move his body. He finally roared out his anger for several minutes. When he finished, Will said, "You're under arrest for the murder of Jolene Carson Butler."

"I'll kill that damn Jim Turner!" he swore, thinking that Jim must have told them where he was hiding.

"No use blamin' Jim," Will told him. "Jim did his best tryin' to keep us from findin' you. He don't know we caught up with you yet." Will looked at Ed then and said, "That's somethin' we'll have to talk about, what we're gonna do about Jim Turner. The only crime we know about for Jim is tryin' to help ol' Long Bob, here, to hide. 'Course, he mighta known who really killed Jolene, too." He was halfway inclined to let Sheriff Leach handle Jim's involvement in this affair. "But right now, I reckon we'd best get on with the hardest part of this arrest."

"What's that?" Ed had to wonder. He was

already thanking his lucky stars that the arrest was accomplished so easily.

"Gettin' this big load of manure onto his horse and carrying him outta here."

"Oh, right," Ed replied. "I reckon we'd best saddle his horse."

Thinking they were ahead of the game at this point, they were reluctant to untie his feet, so he could sit in the saddle. They were also not very anxious to unlock his hands, so he could have them in front of him. Both lawmen agreed that with this particular individual, it would be less risky to transport him across his saddle on his belly. Finally, Will shrugged and said, "We're just gonna have to shoot him. The warrant says dead or alive, and I don't think they really care, one way or the other."

"Wait a minute!" Long Bob suddenly sobered up. "What the hell are you talkin' about? You can't just shoot me!"

"The hell we can't," Will replied. "You resisted arrest. Who's gonna know? Right, Ed?"

"That's a fact," Ed responded. "It'll be a whole lot easier."

"I ain't resistin' arrest," Long Bob pleaded. "I'll do whatever you say. I won't give you no trouble."

Will looked at him and shook his head as if undecided. Then back to Ed, he said, "I don't know, Ed, he's gonna be so much easier dead.

We won't have to dig a hole to put him in. We'll just leave him in this shack and set it on fire. I'm gonna go saddle that bay horse. I know we wanna keep that horse and the saddle, too. Keep your eye on him. We'll decide for sure when I get back."

As soon as Will walked out of the shack, Long Bob started to work on Ed. "I can tell you're a lot more fair-minded man than your partner. I just wanna let you know I can see that you're a more Christian man than he is, and I respect you for it. I swear to you, I ain't gonna give you fellers no trouble at all. I'm really a peaceable man by nature. Anybody will tell you that."

When Will came back in the shack, he had his six-gun in his hand. He broke the cylinder open and checked to see that it was fully loaded. "All right, let's get this thing done."

"Hold on a second, Will," Ed said. "I think maybe we oughta give Long Bob a chance. I've been talkin' to him and I think he means what he says when he promises he'll do what we tell him."

"Hell, Ed," Will replied. "They all say that."

"I think this one means it," Ed declared.

"All right, but I ain't ever seen you go soft on a prisoner before. You can untie his feet, so he can sit in the saddle. But I'm tellin' you one little funny move and he's dead. Let's get him on his horse."

Ed untied Long Bob's feet and helped him up, then walked him out the door. Since Long

Bob's hands were still cuffed behind him, he had to be helped up into the saddle, but he meekly cooperated with Ed's efforts. Will felt the urge to chuckle when he thought of how much trouble he might have been. When Long Bob was in the saddle, Will said, "All right, Ed, you lead us back the way we came. I'm gonna ride behind our prisoner, and he ain't gettin' no second chance. I see anything that don't look right, I'm shootin' him. That's the deal. Understood?"

"That's the deal," Ed repeated. He took the reins of the bay horse and led it up from the riverside, a wide grin on his face that the prisoner could not see.

When they got back to the jail, they found Barney waiting eagerly for their return. He walked out to meet them when they rode up. "Well, I see you got your man. Any trouble?"

"No trouble at all," Will answered. "The sheriff went home, right?" He just wanted to make sure he didn't come back. "Where's Jim Turner? Did he go to Sally Belcher's?"

"No, he looked like he weren't feelin' too good. He didn't go home. He's sleepin' in the office."

"Well, that'll make it a little easier," Will said. "Let's get Long Bob off his horse."

"You gonna put him in my wagon?" Barney asked.

"No, I think tonight we'll put him in one of the

cells, and he'll have a bed to sleep on. We'll load him in the wagon in the mornin'." He went over and helped Ed catch Long Bob when he came off the bay. Then with one of them on each arm, they walked Long Bob up the steps and rapped on the door until Jim was finally aroused and came to unlock it. Still half asleep, he became completely awake when he saw Long Bob. He backed away, totally astonished. "Bring the keys to the cells, Jim," Will said.

"They're by the door, goin' in the cell room," Jim answered, his eyes growing bigger and bigger as he stared at Long Bob, who was staring back at him.

Will took the cell keys off a hook as he walked by. "Put a bucket of water in that cell," he said when he saw that the bucket in there was empty. Jim went at once to the pump. When he brought it back, Will said, "Bring another one and put it in that cell." He pointed to the cell next to Long Bob's. Confused but too amazed to ask questions, Jim went at once for another bucket of water. By the time he came back, Will had locked Long Bob in his cell and removed his handcuffs.

"You want this in that cell?" Jim asked, and pointed to the cell next to Long Bob's.

"Right," Will answered, and when Jim carried the bucket in, Will closed the cell door behind him and locked it. "Sorry we had to wake you up. You can go ahead and get back to sleep."

"Whadda you doin'?" Jim exclaimed. He rushed to the cell door and grabbed the bars in an effort to open it. "You locked the damn door!"

"Right again," Will said. "It takes you a little while, but you pick up on things eventually."

Still finding it hard to believe, Jim looked from Will to Ed in frustration. "You locked the damn door," he repeated.

"Right," Will said again. "That's how you keep prisoners from gettin' out of the cells. Looks like Sheriff Leach would have explained that to you." He and Ed went back to the office. "You boys get some sleep now and Barney will cook you some breakfast in the mornin'," Will said as he closed the door behind him.

"He's outta his mind," Jim complained. "He's as crazy as a coyote."

"You damn fool," Long Bob said. "You led 'em right to me. You didn't have enough sense to know they was gonna tail you."

CHAPTER 23

Barney had coffee in the pot in the sheriff's office the next morning when Sheriff Marvin Leach came to the office. Barney cooked bacon and grits for the prisoners and the deputies before the sheriff's arrival and they were in the process of hitching up the team to the wagon and saddling the horses when Leach walked in the office. When he found no one in the office, he went into the cell room and was stopped cold when he opened the door. "Long Bob!" Leach blurted. "How did you . . . ?" he started but couldn't finish when he realized Jim` was in the cell beside Bob's. "Jim! What the hell?"

"It's that crazy marshal," Jim exclaimed, "Tanner, he put me in here."

Leach was struck speechless for a couple of minutes while he tried to make sense of what he saw in his jail cells. "When did he arrest Long Bob?"

"Last night," Jim answered. "Then he locked me in here. Let me outta here!"

Leach hesitated a few moments but then turned to look for the keys by the door. "Where are the keys?" he asked when he didn't see them on their usual hook.

"Tanner's got 'em," Jim said. That seemed to

383

further confuse the bewildered sheriff, so Jim said, "They're out back, gettin' ready to go."

Leach turned around and went back through the office, out the door, and around behind the jail. "Mornin', Sheriff," Barney sang out when he saw him round the corner of the building. "You lookin' for a cup of coffee?"

"No," Leach answered. "I mean, yeah, I reckon I need one." Will and Ed were tying lead ropes on the Appaloosa and the packhorses. When they saw Leach, they came over to talk to him.

"I left you one on your stove in the office," Barney said while they waited for Will and Ed.

"One what?" Leach asked.

"Pot of coffee," Barney said.

Leach turned and stared at Barney's smiling face. He was still totally confused. "You boys was pretty busy last night," was all he could think to say.

"Mornin', Sheriff," Will offered. "I reckon we need to talk about a few things this mornin'."

"I reckon we do," Leach replied, finally regaining some of his sense of responsibility. "To start with, what the hell's my deputy doin' locked up in that cell?"

"Tell you the truth, it was hard to decide whether we oughta arrest him for slippin' off last night to take food and stuff to Long Bob at his hideout. Or give him a gold star for helpin' us with the arrest. I don't know if we'da ever found

Long Bob if Jim hadn't led us right to him." He could see the concern in Leach's face when he heard that, so he continued. "Ed and I have been talkin' it over and there are two things we could do with Jim. We can take him on back to Fort Smith and try him for aidin' and abettin' a criminal. Or we can just turn him over to you and let you handle it any way you see fit. We thought you might prefer that option, since you obviously know your deputy better than we do. If you need to think it over, best do it now because we're fixin' to take Long Bob out of his cell and transfer him to the jail wagon. All I need to know is whether or not Long Bob's gonna have any company on the ride back to Fort Smith."

The sheriff didn't take any time to make his decision. "You're a reasonable man, Will Tanner, you and Ed both. I understand you're willin' to give Jim a chance, and so am I. I'll deal with him, myself."

"Fine," Will said. "I wish you good luck with him. You might wanna consider that he likely knew Long Bob killed Jolene, too." He turned then and called, "Come on, Ed, let's load him up."

With the sheriff standing by as an extra guard, they moved Long Bob out of his cell and put him in the jail wagon, where he was locked to a chain by an ankle bracelet. Then Will gave the cell keys to Leach and they shook hands. Barney pulled the wagon out into the street and started back the way they had come. Will pulled up beside Ed and said, "Go ahead. I'll catch up to ya."

He wheeled Buster and loped back down the street, pulled up before the Friendly Saloon, hopped down, and went inside. He walked straight through the saloon to the door in the back. When he walked in the kitchen, he found Mabel taking a tray of biscuits out of the oven, her back to him. "Just hold your horses," she said, without turning around.

He had to laugh. "If those biscuits are for sale, I'd like to buy 'em."

"All of 'em?" she asked as she turned to see who said it. A big smile blossomed on her face when she saw him.

"All of 'em," he answered. "Can you put 'em in a sack?"

"Will Tanner." She said his name like it was something special. "I expected you for supper last night."

"I couldn't make it last night, but I wasn't gonna leave town without eatin' another one of your biscuits."

She dumped the whole pan into a paper bag. "Is that gonna run you short on your customers in the saloon?" Will asked.

"They can wait till I bake some more," she said, and handed the bag to him.

"How much I owe you?"

"Nothin'," she said. "I just hope you enjoy them." He reached in his pocket, pulled out two dollars, and laid them on the table. "That's too much," she exclaimed as he rushed out the door.

"Not for these biscuits," he yelled back.

When he caught up with the wagon, he gave everybody a hot biscuit, including the prisoner.

The trip back to Fort Smith was without incident, and like the trip to Clarksville, they took it in two short days. When they made camp after the first day's travel, they unlocked Long Bob's cage and let him out of the wagon for the night. Still locked to the chain, he had the use of his hands and the length of the chain to move about, but one end of the chain was locked around the axle of the wagon. After that night, Long Bob began to regain some of his natural bluster, now that he was convinced the marshals were intent upon delivering him to court, and he was in no danger of being shot for the sake of convenience. Ed was the most vocal in his impatience with the prisoner, but it was Barney who suffered the constant bragging and crowing that was the persona of Long Bob Butler. He complained to Will and Ed about Long Bob's constant claims that Judge Parker might rule for a hanging, but a hanging was never going to happen to him.

"He's a big 'un, ain't he?" Sid Randolph remarked when Ed and Will walked Long

Bob into receiving at the jail. "Was he much trouble?"

"Not a bit," Ed answered him. "But don't let that fool you. We caught him drunk and asleep. We were lucky."

Will and Ed reported to Dan Stone after they left Long Bob at the jail. They both thought Deputy Jim Turner's involvement would come out in testimony before the court, so they discussed the issue with Stone. His initial reaction was that Jim should have been arrested along with Long Bob. But he understood Will and Ed's decision to let Sheriff Leach handle it. "When I last talked to Judge Parker," Stone told them, "he said he planned to move Butler's trial ahead on the docket. So you'll both be in court right away." He smiled when he looked at Will and said, "I know you won't mind stayin' close to home for a while." Will smiled in return, but he was thinking of the boredom of sitting through a court trial. When Will and Ed started to leave, Stone said, "There's still a little matter of a professional killer lookin' for you, Will."

"I didn't see any reason to include that in the report," Will said, "but that issue has been settled." He went on to explain how he came to be the new owner of an Appaloosa gelding.

"Home in time for supper," Sophie remarked when she saw him come in the door. "Now that's more like it." She gave him a welcome hug, then stepped back while she looked him over. "No new bandages, either! Welcome home."

"Yeah, I missed you, too," he said sarcastically.

The trial was scheduled two days later on a Wednesday morning. Will was given the job of delivering the summons to witnesses Loretta Carson and Rayford Pickens. He was paid the usual fee for delivering them, even though Loretta was still right there at Bennett House, and Rayford was in a holding cell next to the courtroom. Will had not had an occasion to see Rayford in the short time since his return from Clarksville with the prisoner. But Loretta seemed to be self-assured and ready to testify. Will credited most of that to her close association with Margaret for the last few days.

When Long Bob was escorted into the courtroom, Will was reminded of the first time he saw him in the Friendly Saloon. Even with two guards to escort him, Long Bob looked larger than life. Walking tall and confidently, he flashed a wide smile at Loretta, and Will thought he detected a look of panic upon the frail girl's face. *Surely, she won't recant at this late date,* he thought. His thoughts were shifted to the door in the back corner of the courtroom when the bailiff called, "All rise," and Judge Isaac Parker walked in.

As Dan Stone had predicted, Long Bob's trial

went fast and smoothly. Much to Will's relief, Loretta faced the jury bravely and told the truth. She said that Rayford had tried to protect her sister, Jolene. But Long Bob killed Jolene, then threatened to kill her if she didn't say Rayford killed Jolene. The jury was unanimous in their decision of guilty, and Judge Parker promptly sentenced Long Bob to death by hanging.

It was done. Nothing could compensate for the loss of her sister, but Loretta had at least seen justice for the man who killed her. And she was the one who had defied his threats and driven the nail in his coffin. Justice was served in everyone's mind but Long Bob's. When his guards escorted him back past the witness box, Long Bob suddenly tore away from them and lunged toward Loretta, his handcuffed hands reaching for her throat. It happened too fast for anyone to react quickly enough to stop him, except for one person. Once again, Rayford Pickens thrust his body between Long Bob and his victim, this time with enough force to knock the angry giant to the floor. Will was quick to assist the two guards as they dragged a frustrated Long Bob from the courtroom. When he came back, he was gratified to see Rayford still locked in Loretta's grateful embrace. *Might be the start of something,* he thought.

William W. Johnstone is the *New York Times* and *USA Today* bestselling author of over three hundred books, including the bestselling series Smoke Jensen: The Mountain Man; Preacher: The First Mountain Man; Flintlock; MacCallister; and Will Tanner: U.S. Deputy Marshal, and the stand-alone thrillers *Black Friday*, *Tyranny*, and *Stand Your Ground*.

Being the all-around assistant, typist, researcher, and fact-checker to one of the most popular Western authors of all time, **J. A. Johnstone** learned from the master, Uncle William W. Johnstone.

He began tutoring J.A. at an early age. After-school hours were often spent retyping manuscripts or researching his massive American Western history library as well as the more modern wars and conflicts. J.A. worked hard—and learned.

"Every day with Bill was an adventure story in itself. Bill taught me all he could about the art of storytelling. *'Keep the historical facts accurate,'* he would say. *'Remember the readers, and as your grandfather once told me, I am telling you now: be the best J.A. Johnstone you can be.'*"

Visit the website: www.williamjohnstone.net

Center Point Large Print
600 Brooks Road / PO Box 1
Thorndike, ME 04986-0001 USA

(207) 568-3717

US & Canada:
1 800 929-9108
www.centerpointlargeprint.com